THE HUSBAND TRAP

NJ MOSS

BLOODHOUND
— BOOKS —

ALSO BY NJ MOSS

All Your Fault

———

Her Final Victim

———

My Dead Husband

For Sally HB,
thank you for all your kindness and generosity

CHAPTER ONE

"Emily, can you come in here for a second?"

Liam looked around the living room, making sure everything was just right. He'd spent a long time scattering the rose petals all over the place. He'd wanted every inch of the flat to be covered. But he hadn't bought enough; it looked more like a rose petal sprinkling instead of the romantic scene he'd imagined.

Still, he wasn't going to mess around anymore. Emily was due to give birth any day and he should've done this a long time ago.

"You know it takes me about ten years to get out of bed, right..."

She trailed off when she noticed the rose petals, the flickering candles, and Liam guessed she was more than a little shocked at seeing him in a suit. He felt like a bit of an arse in the shirt and jacket, but tonight was big.

Emily was wearing her nightie, baggy down to her knees. Her belly was round and beautiful. She always laughed when he said that, but it was true. It reminded him of the future they were going to share. She'd never looked more stunning, especially with her hair all messy around her shoulders.

"What is this?" She took a few steps, faltered, tilted her head like she was expecting a joke. "Liam? You're in a suit." She laughed as tears glimmered in her eyes.

He grinned as he took her hands in his. "We both know there's something I should've asked you a long time ago. If I wasn't such an idiot, I would've done it, say, roughly eight months and three weeks ago..."

Her grip tightened on his. "You don't have to do anything just because I'm, you know, a big walking snowball."

"No, it's not that. Not *just* that. It's you, Emily. It's everything about you. It's the way you cry at adverts and how angry you get when people are rude to waiters. It's the way you can't stop yourself singing along to Christmas songs. It's your kind heart and... It's *you*. It's us. I love you more than I can ever explain."

Liam got down on one knee, and of course that was when Rocky decided to join them. The Jack Russell padded into the room and whined softly, clambering onto Liam's legs with his forepaws like he wanted to get involved. Smiling, Liam stroked the old boy behind the ears, then nodded. "Sit and wait. Hopefully, in a few seconds, we'll have some celebrating to do."

Rocky didn't understand the rest of it, but *wait* and *sit* were known to him. He obediently lowered his butt and watched his human turn back to his other human.

Liam looked up at the woman he wanted to spend the rest of his life with. "Emily Ruth Taylor, will you marry me?"

Her eyes were shiny with happy tears; he could read her easily, one of the many reasons they worked so well. His heart gave a flutter. She was going to say yes. He knew it.

"Um, Liam."

"Yeah?"

"Can you please show me the bloody ring so I can say yes?"

Liam leapt to his feet and wrapped his arms around her, gently because of the baby. He leaned close and inhaled her scent. It was sweat and shampoo and, underneath it all, Emily, his Emily. "Only if you say yes again."

"Yes, yes, *yes*." She looped her arms over his shoulders. "It was always going to be yes. I love you so much."

They kissed passionately, and then Liam quickly took a step back before he got carried away. "Let me do this properly."

He returned to his knee and reached into his pocket, taking out the ring box. In his fantasies, he'd thought about presenting her with a big rock, like on those reality shows she sometimes watched. But he was a dog trainer and didn't make a bunch of money.

Opening the box, he gauged her reaction. It was an elegant piece, he hoped. He'd gone to the shop with one of his mates and his girlfriend, and together they'd picked it out. His mate's girlfriend had assured him Emily would love it.

"Oh, Liam, it's beautiful."

He slipped the ring onto her finger. Standing, he hugged her again. "This is it. The first day of the rest of our lives."

Her hands trailed over his face, into his hair. "You're the best. I mean that. The best, most loving, most loyal man I've ever met."

"Are you done talking so I can kiss you again?"

"Dick." She pushed her lips against his before he could say anything else. They were sinking into it, Emily moaning in that way he knew well, when Rocky gave a whine from beneath them.

"Don't worry, boy." Liam laughed as he reached down to pick the little guy up. "Nobody's forgotten about you."

"How could we, huh?" Emily gave his nose a tickle, looking over his head at Liam. "How did you arrange this?

And when did you change? And how did you know the ring would fit?"

"I've been sneaking around for about forty-five minutes. You were snoring like a right animal..." She laughed, and he grinned as he went on. "You didn't notice me getting changed. As for the ring, I used one of those measurer thingies when you were sleeping."

"Seems like you thought of everything, huh?"

Keeping one hand braced under Rocky's belly, he reached over and tucked a wayward strand of hair from his girlfriend – no, his fiancée's – face. "I'm so relieved right now. You've got no idea."

"Silly. What did you think I would say?"

"I don't know. I wanted it to be special. Sorry it's not a chariot ride to a field full of sparkling puppies or whatever."

"A chariot ride to a field of sparkling puppies?"

"I don't know what I'm saying. I'm just so happy! Hang on. I need to get something."

He carried Rocky into the kitchen and grabbed the non-alcoholic champagne.

Emily had her hands clasped over her middle when he returned, her cheeks wet. "Please let me take a photo of you. I want to remember this forever."

Liam normally didn't like his photo being taken. It wasn't that he had anything against it, particularly, but more that he didn't like the fuss of it all. Emily said it was a man thing. But he didn't care, not tonight; he would've let her take a thousand.

She walked into the bedroom and returned with her phone. She did her funny waddling walk, but the one time he'd shared *that* observation she'd threatened to hit him with a slipper.

After taking the photo, she threw her phone onto the sofa and took the glasses. Liam popped the cork and Emily clapped as champagne spilled out. Liam didn't care that some of it went on the carpet. He'd grown up with a mother who was always ranting about the bills, about how his rowdiness was why they couldn't have nice things, and usually he was the same.

But not tonight. They clinked their glasses together and sipped.

Their eyes met. The corner of Emily's lips twitched. Liam felt his mirroring their shape.

"It's not the same, is it?" she said finally.

"Nope. But not long now."

"Didn't you get yourself some beers or something?"

"I thought about it. But then, like the loving gentleman I am, I thought to myself, Hey, you know what, Emily doesn't want to sit there watching me drink my bodyweight in alcohol, not when she can't have a single drop. Because I'm nice like that."

"You are nice." She grabbed his shirt, digging her nails against his chest. "*Very* nice, in fact. But I won't mind if you want to run to the shop and get yourself some. Honestly. There's no reason both of us should suffer."

Liam shrugged. "I don't need it. I know this'll sound cheesy, but this moment's special enough."

Emily might've mimed being sick at a comment like that... if Liam hadn't just proposed. Now, sarcasm was beyond even her. Liam could tell she felt as high on the moment as him, both floating with happiness. "I know you don't need it. But it might be nice. And if you're really lucky, I might even let you rub my feet later. As a special proposal present. I think you'll want to be drunk for that."

He embraced her, getting as close as he could, short of melting into her. He could feel her breath. He could feel her heartbeat drumming through her body. "I'll be five minutes."

Liam kissed Emily on the lips, gave the bump a peck, and scratched Rocky's head. He only realised he was skipping when one of his neighbour's came walking down the other end of the hallway, carrying two overstuffed carrier bags, a grim set to his lips. When was the last time Liam had skipped? He must've been a kid.

He hurried into the autumn cold and down the street, taking a right into the alleyway that would lead to the twenty-four-hour shop. It was the same alleyway he'd told Emily to never walk down on her own. They didn't live in the roughest place, sure, but it wasn't the nicest either.

There was a homeless man hunched next to a wheelie bin, his blankets laid out. Liam had seen him around a few times. They exchanged a nod, before the homeless man went back to sorting coins.

Nothing could dampen Liam's mood. He knew he'd always remember this: the sharp air and the hammering of his heart and the smell of alley piss and the mewling of a cat a few streets away. Good and bad, it didn't matter; it was all part of it. Of Emily. Of them. Of the future they were going to share.

It was dark here, everything hazy, shadowed outlines.

The man appeared as a silhouette. Liam stood a little straighter, put his shoulders back. The man was blocking his path.

"You good, mate?"

"Hm-mm," the man grunted. He sounded drunk.

"Mind getting out of my way?"

Swiftly there was an arm around Liam's neck.

He hadn't heard anybody sneaking up on him. He'd been too focused on the man... and the man: yes, Liam was sure. He was wearing a mask, a balaclava, like bank robbers wore.

Liam thrashed, his hands darting up to the arm. He squeezed and pulled with all his strength. The arm came loose and its owner grunted. Liam threw his weight back, felt his head connect with teeth, biting sharply into his skull. The shadowy man cursed, advancing with his hands raised. Liam was ready. Mugging him now, of all nights.

"Come on then, let's have it." He backed against the wall, trying to keep them both in front of him.

But there was a third. Liam only knew he was there when he felt the needle go into his neck.

He slurred as he failed to shout. His eyelids were getting heavy. His legs folded and he collapsed against the concrete.

Emily, he tried to say.

And then it all went black.

CHAPTER TWO

H e shouldn't have had so much to drink last night. His mouth was dry and his head was pounding. But she'd said yes; all that worrying, all that wondering, and she'd said yes! Emily was going to be his wife and they were going to raise their child well and–

His thoughts cut off as he fully emerged from sleep. He remembered the men in the alleyway, the sting of the needle in his neck. Opening his eyes, he peered up at an ornately carved pattern. Swirls and shapes had been cut into the wood. When Liam looked to his side, the sunlight was purple, like he was peering through stained glass.

Sitting up, he looked down the length of his body. He was lying on top of silk sheets, in a four-poster bed. The light was coming through the curtains... was that what they were called, in a fancy bed like this, curtains? He wasn't sure. He wasn't dreaming, was he? It felt real enough.

"Hello?" His voice was raspy with dehydration. "Is anybody there?"

Pushing the curtains aside, he climbed from the bed with an effort. He was in what looked like an upscale hotel room. There was the bed, a big wooden dresser with wrought metal handles, rugs draped over the floor; the lights were fitted into sconces on the walls, and there was a door to the en suite off to the side. He stumbled over to the window, struggling to find his footing.

There was a padlock on the window. He grabbed it. Shook it. Nothing. It was solid. He saw a gravel road and a fountain and a long field and a garden and, past it all, a small wooded area, the leaves brown with autumn. The terrain rose in a hill, which, coupled with the trees, blocked much of his view of the wider property. Where the hell was he?

Looking down, he guessed he was at least three floors up. He couldn't judge the drop without opening the window, but even if it was a bush down there – and not stones like the surrounding area – it'd still hurt. He might twist his ankle, or worse, making escape impossible.

He massaged his temples, closing his eyes and focusing hard to remember. He'd proposed to Emily, left to get some beers, and then... the men, this, waking up here.

He was still wearing his suit from last night – if it had been last night; he had no idea how much time had passed – but it was crumpled and reeked of sweat. Hanging from the wardrobe was another suit, this one clean. Was it for him? Why would somebody drug him and then give him a suit?

He marched over to the door, threw it open. So at least that wasn't locked.

To the right there was a staircase, the bannisters wooden with more patterns carved in them. All along the hallway there were landscape paintings, everything looking old-fashioned. It was like the time he and Emily had gone to stay at a five-star hotel in Wales; he had the feeling of being somewhere he didn't belong. Which was true. He didn't belong here. But it was more than that. This was the sort of place which always made him feel poor.

He returned to the room and looked for a weapon. All the drawers had been emptied. He could've smashed the window and used a shard of glass, or maybe the glass in the en suite bathroom's mirror. Otherwise, there was nothing. Maybe he could've pulled off one of the handles on the drawers. But he didn't want to waste any vital time messing around. He needed to get out of here; he needed to get to Emily.

Liam walked down the hallway, trying all the doors: nine in total. Each of them was locked. At the very end, there was a mounted deer's head, antlers slicing into the air, dead eyes watching as he walked back the way he'd come. He stood at the top of the stairs and peered down. He thought about calling out again. But with the haziness of sleep gone, he knew it wasn't a good idea. He didn't want them to know he was awake, not that he knew who *they* were.

"Good morning, sir." A man walked up the stairs. He was around sixty, if Liam had to guess, with a shock of white hair and a prim-and-proper sort of manner. It was the way he was walking, stiff-backed. He wore a servant's uniform. He paused before ascending to Liam's floor. "I'm sure you're confused."

"Where am I?"

"Allow me to introduce myself."

"What is this?"

"I am Bretherton, and I shall be serving as your butler for the time being."

"My butler?" Liam coughed out a deranged laugh. "Did Pat put you up to this? Is this an early stag prank? Because I'm telling you, it's not funny."

Bretherton frowned, deepening the lines in his face. "I agree. There is nothing funny about this."

"I don't know what *this* is."

"All will become clear. I must request, sir – with all due

respect – that you put on the clothes the lady of the house has so kindly provided for you."

"Tried that. Didn't fit."

"The lady was careful to take your measurements..."

"I was joking, dickhead." Liam walked down the stairs, staring hard at the old man. He didn't want to hurt him. "Where's the exit? I'm done."

"Sir, I really wouldn't recommend–"

"Yeah, yeah."

He took the stairs two at a time, almost tripping. There were more paintings on the walls. He crossed the landing of the second storey, ignoring the doors to his left and right, and headed to the bottom floor. The entranceway was massive, the front door big enough to fit four of him. He jogged over to it and took the big metal handle in both his hands, pulling roughly.

It swung open with force, almost sending him flying. Bretherton had reached the bottom of the stairs. He called over. "Sir, there is a civilised way to do this. Please, let's keep this respectful."

Liam turned, glared at the man. "I'm respectfully telling you to go fuck yourself."

His voice stuttered at the end. He silently cursed. He couldn't let the old man see how much this situation was screwing with him. He had to be strong.

But his strength faded when he turned back to the open doorway. Three men stood on the porch. They were fit, built like rugby players, all average height. They wore identical black sweaters, black cargo trousers, chunky black boots, and balaclavas, hiding their faces.

"Please. Come back inside and get dressed." Bretherton had walked over. "You're going to be late for breakfast."

Liam assessed the men. There was no way he'd be able to take all three. He wasn't even sure he'd be able to take one. He'd done some boxing as a teenager and had been in a few scraps in his life, but nothing like this. These men held themselves like they were ready for violence.

Bretherton lowered his voice. "You're going to make them sedate you again. It will make you terribly groggy, and there may even be adverse side effects, coming so soon after your previous dose. Be reasonable."

They'd ambushed him, drugged him, kidnapped him. They wanted him to play dress-up. They'd taken him from his home, his fiancée, his baby, his dog. And they wanted him to be reasonable.

He took a step. The men tensed up. Two of them exchanged glances. Liam took another step, then another, until he was within touching distance.

Behind the men, there were some wooden steps leading down to a wide gravel driveway, the fountain in the middle. The trees were past that; he'd run for them, and then keep running to whatever was beyond.

He leapt to the side, meaning to dive around the man on the right and then vault over the porch railing. But the men were quick and efficient. The nearest dove and threw him to the floor. Liam sprang up, caught one with his elbow. He spat and kicked and he headbutted one of them, but they kept coming, and soon they were squashing his arms against his sides.

Two of them held him, crushing his chest. He kicked and tried to sit down, forcing them to carry him, but it was more of a nuisance than a proper fight.

The man in front softly touched his own face. He was the one Liam had headbutted, if the way he winced was any indication. Maybe that was why there was a glint in his eyes as he reached into his pocket and took out the syringe.

"Don't put that thing in my neck. You hear me? I'm telling you no."

The man pulled off the plastic cap and approached carefully, gaze flitting to Liam's legs. Good. He ought to be scared. Liam would kick him in the balls as hard as possible, and then deal with the other two. But that was a boyish fantasy. He wasn't a superhero, and there was nothing he could do as the needle met with his skin.

CHAPTER THREE

Liam woke with his tongue stuck to his cheek, his dry mouth desperate for water. His arms were sore and his forehead ached from the fight. He rolled over, pushed away the curtains, and stumbled over to the window. The light had shifted, but it was still daytime. His mind whirred; that meant they'd used a lighter dose than the first, which had knocked him unconscious for the whole journey.

He lost his footing. Catching himself on the railing of the four-poster bed, he closed his eyes and concentrated on not falling. If they'd given him a heavier dose for the kidnapping, that meant there had been some planning involved: they knew they were going to take him, knew they didn't want him to remember the journey.

Dropping onto the bed, he buried his face in his hands and tried to remember. The proposal – sweet Emily – the attack in the alleyway, the needle... His thoughts clouded. He concentrated as hard as he could, the same way he did when he was training a particularly stubborn dog.

Flickers of memories taunted him. He was in a van; his

hands were bound. He was bumping up and down. Male voices discussed him matter-of-factly, but he couldn't make out the words.

And then there had been the fight this morning... unless he was wrong, and it wasn't the same day. No, that didn't feel right. He would've felt much more sluggish.

He forced himself to his feet, into the en suite. After gulping so much water from the tap he felt like he was going to be sick, he returned to the bedroom.

The door was locked. He pushed harder, leaned his weight against it, driving with his shoulder. It felt sturdy, not at all like the hollow doors in his and Emily's rental flat. Stepping back, he judged the distance and gave it an experimental kick.

The impact reverberated up his leg and he quickly balanced himself. Maybe if he went at it for an hour, or he had an axe or something to break apart a section of it, he could get free. But that was only if the key was in the lock on the other side. It didn't matter; he had nothing to break the wood with.

If he decided to kick it in, how long before the guards came?

"Sir." It was the butler, Bretherton, standing on the other side of the door. "I would advise against trying to break the door down. The entire estate is under guard. You will only be making things more difficult for yourself."

"Why am I here? I don't understand any of this. What's happening?"

"You are here because the lady of the house wishes you to be."

"Who is she? It doesn't make any sense. I've never met anybody who'd... who lives in a place like this."

"That's right, sir. I don't believe the two of you have officially met yet. But she is excited to make your acquaintance."

Liam groaned. "But why?"

"That is not my place to say."

Liam slammed his fist against the door. Big mistake. His knuckles cracked and agony bit up his arm. "Dammit."

He reeled across the room, pacing, looking for something to break. He thought about smashing the window and dropping down. But his previous assessment had been right; the drop was far too steep. He'd be lucky to only twist an ankle. If he fell wrong, he might break a leg. He could even die if he was incredibly unlucky.

"Are you quite all right in there, sir?"

"Yeah, fine and dandy. Having the time of my life."

"I suppose sarcasm makes this easier. I would advise against it when you meet the lady, however. She is quite serious about this whole affair."

"What affair?"

"That is not my place to–"

"If you can't tell me what's going on, and if you won't let me out, piss off."

Bretherton let out a sigh. It seemed designed for Liam to hear it, loud and disappointed, like a teacher who didn't know how to handle an unruly student. Then he was gone, footsteps receding.

Liam explored the room fully. There were no coat hangers in the wardrobe. There was nothing under the bed. Every drawer was empty. There was just the suit they wanted him to wear, and a folded-up piece of paper on the bedside table.

He took it, unfolded it.

Naughty boys deserve empty bellies. Be good and I'll see you tomorrow for breakfast.

Liam tried to think of anybody he'd ever met who would want to do this to him. He hadn't made many enemies in his life. When he was a teenager, he'd been a bit of a dick, drinking too much, getting into fights, but no long-term damage had been done. He'd never abused any of the dogs he trained; the thought was ridiculous. Had one of Emily's ex-boyfriends somehow arranged this?

But why?

There were too many questions. He didn't have the information to make sense of it.

"Naughty boys deserve empty bellies." He slumped to the floor, resting his back against the wall, crumpling the note in his hand.

Psychotic kidnappers deserved much worse.

They left him there all day and all night. Liam couldn't sleep for most of it. He ran his hands through his hair and closed his eyes, waiting for it to be over, wanting to trash the room when he opened his eyes and saw it was still happening. This was his new reality. This was his life.

He touched the back of his head and a spot of blood came away on his fingertips, probably from when they'd abducted him and his skull had bashed into the attacker's tooth.

Finally, he fell into a fitful rest.

Shimmering dreams tempted him. Emily was laughing and her wedding dress was white and shiny, and Rocky sat at her feet with his grey beard and his tongue hanging out; a baby was crying, his son or daughter. They hadn't wanted to know the gender. But, as a knocking pounded in some faraway place, he wished they'd asked. He didn't want to die without knowing if he had a little boy or girl. Or that the birth had gone well. Or that Emily knew he loved her, always would, and he hadn't abandoned her.

The knocking got louder and Liam opened his eyes, staring up at the patterns above.

"Sir, it's time for breakfast."

Liam sat up and walked over to the suit. He needed to find out what was going on.

CHAPTER FOUR

B retherton led him down the stairs. Liam studied the old man's head, the wispy hair across his balding pate, and thought about cracking it as hard as he could. Or maybe he could snap off the deer antler on his cell's floor, use it as a shiv, take somebody hostage to leverage his escape.

But attacking an old man from behind was wrong. Even if he was part of this madness.

Chunky padlocks were on all of the doors. Liam paused and studied one, giving it a shake. It felt as sturdy as the ones upstairs.

Bretherton paused. "The lady only wishes to make use of certain parts of the estate."

Liam tugged on the padlock again, mostly just to annoy the butler. It worked. Bretherton spun and stared up at him. Liam was sure he detected a glint in the man's eyes, cruel, and a smile tugging at the corner of his lip. It was like he was enjoying this. "I'm sure you're dreaming up all sorts of evils beyond those locked doors. But the truth is much more ordinary. Large houses like this are bothersome to maintain. It's easier to leave certain areas ignored if they are not required."

"It's hard to believe anything you say when you won't even tell me why I'm here."

Bretherton gestured down the corridor. "Shall we?"

Liam followed. It was obvious nobody was going to tell him anything until he'd met the lady of the house. He was going to get answers from her, no matter what. He wouldn't play this sick game.

They walked down another long corridor, with more locked doors. This place was confusing. He tried to remember where he was in relation to his bedroom as they passed large paintings in gold-coloured frames and more animal heads; there was even a bear, mouth open in a primal scream. Liam could relate.

Bretherton gestured to an open door on the left. Liam debated telling him no. Whatever was waiting for him, he knew it wouldn't be good. But he didn't have a choice.

He walked into a dining room. Or more like a dining cavern. It was massive, with a domed ceiling, with Biblical artwork painted all over it. A chandelier hung and glittered as sunlight shafted through the tall windows at the back. The table was absurdly long, with at least twenty chairs. A woman sat in the one at the very end.

She was around Liam's age, with a bob of blonde hair, pearls at her neck and a bracelet on her wrist; it jangled as she reached for her glass of orange juice. Pastries were laid out before her. There was no cutlery, Liam noted, but the glasses and the plates were real, not plastic. They could do some damage.

"Please, sit." The woman gestured at the seat next to her, where another glass of orange juice sat. Her voice wasn't as posh as he'd guessed it would be. It was like she was doing a bad impression. "Liam, let's not make this nasty. Please."

"Who *are* you?" Liam walked over. There were no guards in here. Were they waiting in the corridor, or in one of the adjacent rooms? "They said I had to wait until I met the lady of the house until they'd tell me anything. I'm guessing that's you. So please tell me what the fuck's going on."

Her upper lip curled. "I do not like being cursed at, Liam."

He stood behind his chair. She had a placid smile on her face, acting like nothing was wrong; her lips widened the more he stared. She thought he was admiring her, he realised. He purposefully looked away.

"My name is Rebecca, but you can call me Becky."

"Lucky me. Why am I here?"

"It's so boring when somebody asks the same question over and over. Let's enjoy our breakfast. The suit looks lovely, by the way."

"Why. The fuck. Am I. Here?"

Rebecca's eyes widened as they flitted to the corner of the room. He followed her gaze; a camera watched them from the very top, red light blinking. "If you keep cursing, I'll be forced to call the guards. I don't wish to cause any more fuss."

"Fuss? Your men attacked me in an alleyway. I'd just proposed to my girlfriend–"

"You do not have a girlfriend."

The comment was deranged. He laughed reflexively. "What?"

She sat up straighter. "You have no girlfriend. You're single, looking for love, the same way I am."

"Wait. Is that why I'm here?"

She toyed with her pearls. Liam sensed she was trying to look shy and attractive, flirty, as if he'd be remotely interested in that. Even if she hadn't kidnapped him – or ordered it – he loved Emily. "I suppose we'll have to see. But I would like to get to know you."

Liam threw his head back and laughed.

"Stop it."

He didn't care if he sounded like a madman. He kept laughing. Surely this couldn't be it. Surely he hadn't been brought here to, what, *seduce* this woman.

She stood quickly, aiming a manicured finger at him. "You are being very impolite. I've had this lovely breakfast prepared and you won't even sit down. And now you're telling horrible lies about having a girlfriend, and laughing at me, and..."

Liam stopped, taking a step closer. She reeked of perfume. "I do have a girlfriend. A fiancée, actually. If you've brought me here to be your sex slave or your Romeo, you're in for a big shock, darling."

"Do *not* call me darling."

"No?" Liam grinned. "Sorry, darling."

"I'm warning you."

"Darling, darling, darling."

She smoothed her hands down her dress, closed her eyes, as if summoning her patience. When she opened them, her smile returned. "Let's put all this nastiness behind us and enjoy our pastries. I was thinking afterwards we could–"

Liam grabbed the glass and threw it at the wall. Hard. It shattered loudly and juice sprayed everywhere, the shards clattering against the hardwood floor.

Rebecca cringed away, covering her face with her hands. "Guards! Guards! He's gone wild!"

"Maybe I have."

Liam threw the other glass. He smashed the plates and picked up a chair, using it as a weapon as the guards rushed into the room. He didn't give a damn. He wouldn't do what they wanted him to.

Five of them approached, dressed in black, balaclavas on their heads.

"Don't be stupid," the one at the front said. His voice was

deep and gravelly. His eyes had a matter-of-fact seriousness about them. He was ready for whatever Liam was going to do. Liam guessed he was the leader. "There's no way you can win this. You're just causing yourself more hassle."

Liam brandished the chair as the man approached. "Maybe I *want* hassle."

"You're disturbing the lady of the house."

"Maybe I want that too."

He did his best to fight them off, but it had been a losing battle from the start. The only thing which might've helped was taking Rebecca hostage. But that opportunity had passed; as Liam had been talking with the leader, two of the guards had walked around the table, putting themselves between her and Liam. The three remaining guards swarmed him. He struck. He spit. He bit. He elbowed. He fought.

But eventually they wrestled him to the floor, slamming him onto his front. A knee drove into his back. His belly was winded.

"He has to be a good boy," Rebecca called over her shoulder as she left the room. "Tell him he has to be good. Or he'll starve."

"Hear that?" It was the leader again, his voice close to Liam's ear. "Stop messing about. Do what she wants and your life will be a hell of a lot easier."

"You're a piece of shit. You know this is wrong, but what, she's paying you so much you don't care?"

The leader said nothing. They hauled Liam to his feet and dragged him up the stairs. When he tried to wrestle from their clutches, they aimed stiff strikes at his belly. He coughed, vomit burning up his throat, dribbling down his lips.

They threw him into the bedroom and slammed the door. A heavy padlock closed and he rolled onto his side, drawing his knees to his chest, trying to suck in enough air. His belly was cramping.

Closing his eyes, he thought of the day they'd found out Emily was pregnant. He'd been on his laptop in the living room, arranging some one-on-one dog training sessions, when she appeared in the bedroom doorway. She was wearing her dressing gown and she held the test in her hands.

He hadn't even known she'd bought a test. They hadn't planned to get pregnant. But the second she told him, he threw his laptop aside and pulled her into his arms. They spun around and around the living room, Emily crying as he told her he was always going to be there; he'd never let her go. He was going to be the best father he possibly could. And he knew she was going to make an incredible mother.

Fine, they didn't have all the money in the world. But Liam had struck out on his own after working a few odd jobs over the years, training in a new career, and now he was finally starting to gain some traction. Emily worked in a call centre, which wasn't the fanciest job in the world, but she liked her colleagues and she was thinking about doing an online course on the side.

"Whatever happens," he'd told her, "we'll make it work. Our child will always know they're loved."

Once the pain had mostly passed, Liam climbed onto the bed. His belly rumbled. He hadn't eaten since the morning of the kidnapping. He'd been so anxious about asking Emily to marry him, he hadn't been able to stomach any food. He wasn't sure how long he could go before he was forced to cave and eat breakfast with Rebecca.

He thought about what she'd implied: she wanted them to develop some sort of relationship. He hadn't missed the anger when she sternly told him he didn't have a girlfriend.

So that was it then. He was a toy, a plaything for this crazy rich lady. Maybe this was her fetish or maybe there was something else going on. He couldn't afford to care. All he could think about was escape.

Their baby was due in a week... no, it would be five or so days now. If he didn't find a way out, he was going to miss the birth of his child.

CHAPTER FIVE

I knew Liam wasn't going to succumb to his situation easily. He was a tall strong man, six foot with wide shoulders, with short naturally spiky black hair and a dusting of black across his jaws. There was nothing effete about him whatsoever; everything was rugged, animalistic. So it made sense he'd growl and spit and smash the bars of his cage.

He'd been like a beast at the breakfast table, shattering those glasses. A spark of annoyance had touched me. I wanted certain parts of him to be beastly – his passion for me, his dedication, his protective instincts – but there was a time and place for such displays. But I felt certain he would learn his lesson.

Soon, we would begin our romance in earnest. He'd made some silly comments about having a girlfriend, but he was confused. He lived in a dingy flat with a mediocre-looking woman. She was frumpy, not at all stylish, with a vacant expression. And she worked in a call centre, I'd been told... what a miserable existence that must've been.

Liam would learn how much better his current position was. He had a beautiful, elegant woman willing to lavish her attentions on him, when the time was right. He was staying in a manor he never could've dreamed of before I'd chosen him. He was going through a natural transitional period, but with time he'd forget about his so-called girlfriend and his wretched former life.

This was it. I felt sure. I had found my Prince Charming.

Father would laugh if I phrased it in such terms. But it was the truth.

There is nothing purer and nobler than the search for true love. And, as any romantic knows, it is the rarest of things; a delicate flower which has to be plucked carefully, lest the thorns sting or the petals blow away in the wind. I was up to the challenge.

Materially speaking, I had everything a person could wish for, and yet I felt hollow, as though I was searching for something. Maybe, just maybe, Liam was that something.

I deserved happiness. I deserved to be complimented and adored, to be doted on and desired. I deserved a romance that would make others jealous – not that I'd tell anybody how our relationship began – and a finale that would end in love, not blood.

I deserved my happily ever after.

CHAPTER SIX

Hunger won.

Liam told himself he needed to keep his strength up; he wouldn't be able to fight his way back to Emily and their child if he starved. But maybe that was an excuse. Hunger cramps had started to make his belly tight. A few of his mates did intermittent fasting, where they sometimes went up to three days without food, but Liam had never tried it. His thoughts had started to fill with nothing but food. He dreamed of the pastries from the previous morning.

When Bretherton knocked on his door and told him to shower and get changed, he complied. But he'd only do what was necessary until his belly was full. And he would watch everybody, everything, waiting for an opportunity to escape.

His head swam as he stood under the shower, blasting himself with the highest pressure setting, turning the heat up. His body was a patchwork of pain, but he ignored it. His comfort didn't matter. It had been three days since they'd taken him; Emily would be driving herself crazy wondering what had happened.

At some point between Liam entering the en suite and

leaving it, Bretherton had unlocked his bedroom door. The butler offered a tight smile. "You look rather dashing, sir, if I may say so."

Liam had looked at himself in the mirror. His jaws were covered in a thickening black beard, his hair was messy. His eyes were like a caged animal's, waiting for his chance. "How kind of you."

"The lady is waiting. Shall we?"

"Sure."

Bretherton led the way and once again Liam thought about attacking the man and taking him hostage. But if they felt like they could leave him and the butler alone, that surely meant they didn't care if Liam hurt him. He must've been expendable.

"How long have you worked here?" Liam asked as they descended the giant staircase.

"A number of years."

"Do you like your work, kidnapping innocent men and forcing them to play messed-up games for messed-up rich ladies?"

Bretherton paused. "You should choose your words more carefully. That sort of talk will do you no favours."

"I guess they pay you double what you'd usually get. Or triple. And you pretend this is all okay."

"I merely serve the lady. It is not my place to pass judgement."

"Like a Nazi guard."

Bretherton shrugged. "If thinking of me like that makes it easier for you, then by all means... Shall we?"

Liam walked down the long corridor with the tall ceilings, towards the dining room. He'd purposefully remembered the way this time. They'd taken a right at the bottom of the stairs, and then another right, and the dining room was at the top left.

He wasn't sure if that knowledge would come in useful. But he had to remember everything.

Rebecca was once again sitting at the head of the table. The red light of the camera blinked, and angels and devils and a white-bearded God stared at them from above. Rebecca was wearing a sparkling white dress and a forgiving smile, like she was ready to give Liam a second chance. It made him feel like one of the dogs he trained.

His gaze moved to the pastries, his mouth watering. He dropped into the seat, grabbing the food with his hands and stuffing it into his mouth.

"It's a lovely morning, isn't it?" Rebecca chattered.

Liam chewed and swallowed quickly, ignoring her. Nothing else existed but the food. There were chocolate-flavoured ones, butter, and something with raisins in. He didn't care; he wolfed it all down, barely swallowing before stuffing another into his mouth.

"Did you look across the grounds? It's wonderful this time of year. The dew makes the whole world glisten."

Liam wasn't sure if he had it in him to take a woman hostage, but surely the guards must've known it was a risk. He had assumed Bretherton was expendable... but what about Rebecca? There was no cutlery, and this time the glasses were plastic and the plates were paper. But, as far as the guards knew, he might grab her and wrap his hands around her throat.

Something wasn't right. It was niggling at him.

"What do you think? Isn't it beautiful?"

Liam crushed the last pastry between his teeth. He took his plastic cup of orange juice and necked it. Sugar rushed around his body. He already felt stronger.

"Is there more?"

Rebecca glanced at the camera. She looked like she was

about to have a temper tantrum. "I'd love to be able to paint the garden, but I'm afraid I don't have the patience for it."

"Are you going to eat that?" Liam gestured at her plate, piled high with pastries.

"I, uh, I'm not sure."

"May I?"

Without waiting for an answer, Liam grabbed her plate and glass of orange juice. He pulled them over to him and started wolfing down more food. He didn't care if she wanted to prattle on; as long as the guards left him alone and he could fill his belly, he'd consider this morning a success.

Rebecca huffed. "I must say, you're not making for very good conversation."

He ate her food as quickly as he could, conscious he might not get another chance. Washing it down with her orange juice, he sat back.

Footsteps creaked behind them. Two guards had entered the room. Liam studied them; there was no way to recognise if one of them was the leader from before, the one who'd warned Liam to go along with this.

The threat was clear. He was going to have to talk to Rebecca, in the way she wanted, or they would hurt him again, maybe inject him. He assessed the men. Could he take them? Probably not. And even if he could, it didn't matter; there were more guards in the next room, he guessed, or waiting in the corridor.

"Have you ever tried your hand at painting?"

Hating himself – and silently telling Emily he was sorry – he shook his head. "Nope."

Rebecca's eyes lit up. *Good boy, oh what a good boy,* Liam imagined her thinking. "I was quite obsessed when I was a girl, but I'm afraid I didn't have the knack. It takes a certain inherent quality, doesn't it?"

"Sure."

"Do you have any artistic interests?"

"No, Emily sometimes does these paint-by-number—"

A fist smashed into the side of his head. Liam yelled and fell sideways, the chair slamming to the floor, his shoulder pulsing in agony. He groaned as hands grabbed him and hauled him upright, then the guard stepped away, leaving him to slump in his chair.

"I'm sorry." Rebecca narrowed her eyes. "I'd rather not talk about imaginary people."

He touched his cheek, winced. The bastard had sucker punched him. His fists clenched and the urge to do something boiled through him. But the pain was too much. It was like there was a golf ball lodged in his jaw.

"What do you think about the fresco?"

"The what?" Liam forced the words out.

Rebecca tittered. "The ceiling painting, silly. I think it's a little extravagant, but Father adores it."

"It's fine."

"What's fine about it?"

Liam had never hit a woman. But right then, he thought about it. She was enjoying this too much. "I like the detail." He probed at his jaw, cringing as a jolt bit sharply through him.

"Didn't your mother ever teach you not to touch your face during mealtimes?"

His hand dropped. It was a reflex. He was achingly aware of the guards standing right behind him. If they struck the same spot again, they'd do serious damage.

"That's better. I suppose a man like you is more into physical pursuits, hmm? If those muscles are any indication."

Invisible worms crawled over his skin. She was leering, showing her teeth, her eyes wide. He felt like a specimen in a zoo. "I try to go to the gym as often as I can. And sometimes I go to boxercise classes."

"Boxercise?"

"It's a circuit training boxing workout."

"How exciting. So you punch people?"

"No, not at the exercise class. You hit the mitts. You do push-ups. It's a good workout."

"I bet you're devilishly sweaty afterwards."

Her fingers were clawing across the table, as though she was going to hold his hand. He quickly placed his hands under the table, hoping the guards didn't take this as a sign of disrespect.

"I can imagine you now, your shirt stuck to your big strong body, all full of vim and testosterone."

"It's a good workout."

"You already said that," she snapped.

Liam waited; he didn't know what else to say. Rebecca drummed her fingers. "I think this has been quite lovely, don't you?"

Liam nodded.

"Don't you?" she pressed.

After a pause, he said, "Yes."

"Excellent. Yes, a vast improvement over your episode yesterday. I'm almost tempted to let you kiss me."

No, that was too much. Make some small talk, fine. But not that.

She sniggered as she stood. "But I'm a lady. I don't think it would be appropriate so soon."

She walked to the door, her heels clicking. Then she paused. "You might want to watch me leave, Liam. It's called flirting."

Liam turned in his chair and watched as she melodramatically swished her hips. She looked over her shoulder, pouting, like this was a big moment for her. Liam felt sick; he'd eaten the food too fast, and this performance wasn't making it any better.

"You did well, sir," Bretherton told him, when they were walking back up the stairs. "The lady seems most pleased."

"You know they don't care about you. I could drag you in there, smash the window, slit your throat with a shard of glass. They wouldn't care. Have you thought about that?"

Bretherton's eyes glimmered; it was like he was going to say something. Maybe he was going to agree with him. But then he sighed. "If you will, sir."

Liam walked into the room, the cell, and the butler locked the door behind him. Liam stood at the window and looked over the grounds. Rebecca was wrong. They weren't beautiful. They were ugly, too much emptiness. He would've taken his and Emily's one-bedroom flat any day.

CHAPTER SEVEN

L iam was bored.

He hadn't expected that, but with a full belly and once the pulsing in his jaw had stopped, the thought of spending all day locked in this room made him want to roar.

Emily always joked that Liam only had one gear: go, go, go. It was true. He liked to be active, to take Rocky on long walks... or he had, before the old dog started to slow down a little. But even then, he'd walk his auntie's German Shepherd and one of his neighbour's Dachshunds. He rarely allowed himself to slow down. He hated sitting still, with nothing but his own thoughts.

Lying in bed, he wondered what Emily was doing. He hoped she knew he hadn't left her. He hoped she knew he loved her, and he'd die before he abandoned her and their child. He wanted to hold her most of all, pull her close, inhale the scent of her hair.

In the afternoon, a knock came at the door. "Lunch, sir."

Liam walked across the room, tested the handle. They'd unlocked it while he was daydreaming.

Opening it, he took in the sight of Bretherton and the two guards. One of the guards was new. Taller than the rest, and there was something about his eyes... While the first stared at Liam like he hated him, the other looked at the floor. He seemed younger, though Liam couldn't have said what made him assume that.

Bretherton stepped forwards with a paper bag in his hand. Liam resisted the urge to lick his lips. It smelled like meat. "The lady thinks you deserve a treat. Isn't that nice?"

The guards were standing right there; he couldn't speak as freely as he had with Bretherton. And, really, talking openly to the butler was probably a mistake. "Yeah, very nice."

"She has requested your presence later this evening. She wishes to go bowling."

An outside trip? Surely they wouldn't be that stupid. But this was his chance. He'd go along with it, wait for his opportunity.

Bretherton frowned, as though reading Liam's thoughts. "Apologies, sir. That was poor phrasing on my part. We have a bowling alley here. The lady wishes to make use of it this evening." His hand tightened around the paper bag.

The message was obvious. Liam had to agree or he wouldn't get any lunch. "Then I guess I'm going bowling later."

Liam snatched the paper bag and returned to the bedroom. The door closed behind him and he tore the bag open. It was a rump steak, the juices seeping through the bag and dripping onto the floor. He grabbed it with his hands and tore into it with his teeth, telling himself with each bite he was doing this for Emily. Whatever he did, whatever games he had to play, it was all for his fiancée.

***

He'd hoped to get a better sense of the geography of the house when they took him to the bowling alley. But when Bretherton came to collect him later that day, he was joined by three guards. One ordered him to turn around so they could cuff his hands behind his back; another shoved a black bag over his head.

"You're making the right choice." It was the leader's voice, from the previous morning, deep and gravelly.

"It doesn't feel right."

"Enough chatter," Bretherton said. "The lady is waiting."

They frogmarched him down the hallway. They took him down a set of stairs, Liam focusing not to trip over. And then he lost all sense of direction.

They turned several times, entered and left half a dozen rooms, went up another set of stairs, through another door. And then, after what felt like around ten minutes, they removed the bag from his head.

Liam took in the scene. It was completely at odds with rest of the manor. They were in a windowless room, neon lights glowing blue, with two bowling lanes and a bowling-ball dispenser. His heart ached when a memory struck him, like a physical blow; one of his and Emily's earliest dates had been at a bowling alley.

The guards uncuffed him and Liam turned. Bretherton was gone. It was just the two guards. One was taller, the one Liam sensed was younger than the others. Liam purposefully stared at him, but the kid wouldn't meet his eye.

"We're going to be just over there." The leader gestured to a seating area at the rear of the room. "Remember your manners. The lady of the house will be here soon."

"Do you feel good about this, either of you?"

"There are cameras, and the room is bugged." The leader backed away to the chairs. Good, let them be wary. Just because he was playing nice, it didn't mean they'd beaten him.

Liam wandered over to the bowling alley. There was even a

screen with a scoreboard. Liam and Rebecca's names had already been added.

"Sorry I'm late." Rebecca closed the door before Liam had a chance to see the corridor. She'd changed from earlier, hair freshly styled, wearing black trousers and a suit jacket.

Liam might've felt self-conscious about his body odour and his bad breath – they hadn't given him deodorant or toothpaste – but he wanted to be as disgusting to her as possible. He wanted her to leave him alone.

She approached. "Have you been waiting long?"

"No."

"I bet it's been horribly tempting to start without me."

"Nope."

"You aren't getting grumpy with me, are you? Bowling is supposed to be fun."

Liam bared his teeth in an intended smile. "I'm ready."

"Excellent. Oh, and look. It seems I'm going first."

From the way she hefted the bowling ball, Liam could tell they were real. Which meant they either trusted Liam not to cave her head in before the guards could reach him, or they didn't care if he did. But of course they cared; they were doing everything in their power to make him satisfy this lunatic. It had to be that they didn't think he'd hurt her.

When he and Emily had gone on their bowling date, it had been the most fun he'd had in months. She'd danced up to the lane every time, shooting him enticing looks, and Liam had grinned as her ball rolled into the gutter. "It's not fair. We should've put the barriers up." He'd kissed her cheek softly, jokingly telling her to stop complaining.

"Liam." Rebecca was standing close. "It's your turn."

He hadn't even realised she'd taken hers. The mechanism was clearing away her remaining pins and replacing them with ten new ones. She'd scored a seven.

Liam grabbed a bowling ball. It was heavy, and he wondered if he could take the two guards with it. The leader would be the biggest problem. And there was the matter of not knowing if they had weapons. Those cargo trousers they wore had big pockets. They could have pistols, tasers, maybe police batons. And they had the syringes; he couldn't let them drug him again.

He threw the ball and scored a strike. Rebecca tittered and clapped her hands. "Oh, what a lark this is."

A lark. Bloody hell.

They played for a while and Liam did his best to play his role. But every time she met his eye, he wanted to spit in her face. It was the way she was looking at him. *See, it's not hard to be a good boy, is it? It's not hard to do as you're told.*

She reminded him of a client he'd worked with once, a woman who was determined that her whippet was beyond training. She'd told him – with a note of pride – that her dog was too wild to do as he was told. Liam had assured her he would try his best, and, after an hour of solo time, he'd returned to the woman's house with the dog already calmer, more receptive, and ready for the next session.

The woman's cheeks had coloured when she saw how patiently her dog sat on the doorstep. "I suppose you want a medal, do you?"

After dragging the dog inside, she'd slammed the door in Liam's face. Liam had ranted about it to Emily for days afterwards. "Some people don't want to help their pets. They just want to be told they're beyond help, so they can play the victim. So they can tell themselves they did everything they could. But it's bullshit."

Liam hated bullshit. He hated pretending.

Rebecca threw her hands up when she scored a strike, giddy

as she skipped over to Liam. She moved to wrap her arms around him in a celebratory hug.

He didn't think. He stepped back, raised his palms, not touching her but keeping a distance.

"Rude." She tried again, and Liam stepped back. "Why are you being so silly? I just scored my first strike!"

"I know. Well done."

She stepped close, and Liam moved away again. They were doing a strange dance.

"You're embarrassing me. Didn't you see? I feel like you've been somewhere else for the whole game. But you *must've* seen. I scored a strike."

How many times was she going to say that?

"I saw. And I said well done."

"But you won't give me a simple hug."

Behind him, the guards rose to their feet. He heard the rustling of their clothes. Footsteps approached him. Liam tried to make himself embrace her; it was a simple enough thing, like she'd said. All he had to do was wrap his arms around her body, squeeze for a moment, then let her go.

The pause lengthened. Rebecca lowered her voice. "Please."

The desperation seemed more human than anything she'd said yet. He almost felt sorry for her. He was being an idiot. He knew that. If Emily were here, she'd tell him to go through the motions so he could return to her.

"No."

Rebecca marched from the room and slammed the door. Liam watched the guards, hovering a few feet away. The lanky one was all jittery energy, foot tapping, hand opening and closing.

A radio buzzed from the leader's pocket. He took it out and pressed the button. "Yeah?"

"The lady has a request." The voice was crackly, but Liam felt sure it was Bretherton. "Cell."

The leader nodded, replacing the walkie and glaring at Liam. "You're an idiot. Why didn't you just hug her?"

"Cell, what does that mean?"

But Liam could guess easily enough what it meant. They were going to take him to a prison of some sort. He looked around, judged the distance between him and the nearest bowling ball.

"Fight if you want. It won't make any difference. There are half a dozen guards waiting outside that door. You've got a choice. Come with us and spend the next few days shitting in a bucket... or spend the next few days shitting in a bucket, with a few broken bones and a concussion to go with it."

Liam wasn't a coward. At least he hoped he wasn't. But what was the point in attacking these two men? He'd already learned what would happen. He knew the leader wasn't lying.

"I guess I'll take option one."

"Good. Turn around. We need to cuff you."

CHAPTER EIGHT

They handcuffed him, put a black bag over his head, and frogmarched him through the house. Liam did his best to act like none of this was bothering him, but the word *cell* was bouncing painfully around his mind, along with the head guard's words about shitting in a bucket.

They walked up and down a set of stairs, along what must've been a long corridor, and then down another flight of stairs. He felt cool air on his face as they took him outside, their footsteps squishing in wet grass. And then they were inside again, walking along another corridor. From the way the guards were holding him, Liam sensed this one was narrower than the last. Were they underground?

Whatever happened, he wouldn't let them see how badly this was messing him up. He couldn't let them know he felt like crying; he forced the tears away, told himself to get his act together. He wasn't going to break. He thought about Emily. She'd been his rock ever since they'd started going out.

A heavy rasping sound let him know a metal door was being opened. The sound stopped, and the guards pushed him inside.

They removed the bag and Liam blinked in the harsh white lights. He was standing in a windowless cell, the walls bare stone, with a plastic bucket in the corner and one roll of toilet paper.

As one of the guards fiddled with his handcuffs, Liam couldn't hold it back any longer. "Don't leave me here. Please."

"Hurry up, lad."

It was the leader's voice; he was talking to the tall one. He'd said lad. That meant Liam was right. He was younger than the others. Liam was thirty-one, and he sensed that the tall guard was younger than him, though this was a feeling rather than anything concrete.

"Please," Liam whispered, wishing he didn't sound so pathetic, so helpless.

The cuffs came away and his hands were freed. He spun. The lanky guard took several quick steps back, standing in the doorway with the leader.

"You should've hugged her," the guard said, in a boyish voice.

"Come on." The leader grabbed the other guard's arm and led him from the room.

The door slammed shut. It was metal, like Liam had guessed. It looked thick and sturdy. Liam paced the cell. It was smaller than the boiler room in their flat; he could cross it in six big steps. They hadn't left him a blanket or a pillow or anything, just the bucket and the toilet roll.

He thought about pounding on the door. He thought about roaring at them to let him go. But there was no point. He was learning that whatever Rebecca wanted, they gave her, and she'd ordered him to be brought here. A few days, the leader had said, but was that a guess? What if it was longer?

Slumping against the wall, Liam sat as gently as he could,

careful because of his injuries. That was the only reason he hadn't fought, he assured himself; he couldn't keep giving them reasons to hurt him. As it was, he was doing okay. His body was a little sore from the fighting. His head was still aching. His mouth was the worst, feeling disjointed after the sucker punch.

With nothing to do, Liam closed his eyes, steadied his breathing. Tears tried to break through his resolve and he quickly beat them down. He'd never been much of a crier, but this was turning into hell. He didn't let himself think about the moment when he'd have to use the bucket.

With the light always on, it was impossible to tell how much time had passed. But it had clearly been a few hours. The fact he was awkwardly squatting over the bucket with his trousers around his knees was evidence of that. He wiped and then dropped the dirty toilet roll into his mess. He'd already had a piss, and that wasn't too bad. But this was awful. The stink of it, the fact of it.

When he was done, he went to the opposite corner. It made no difference. The stench followed him. He gagged and closed his eyes, dreaming he was someplace else. He was with Emily, in the pub with her mum and dad. It was the day after they'd learned about the pregnancy.

Emily's mum had a big glowing smile on her face. She'd been dropping jokey hints for years about when they were going to start a family. It wasn't like they didn't have time. Emily was twenty-eight when they'd learned she was pregnant. But now the moment had come, and all of them were grinning like loons, so happy they could burst.

The guards came twice per day to give him a tray of food

and empty his bucket. At least, Liam assumed it was twice per day. He tried counting the hours, but he grew tired after three minutes. The first meal was a plate of pastries or toast, so Liam marked that as breakfast. The second was meat and potatoes and vegetables, so that must've been dinner; they never gave him any cutlery. He scooped peas into his dirty hands and into his mouth. He gnawed on lamb or steak, relieved they weren't starving him.

When the guards entered, they told Liam to stand on the other side of the room and face the wall. Several times he debated fighting them. But it was so obviously pointless. He should've taken Rebecca hostage when he had the chance. When he got out of here, that was what he'd do; he'd wrap his arm across her throat and use her as a human shield, moving across the estate, until he came to an exit.

But was there a wall around the estate? He hadn't been able to tell from his bedroom window.

Why hadn't Liam just hugged her?

That was a question he asked himself time and time again. Using the meals as a marker, he judged three days had passed since they'd brought him here. Three days in a cell, not being able to sleep because the light glared too brightly, and all because he hadn't been able to hug her for a second.

In his younger years, he'd flitted from relationship to relationship, or one-night stand to one-night stand. In those days, being physically intimate with strangers hadn't meant anything to him. He'd gone to nightclubs specifically to hook up with women he didn't know. But once he found Emily, the idea of touching another woman repulsed him. It was Liam and Emily, forever; he didn't need or want anybody else.

They'd been together for six years and he wanted to be with her for sixty.

He kept thinking about what he'd want Emily to do in similar circumstances. If some rich psycho kidnapped her and ordered her to hug him, Liam would tell her to do it. He'd hate it. He'd make it his life's mission to hunt the bastard down and hurt him. But he'd still tell her to do it.

His back was aching from the hard stone floor. His shoulders were burning from trying to find a comfortable position. The room stank, even after they replaced the bucket. The odour lingered, got into Liam's clothes, his hair, everything.

On day four – if he was right about breakfast and dinner – he realised something. It was Emily's due date. She was out there somewhere, ready to give birth to their child. Due dates weren't completely accurate, and maybe he had some time. But how long? And if it was correct, it meant he was going to miss his child's birth, little Jamie or Hazel; he'd always be the man who wasn't there when his fiancée and his child needed him.

Whatever happened, he couldn't stay there much longer. His lack of sleep was making him feel raw, exposed. His mind went over the smallest incidents and made them massive. He remembered when Emily had come home drunk one night, stumbling into bed. She'd prodded him, giggling. "*Liiiiaaaaaam,* can you give me a hug?"

Liam had been in a bad mood. It was before he'd started his dog training business and he had just finished a double shift at the warehouse. He'd pretended to be asleep, silently wishing for her to shut up and leave him alone. He didn't want to argue. But he didn't want to hold her either.

In the cell, with nothing else to think about, he remembered it over and over, how angry he'd been with her, how sulky the next day, even if it wasn't her fault he was in a job he hated. He tried to direct his fitful dreams to that night so he could fix it.

He'd roll over, he'd laugh with her; he'd hold her.

He had a plan. Get out of here, act like they'd broken him –

which they hadn't; they never would – and get his hands on Rebecca. They clearly weren't expecting him to go to such extremes. He'd have the element of surprise.

Next time the metal door whined open, Liam stood facing the guards. He didn't recognise them. He'd been hoping for the lanky kid, or maybe the leader; they seemed more human than the others. But this would have to do.

"Tell her I'm sorry. Tell her I want to make it up to her."

It was difficult to be sure with the balaclava covering his mouth, but Liam thought he saw the man smile; the material shifted in a certain telling way.

Instead of entering the room, cuffing him, and then collecting the bucket, the man shut the door.

"Will you tell her?" Liam ran over to the door, slamming his fist against it. He'd assumed they'd take him at once. "Tell her I'm sorry!"

There was no reply. He slumped to the floor.

But then, a while later, a voice came from the other side of the door. It was Bretherton. "Sir, I think you're making an excellent decision. The lady wishes you to remain in here a day longer. But tomorrow, you will be allowed to shower and groom yourself. And at your next meeting – these are her words, sir – you're going to be a good boy, aren't you?"

Liam cringed, but reminded himself this was part of the plan. "Yes."

"Sir, she is listening on the walkie-talkie. Can you please speak louder? And she would like you to use her specific phrasing."

"She wants me to tell her I'll be a good boy?"

"That's right."

Liam's hand flew up instinctively. He was going to pound his fist against the wall. At the last second, he stopped himself. Any outbursts might result in another day, week, month. Year.

47

He breathed as steadily as he could. "I will, tell her I will."

"Sir..."

He thought of Emily, of her drunken giggle, of her warm body pressed against his back. Raising his voice, he spit the words out. "Tell her I'll be a good boy."

CHAPTER NINE

I was proud of Liam for finally seeing things my way. Proceedings would be far nicer from now on. He would engage in the process enthusiastically, and when I offered myself to him, he'd realise how much better I was than the slut he'd spent far too long living with. I knew she was a slut because I'd had Father's men do some digging before they brought Liam here.

Through a series of posts on social media, it was revealed that Emily Taylor had been a complete whore in her youth. She'd spent her teenage years drinking and hanging around with boys in parks; in one photo, she had one arm around one boy as another kissed her on the cheek, and she stared at the camera, smiling like a moron: *Look at me, I'm going to get gang-banged in a dingy park by a bunch of reprobates who'll forget I exist in a few days.*

Liam wasn't educated in the ways of the world. He didn't understand how much better a lady like me was. I'd had a few dalliances over the years, fine, but I would never degrade myself the way she had. Even more recently – when she and Liam were supposedly in a relationship – there were photos of her dressed like a prostitute, her face plastered in make-up as she posed in a nightclub.

Liam deserved a romance, to adopt the role of a suitor, to know what it meant to chastely kiss and to nervously make love and to tenderly embrace afterwards. He didn't want a skank who'd spread her legs for anybody.

One day, we would look back on these days and laugh. As I curled up in his arms and our precious babies played in the light of the crackling fire, he'd thank me for showing him how much better life could be. We'd make jokes about this Emily woman. "I can't believe I was ever with her," he'd say.

"I know, my love. But you didn't know any better."

"But still..."

His fingers would make tickling patterns across my scalp, sending starry reverberations through my body.

"She was a whore. I should've known it from the start. And she was so common, so basic. There was nothing exceptional about her whatsoever."

He would see. I knew it. He was going to be a good boy from now on.

CHAPTER TEN

Three guards waited in the bedroom as Liam guided the razor across his jaw. He winced as the blade probed the place he'd been hit a few days ago... no, almost a week ago. Time had done strange things in the stone cell. He could still smell the reek of shit and piss, and he flinched every time the floorboards whined outside the en suite's door.

He looked terrible. His eyes were sunken and his skin looked faded, maybe from lack of sunlight. The scraggly facial hair didn't fit with his face. He rarely let his beard grow beyond stubble, and he felt cleaner once he'd shaved it all away, even if it left him looking boyish and vulnerable.

A guard pounded on the door. "What's taking so long?"

He hadn't recognised any of the three who'd dragged him from the cell back to his room, with a black bag over his head. The lanky kid and the leader weren't there; maybe they were out in the world someplace, finding more innocent men to kidnap and drag back to this nightmare.

"I thought she wanted me to take a shower," Liam said.

"Just hurry up. And don't do anything stupid with that razor."

It took a moment for Liam to understand what he meant. They thought he was a suicide risk. That was never going to happen. No matter what they did to him, he'd never lose hope. He'd always remember Emily.

No, of course it wasn't that. They didn't give a shit what happened to him. They just didn't want him using it as a weapon against that madwoman.

After showering, he wrapped himself in a towel and knocked on the door. "I need my clothes."

The guard grunted and pushed the door open, a hand snaking around the edge, clasping a hanger with a suit draping from it. Liam studied the hand. He could slam the door: shatter the wrist. But then they'd run in here, beat him, and throw him back in the cell. He took the suit and got dressed.

After taking the razor, they left him in the room, informing him he'd be having lunch with Rebecca. He had to be smart about this. He'd make her believe she'd broken him, and then, when her defences were down, he'd get his hands on her. He wouldn't hurt her, but he'd make the guards believe he would.

The bed felt softer than he could believe. He lay back and closed his eyes, the mattress soothing the aches the hard floor of the cell had driven into him.

A dreamless sleep carried him away, and he woke to a hammering on the door.

"Sir," Bretherton called. "It is time for lunch with the lady."

Liam climbed out of bed. "I'm ready."

"Excellent. The lady wishes to dine on the balcony, which I'm afraid necessitates the need for certain measures."

"What?" Liam wished the man could just speak simply.

"We cannot let you learn the geography of the house. You understand."

"You want to put a black bag over my head again."

"That's correct."

He almost made a sarcastic comment, but then he remembered the guards' walkie-talkies, and how word might get back to Rebecca. "That's fine. I'm just looking forward to seeing Becky."

She'd said her friends called her Becky; Liam needed her to believe he was a friend.

"Excellent. Face the wall and put your hands behind your back."

Liam did as he was told, wondering if this was what it felt like after a week in prison. It was starting to feel far too routine. But it was only for a little longer. Grab Rebecca, use her as a human shield, drag her past the trees and to whatever was beyond: force them to open a gate if there was one. And then run.

After cuffing him and pulling the bag over his head, they frogmarched him through the building. He didn't bother to track where he was going this time. There was no use. The route made no sense, as they looped back on themselves, went in and out of rooms for seemingly no reason; they were purposefully disorienting him, he guessed, and it worked.

He blinked in the midday sun when they pulled the bag off. He was standing on a large balcony, overlooking the rear of the house; at least he assumed it was the rear. This place was so massive, it could've been a side area. Long lawns stretched towards a pond, and past that, tall conifers blocked the horizon. Liam tried to make out the distance: hills, motorways, anything that would give him a sense of where he was. But this place was like its own universe.

"So nice of you to join me." Rebecca smiled up at him from the table, pastries and juice laid out in front of her. The plates were paper again, the cups plastic.

His plan had a fatal flaw. He had no idea where he was in the house, and there were no weapons to use. He would have preferred to be in the dining room; he knew his way to the front door from there.

She stared at him expectantly, this lunatic in a zip-up autumn jacket, a brand name over the chest, her hands wrapped around a paper cup of steaming coffee.

"I was happy you asked to see me." Liam made himself say the words. "Is there any more of that?"

Her smile made Liam want to throw her off the balcony. It was a second storey one, and the drop probably wouldn't kill her. Which made Liam wonder if he should jump. Maybe this was the best chance he'd get. But without Rebecca as a hostage, there was nothing to stop the guards from hunting him down. He decided to wait for a better opportunity. He'd only get one chance.

"Bretherton," she called over her shoulder. "Please get the good boy a cup of coffee, would you?"

The area beyond the glass looked like some sort of living room, with a piano and tall bookshelves. Bretherton hovered close and, just behind him, two guards stood, cold eyes staring from their balaclavas.

"Please, sit." Rebecca waved a hand at the chair opposite.

Liam dropped into it.

"You might want to ask me how I've been." Rebecca stared. "Since the embarrassment in the bowling alley."

He fought his every instinct, forcing himself to ask the question.

She huffed melodramatically, placing her cup down. "Not well, in all honesty. I was so hurt by your rejection. I thought we were having a fantastic time. It was so fun. And when you refused me a simple hug, it was like you weren't at all interested. But you are, aren't you?"

"Yes. I am. I was just confused."

He silently apologised to Emily, but he knew she'd want

54

him to do this. He had to if he was ever going to see her again. Eight days, by his count; that was how long it'd been since they'd kidnapped him. Emily was either in labour or recovering from labour. His child might already be in the world.

"Confused like when you said you had a girlfriend? That sort of confused?"

The balcony door opened and Bretherton laid the cup down, backing away quickly, as though not wanting to intrude on this tender scene.

"I was confused," Liam said.

"About what?"

Wasn't that enough? But no. She needed him to say it.

"About having a girlfriend."

She nodded. "It was such a strange thing to say. We're both looking for love."

"Yes, we're both looking for love."

Grabbing his coffee, he knocked half of it back in one gulp, not caring when it scalded his tongue and burned down his throat. The caffeine flooded into him, pumping through his veins. His head rushed. He normally drank at least three mugs a day, but he hadn't had any since coming here.

Rebecca giggled when he finished the rest of it. "You eager boy. So, Liam, tell me about yourself."

He stifled a groan. "What would you like to know?"

"Everything. I think that's a good place to start."

"That might take a while."

"Have you got somewhere to be?" she snapped.

"No, I was just saying." He flinched when her tone changed. If the guards heard their lady displeased, maybe they'd run out here again. "I was born to pretty regular parents. My dad cheated on my mum when I was twelve, and they split up. I lived with my mum, and I left home at eighteen. I lived with a few mates and worked a bunch of odd jobs. I..."

I met Emily, he was about to say, but he quickly moved on.

"I decided to become a dog trainer and I've worked as one ever since."

"How interesting. Why a dog trainer?"

"I've always loved dogs. When I was a teenager, I got this dog, Rocky. He was six months and I'm sure he'd been abused in his early life. He was so scared of everything. I helped train him out of that. Later, when I was sharing a house with my mates, he lived with my mum. But when I..."

When I moved in with Emily.

"When I got my own place, I brought him with me."

"You must have a kind and loving spirit." She reached across the table, fingers searching for his. "Perfect father material, some might say."

Was she head-fucking him? Did she know Emily was pregnant?

Her fingers met with his. Liam cringed, but then he held hands with her. Her touch was cold and clammy.

"What about you?" Liam asked.

She tightened her hold. "What *about* me?"

Liam grinned. It hurt his cheeks. "I've given you my whole life story, basically. What about yours?"

"Oh, it's terribly boring. And you're going to have to work a lot harder to get inside my head... and other places, if you're lucky."

Nope. He'd rather stick his dick in a woodchipper. "Fair enough."

"Let's eat and enjoy the view."

She removed her hand, and thankfully she seemed okay with eating in silence. Liam was careful not to shovel the food down. He needed to seem civilised.

She stood once they were done. Liam quickly followed suit.

"I think this has been rather lovely, don't you?"

He nodded, ordering his legs to stay still as she approached. Her perfume washed over him. It smelled worse than his cell had. It repulsed him.

"I've got half a mind to let you give me a kiss. How would you feel about that?"

His hands tried to clench into fists; his lips tried to shape into a sneer. He fought it all. "I'd consider myself a very lucky man."

"Oh, *you*." She turned her face to the side. "Only on the cheek. You haven't quite earned the real thing yet. But you're getting close."

Liam leaned down and pressed his lips against her skin, and then stepped back.

She narrowed her eyes, as though she hadn't deemed it passionate enough.

"I don't want to get carried away," he said quickly.

"You really are a wild man, aren't you?"

After dragging her fingers along his chest – digging her nails through his shirt, against his skin, in what Liam guessed was supposed to be a sexy way – she headed for the door.

Liam let out a long breath. He'd made progress, even if it sickened him.

CHAPTER ELEVEN

B ack in his room, Liam was thinking about the first time he and Emily had viewed their flat. It was a private rental and he knew the landlord through a friend; he was okay with Rocky living there. "But if he pisses on the floor, you owe me a new carpet."

Liam had agreed, too exhilarated at this new chapter of his life to care. The place wasn't fancy by any means: one bedroom, an adjoined kitchen and living room, and a small bathroom and boiler cupboard. The wallpaper was faded in places and the carpet looked like it had been there since the nineties. But it was theirs.

They'd worked hard to make it a home. Liam had replaced the wallpaper and rented a carpet cleaner, and Emily had taken a trip to the shopping centre with her mum, returning with several canvas paintings, ornaments, cushions, and little knickknacks Liam never would've thought to get: a dog-themed toilet roll dispenser, a wooden bread bin with a motivational quote carved across the front, an antique-look bowl for their keys.

They were saving for a mortgage, but it was tough these

days, especially with Liam trying to get his dog training career off the ground. But lately he'd made something of a name for himself in the local community; clients sought him out, instead of the other way around. His Facebook page had over three thousand likes.

They were well on their way to the future they both wanted, and the baby had sped matters up. Their savings were almost enough for a deposit on a modest property. Little Jamie or Hazel would have to stay in Liam and Emily's bedroom for a year or so, but after that, they'd be able to move into a place all their own.

He missed Emily so badly it hurt. Rolling over in bed, he closed his eyes and willed himself to fall asleep, so he could disappear into dreams. But the caffeine was still buzzing around his body.

Later, a knock came at the door. "Sir, the lady has asked if you have any special requests for dinner. She seems most pleased with you, and thinks you deserve a treat."

A treat. Like the good boy he was.

This was a chance.

"Can I have a rump steak? Cooked rare. I like it chewy."

They'd forced him to eat steak and lamb and other meats with his hands, both in his bedroom and the cell, but surely they wouldn't want Rebecca to see him like that. Was it possible they'd give him a steak knife? If they were eating in the dining room, that meant Liam would know the quickest route to the front door.

"Very good. I will collect you when it's time."

A while later – hours, Liam guessed, but it was difficult to gauge – Bretherton knocked on the door again.

There were no guards as the butler led him down the stairs, past the paintings and the locked doors, the dead eyes of the bear staring when they reached the dining room.

Liam's belly dropped when he entered the room. It was good and bad.

There were real plates on the tables, with a sharp steak knife laid next to his regular cutlery. The bad news was there were five guards standing at various places in the room, all of them watching as he made his way over to his chair. He recognised the tall kid; he was shifting from foot to foot, as though he felt as caged as Liam.

The nearest guard was behind Liam, but several paces away. Liam would have enough time to grab the knife and leap across the table: get his hands on Rebecca, hold the serrated edge of the blade to her throat, and roar at the guards that he'd kill her if they tried to intervene. Yet something was niggling at him. One lunch where he'd said and done what she wanted, and now she was willing to give him a weapon?

That was fear talking; that was the thought of the cell and the stink of the bucket and the simple fact he didn't want to be hit again. His child was out in the world, waiting for him. Emily needed him.

"I hope you don't mind the company," Rebecca said. "It's an unfortunate necessity. But I'm sure, one day very soon, we can dine more privately."

"I understand. My behaviour hasn't been the best. But I hope I can prove how much I've changed, Becky."

She giggled, smoothing a hand over her bob of blonde hair, as though putting a strand back in place. But her hair was flawless, cold and clinical. "You're so lovely. Where has *this* Liam been hiding?"

"I guess I needed some encouragement."

"Let's not make a habit of it."

"I think we can agree on that."

She rested her chin on her clasped hands. "I'm so pleased you've decided to do away with all that silliness. I was starting to think you weren't attracted to me."

She wasn't an ugly woman. She had an athletic build and her hair was neat and she wore carefully applied make-up. If he'd seen her in a nightclub back in the day, he knew she'd appeal to him. But he wasn't attracted to her. She wasn't Emily; she was making him say and do things he didn't want to say and do. He hated her.

"Of course I'm attracted to you."

She beamed. "Oh, really?"

"Yes." He swallowed. His throat was dry. "Really."

"What's my best feature then?"

Behind him, the guard shifted. Liam wondered if the motherfuckers were silently laughing. Maybe they had barracks where they all made jokes about him.

"Your eyes. They're the sort a man could get lost in."

She ate it up eagerly. "How lovely."

"So, have you had a nice day?"

"I've been trying to paint the grounds. But like I mentioned before, I'm woefully inept."

"I'm sure you're not giving yourself enough credit."

"Perhaps I'll paint you one of these days, and you can see how truly dreadful I am. Wouldn't that be a lark?"

A lark. There was that word again. It sounded ridiculous, so high-pitched and posh, like she was playing a role. But Liam had never been around many upper-class people; maybe this was just how they talked.

"I doubt you could make me any uglier," he joked.

She frowned. "You're not ugly. You're a very handsome man."

"Thank you." Liam eyed the steak knife. "That means a lot."

There was a pause, and she stared meaningfully.

"You're very beautiful, Becky."

"What a delightful thing to say! A compliment as a starter. Could a lady ask for more? I heard you asked for steak for dinner. Bloody and chewy, you said. That's rather animalistic."

"Maybe there's a little animal in me."

"I bet there's more than a little."

She laughed in that annoying way, like she was so pleased with how things were going: like they were having one hell of a *lark*.

"Are you hungry?" she asked.

"Very."

"Then let's eat."

He needed to stop delaying. She must've known there was a risk of him grabbing the knife, hence the guards, but he guessed she didn't think he'd attack her. Otherwise they would've been standing closer, or she would've refused his request for steak.

"Becky, can I tell you a secret?"

Her eyes widened. Excitement, fear? It looked like a combination of both. But he couldn't work out why she'd be scared, unless she thought he might hurt her... in which case, he was back to his original problem. They'd given him the knife.

"A secret?" she murmured.

"Yeah, just something for me and you. I don't want the... our company to hear."

He'd been about to say *the guards*, but he guessed she wouldn't like that. She wanted to believe he'd chosen to be here.

She glanced at the camera in the corner, red light blinking. Liam wondered who was watching. She'd mentioned her father before, when they were discussing the ceiling painting. Maybe it was him. Turning her gaze back to Liam, she said, "If you insist..."

She leaned close. Liam did the same, subtly moving his

hand nearer to the steak knife. Soon she was bent across the table, head twisted, offering him her ear.

He moved quickly, wrapping one hand around her wrist and his other gripping the handle of the knife. He leapt to his feet and dragged her after him, into the corner of the room, as the guards yelled and pounded towards him with heavy footsteps.

Liam spun and brought the point of the knife to her throat. He pressed his forearm against her chest, trapping her. She was panting like she was about to have a panic attack. Liam pushed away any guilt, any pity, anything other than survival instinct.

The guards gathered a few feet away, exchanging glances.

"I'm leaving." Liam pushed the knife a little harder against Rebecca's throat, but he was careful not to break the skin. He wished she'd stop whimpering and blubbering. "I don't want to hurt her, but I will if you force me. Get out of my way. Now. I'm not messing around."

CHAPTER TWELVE

"I did everything you asked."

Liam froze when Rebecca spoke, pushing past her sobs. Her voice sounded completely different. She'd been posh in the extreme before: a bad impression. Now she was suddenly transformed into a regular woman, with a London accent. Her tone was far deeper than it had been just a minute ago.

"Please don't let him hurt me. Please. I did *everything*."

"What are you talking about?" The knife suddenly felt foolish in his hand. The guards were still exchanging glances, as though waiting to be told what to do.

"Don't hurt me, Liam. Please."

"I don't understand."

"I'm a prisoner, like you. I'm sorry for all the things they've done to you and I'm sorry you feel like you have to do this, but please, believe me, it won't make it any better."

"Why are you talking like that?" His head felt slow and cloudy. It had taken a lot for him to lay his hands on a woman, and now it seemed he'd read the situation wrong. Her words finally slammed into him. "You're a prisoner too."

"Yes! So you see, if you hurt me–"

"This is a trick. You planned this. If I hurt you, put on a fake voice, feed me some horseshit, and I'd let you go. It's not going to work."

"I was using a fake voice before, not now."

"What should we do?" the younger guard said.

"Quiet." It was the leader, his gravelling voice unmistakable.

"But he's—"

"I believe he told you to be quiet, young man." A woman spoke through the walkie-talkie. She sounded breathy, sleepy almost, like this was a boring chore. "He's waiting for my instructions. Well, big boy, here they are: take Liam and return him to his chair."

"But what if he hurts Becky?" The kid's voice trembled.

"He won't. He doesn't have it in him. Do as you're told. I won't ask again."

The kid made to speak, but the leader grabbed him by the shoulder and shook him harshly. "Fan out, lads. We'll surround him and approach from all angles." He turned to Liam. "You're not going to hurt her, are you? Realistically speaking, you're not going to slit a woman's throat, especially since it'll get you nothing."

"He's not going to hurt me," Rebecca whimpered. "Are you? Please."

Liam felt her attempting to turn, but it was impossible with his arm across her middle. He felt his grip relaxing on the knife. He didn't know what to do; his plan had turned to shit. The entire thing relied on the guards caring that he had the lady of the house, but apparently Rebecca wasn't important at all. The woman's voice over the walkie... was she the *real* lady of the house?

But it was also possible he'd been right. This was a trick. That woman on the walkie was somebody they'd hired just in case he tried anything like this.

He backed against the wall, dragging Rebecca with him, putting himself in the corner so they couldn't surround him. Applying more pressure with the knife, he bared his teeth, staring at the guards as they slowly approached. "Stay where you are. I mean it. I'll kill her."

"They don't care if you kill me." Rebecca wriggled against him. "Don't you get it? I'm nothing to them, just like you."

The guards were relentless. Liam spun Rebecca, using her as a human shield as he stared them down, but they kept coming; it happened almost like they'd rehearsed it. One guard approached from the right and one from the left.

Soon they were so close Liam had to make a choice. Let them grab him or go through with it, kill this woman, who may or may not truly be his captor.

The guards reached out, one for his knife hand and the other for his shoulder. The other three stood directly in front of him, fingers twitching. The tall one stared, his dark brown eyes filled with misery.

"You're not going to hurt her," the leader said, staring past Rebecca at Liam. "But maybe you're thinking about attacking us. It's true, you'd be able to get a few good shots in. But you won't get us all. And the worse you hurt us, the worse it'll be for you. What's it going to be?"

A guard's hand was on his wrist, carefully pulling the knife away. The other gripped his arm and pulled on him. Liam let it happen. He wasn't going to kill anybody, especially not a woman. And the leader was right; if he lashed out now and cut one of the guards, they'd drag him back to the cell, maybe for another week, or a month. He couldn't risk it.

Rebecca fell away from him, collapsing against a guard and sobbing. Another guard guided Liam back to his chair and forced him to sit. He felt detached, like he was watching everything unfold.

"Thank you." Rebecca rubbed tears from her cheeks, gazing around at the guards. "I'm sorry. I know I shouldn't have said anything. But I was so scared, and... and..." She started sobbing again, burying her face in her hands.

Liam studied her, his thoughts spinning. She didn't look like she was faking it. Which meant somebody had forced her to pretend to be his kidnapper. But why? He sighed and laid his elbows on the table, resting his face in his hands, groaning as the full magnitude of the situation hit him. He'd ruined his one chance.

A weird calm came over the room. Rebecca slumped against the wall, crying, as the lanky kid offered his arm for her to lean on. Three guards stood with their hands crossed in front of them. The leader was gathering the cutlery at the far end of the giant table; he'd collected it when Liam had been wasting time, sighing and groaning, feeling sorry for himself. Now all his weapons were gone.

The door creaked open. A woman walked into the room. She was thin, wearing a dress that hung from her shoulders and went right down to her knees. Her hair was black and straight. She wasn't wearing any shoes, making her seem feral somehow; it matched the look in her eyes as she stood at the far end of the table, gripping the back of a chair.

"Miss, we've collected all the potential weapons."

"Yes, I can see that. Excellent job, Smith."

The leader was called Smith; Liam stowed that piece of information away. "What's happening? Are you the *real* lady of the house? What's going on?"

"You do love your questions. This was a rehearsal. I wanted you to accept the realities of your situation before I introduced myself. But *this* naughty ducky spoiled everything." She turned to Rebecca. "And she's still blubbing. What a mess."

"I'm sorry." Rebecca shrugged the young guard's hand away.

"Miss, I didn't mean to. But I was so scared and I thought he was going to kill me and..."

"Hush, it's okay." The woman opened her arms, pulling Rebecca into a hug. "You don't have to apologise. We all make mistakes."

"You said I could never break character. I promise I didn't mean to."

"Shhh." The woman stroked Rebecca's hair, staring at Liam over her shoulder, an odd smile peeling across her face. It stretched wider and wider, until she looked almost comical. "Smith, be a dear and fetch me a knife."

Rebecca gasped when the woman grabbed a thick bunch of her hair. "Please, no—"

"Shut up. I won't ask again, Smith."

Even the head guard seemed unsure. He looked around the room, as if searching for a way out. But then he sighed and grabbed a steak knife, handing it to her.

Liam jumped to his feet. "Don't do this. You don't have to hurt her."

"I know I don't have to."

She wrenched a big bunch of hair in her hand, causing Rebecca to whine and twist sideways, exposing the nape of her neck. Liam roared and the lanky guard yelled and covered his eyes, but the other four didn't react, merely standing there as the woman stabbed Rebecca. She speared the knife into her neck, and then – as Rebecca coughed and wheezed – she stabbed her in the belly.

Liam rushed forwards. The guards grabbed him, dragged him away, as he shouted at her to stop. But she wouldn't.

Rebecca fell and the woman collapsed atop her, raising the slick knife, screaming as she stabbed over and over. The flesh made a sickly squelching noise, like boots in sludge, and the coppery stink of blood reached him even across the distance of the table.

Liam thrashed. His first thought was to save her. He forgot about Emily and his own safety and his need to play their game. A woman was being stabbed in front of him. She was going to die. She might already be dead. He had to do something.

But the guards held him steadily.

The woman rose. Her face was spattered with blood. Her black hair glistened with it. Her smile had been replaced with a disappointed look.

Liam cringed as she walked around the table, the knife still in her hand. He tried to push against the guards. But they were two beefy bastards. There was nothing he could do as she stopped right in front of him, so close he gagged with the stink of the blood. Her dress was soaked with it.

Raising her hand, she dragged warm, wet fingertips across his face. "See you soon, lover boy."

And then she left the room.

CHAPTER THIRTEEN

I'd often thought about what it would feel like to take a life with my own hand. As a girl, Father had involved me in all kinds of games with the servants.

He would pay them the most pathetic sums – a few thousand pounds – and they would do whatever he wished. He'd string them up by their hands and have me beat them, watching with a smile on his face, his eyes glassy with whisky.

He'd have me scatter pins over the floor and we'd laugh as the silly men and women tried to navigate to the other side of the room, where their prize awaited: an envelope filled with money. We would spectate as two male servants fought each other, viciously punching and scratching and spitting, all for the price of a mid-range handbag.

As the games progressed, I would imagine what it would be like to take the next logical step. I never voiced any of this to Father. We had an uneasy relationship. I'd always felt like he'd blamed me, in some weird way, for my mother's death; it wasn't as though she'd died in childbirth, so this feeling made little sense.

And yet it was there all the same. Or perhaps he'd never

wanted children, and my very existence was a stain. The games with the servants were the closest to a father-daughter connection we ever formed.

But I thought about it. A lot. I imagined the life fading from their eyes and the blood spurting down their bodies.

And now I had finally done it. My first kill.

I hadn't intended to kill Rebecca, but she had outlived her usefulness. I knew nobody would miss her. She was a heroin-addled whore. She had performed her job well, up to a point, but she'd wavered at the most important time. She'd broken down without a fight, forcing me to reveal myself sooner than I'd planned.

I had taken control, fixing the Rebecca problem while showing Liam the true magnitude of his circumstances. Watching the dinner scene unfold on my phone – linked to the security system – I had been rather proud of him when he made his move.

But I knew he wouldn't go all the way; my man might be forced to place his hands on a lady, but he'd never truly harm one. He didn't have it in him. His chivalrous and protective instincts were one of the reasons I knew he was going to make such an incredible life partner. If he proved himself, that was. If he didn't become tiring.

It was time for Liam to meet the real lady of the house, not the caricature Rebecca had presented. She'd done a fine job, considering who she really was; she'd managed to get rid of that awful grisly accent, and if her new voice had been somewhat comical, it was still an improvement.

I'd had the ever-resourceful Smith hunt for Rebecca. He'd found her under a bridge, wrapped in a dirty blanket, like a fucking cliché. It turned out her parents had kicked her out when she was a teenager and she'd never recovered from it; she was nearing thirty, so that seemed like a pathetic excuse to me.

But she stuck to her story. Her daddy touched her or some such nonsense, she told me, as though I was going to feel sorry for her.

But her daddy hadn't forced the needle into her veins; he hadn't forced her to sell her body for the next hit. Smith had lured her here with money, which was easy enough. Once she'd arrived – in preparation for this most special game – I had schooled her so she would seem believable to Liam. She'd been a slow learner, but it was easy to incentivise her. All it took was a needle, or sometimes even a marijuana cigarette, and she would do whatever we asked. Pathetic.

There was a nagging issue: Liam's reaction. He'd yelled and tried to stop me from killing Rebecca, as though he thought her life was in some way valuable. And when I'd stroked my fingers along his face, he'd looked sick, like he despised me.

But this would only add to the challenge. Liam may resent me for a while, but as the days and weeks and months and years passed, he would grow to love me. His love would be all the stronger for overcoming his moment of weakness: the moment when he'd chosen Rebecca's life over my wishes.

Yet I was sure I'd spotted something else in his eyes as I painted his cheek with Rebecca's blood. He would deny it. But I had seen a glint of excitement before he'd remembered he was supposed to be outraged and appalled. The only regret I had was not checking to see if he'd been hard, because that was one thing that couldn't lie. Men's cocks always tell the truth.

It would be time to officially meet soon. No more watching on my phone. No more touching myself as I closed my eyes and imagined all the things he was going to do to me. No more sitting at a window, staring over the grounds, imagining them teeming and vibrant with our family, our future.

We were halfway to falling in love. He just didn't know it yet.

CHAPTER FOURTEEN

Harrison Bennet couldn't take the stuffiness of the balaclava anymore. He pulled it off roughly, dropping it onto the dashboard as Smith drove them away from the manor. The four-by-four bumped as they left the gardens and crossed the fields. This place was huge; it boggled Harrison's mind that it all belonged to a single family.

"You know we're not supposed to do that, lad."

"Who cares? We've seen each other's faces."

"Just don't do it around the other men."

Smith pulled his balaclava off and tossed it beside Harrison's. The other guards would always be unknown to him; that was part of the lengthy contract he'd signed when taking this position. They stayed in a stone building, locked in their rooms at night by Smith, and if they were caught speaking or exchanging information their contracts would be terminated and they'd sacrifice their fee.

After what Harrison had just witnessed, he thought again of those words. Terminate. Sacrifice. Suddenly he realised they might mean a lot more than a pay cheque.

"Try not to dwell on it," Smith said.

Harrison scowled at him. He was a middle-aged man, grey around the temples, with a hard face and unflinching eyes. He reminded Harrison of his old commander, back before a hand injury had seen him medically discharged from the Army.

"You didn't tell me she was going to kill anyone."

Smith – almost certainly a fake name – sighed. "I didn't know she would. She never has before."

"Before? What happened before?"

"Other games."

"So this is a game, is it?"

"Not my word. Relax."

"This is fucked."

Smith said nothing as their car crossed the edge of the property. Harrison thought about when Smith had first approached him, a few days after he'd left the Army.

Smith had emailed him, saying he was aware of Harrison's military record and wanted to meet in person to discuss a job. The number he'd quoted had been absurd, more than Harrison had made during five years in the Army, doubled. They met in a café and Smith explained that he worked for a very powerful family; they needed men who weren't squeamish to carry out guard duty for special events.

Harrison had been a naïve prick, assuming he was talking about balls and charity functions and whatever else rich people did. He'd been even more idiotic when he agreed to the final term in his contract: the blackmail clause.

To secure his position, Smith had ordered him to record a confession in which he admitted to working with the enemy. As the story went, his unit had been ambushed not because of bad luck, not because it was the nature of battle, but because he'd made a secret alliance with the enemy and had made them aware of his squad's position.

He'd known it was wrong as he was doing it, but pound

signs were floating in front of his vision. The job would take no more than six months, and he would earn two hundred and fifty thousand, plus the initial deposit of fifty thousand, which was already in his bank account. That was a far better prospect than trying to scrounge out a living doing something he hated. And at least, he'd told himself, this was sort of related to military work.

He'd assumed they were just being careful. But now he was screwed.

Harrison came from a military family. His father had been in the Army. So had his grandfather. His great grandfather had served in World War Two. Everybody had been so proud of him when he announced he was going to serve overseas. And even after being the sole survivor of an ambush – a miracle which had involved him hiding in a family's home before the cavalry arrived – his family had stood by him. Everybody else whispered; it didn't look good. Sons had been lost that day, and Harrison escaped with nothing more than an injured hand.

If that video was released, his family's history would be disgraced. He would become an ugly stain on an otherwise stellar record of service. But it was more than that. After seeing how casually the lady of the house had killed Rebecca, he knew the same could happen to him.

As far his friends and family were concerned, he was working on an oil rig, a convenient lie. Maybe the lady of the house would decide to order the other guards to hold him down as she brought a blade to his throat; they could tell his parents he'd fallen over the side of the rig, an unfortunate accident. These people had connections. They'd be able to sell the lie.

"What happens if I try to leave?" Harrison asked, as the car came to a stop. It was getting dark already. The headlights shone on the tree trunks, those closest to the property's edge.

Smith clenched his jaws. Harrison could see them jutting out of the older man's hard face. "That wouldn't be smart."

75

"I'm asking anyway."

"The video would be released. The wives and mothers of your old squad mates would believe it, because they want to; they need somebody to blame. The wider world might believe it too. These people, our employers, they might even be able to get a few of the top brass to go along with it. Your life would be over, marked a traitor forever. And that's if you were *allowed* to leave."

"Would you kill me yourself, or get one of the others to do it?"

"For fuck's sake." Smith thumped the steering wheel. The horn rang out over the silence. "What did you want me to do? She's never killed anybody before."

"And now that she has?"

"You ask too many questions."

"Who are the family?" Harrison said, ignoring him.

Smith had originally picked Harrison up in a van, ordering him to sit in the back with a bag over his head. He'd arrived at the estate with no clue who the family was, or where exactly he was.

This afternoon was the first time he'd ever seen the real lady of the house. He'd only learned Rebecca was a fake when he overheard Smith mention it to one of the other guards: something about not risking their necks to save her, she was disposable.

Harrison had only agreed to any of this because of the fee. In hindsight he could see how stupid he'd been. He wished he'd listened to the old saying about things too good to be true.

"Smith, I asked you a question."

"How old are you?"

"I turned twenty-five a few days ago."

"Happy bloody birthday. Listen. This is all going to be over soon. And when it is, you're going to have to learn to keep quiet.

You'll never be able to tell anybody. Even when you meet a nice girl and have a family and find the career you want to go after, you'll have to keep it to yourself. You might as well get used to it."

"But–"

"And think of the money. When you leave, you'll have more than most men your age can dream of. You'll be able to put a sizeable deposit down on a house. You'll be able to help your family. You'll be able to *live*. Stop whining."

"You targeted me because you knew I was desperate. You knew I couldn't let all that work in the Army go to waste. You knew I'd jump at the chance to use my skills, even if it wasn't exactly what I wanted to do. You knew all of that."

Smith stared at him, seeming like he was about to say something. But then he shook his head. "Put your balaclava on."

"Why? Nobody's around."

"You're getting way too chummy."

Harrison pulled on the stuffy mask and climbed from the car. He and Smith went to the boot.

"Open it," Smith said.

"You do it."

Smith squared up to him, shoulders wide. Harrison was tall, but he was built on the thinner side. He'd been told he had a deceptive strength, since he looked so skinny and could lift a fair bit, but he wasn't sure of his chances against Smith. The man might be nearing fifty, by Harrison's guess, but he was built like a brick shithouse.

"I won't ask you again."

Harrison opened the boot, taking out the shovels and laying them on the ground. Rebecca stared at him when he pulled back the tarpaulin. She stank of blood. He'd seen dead bodies before, dozens of them – his friends, men, women, children – but this one hit harder. Those deaths hadn't made sense, exactly, but he'd expected them; he'd known something might happen. This was something else. This was mayhem.

"I'll take her shoulders. You grab her legs. The ground's not too hard. If we work solidly, we'll be done in a few hours. She wants it deep."

"What's her name, the murderer?"

Smith's eyes narrowed in the balaclava. Harrison wondered why he'd put his on too. Maybe he didn't want Harrison to be able to see his face, the shame or lack of shame.

"Hurry up," Smith said, leaning into the car.

They carried Rebecca into the glare of the headlights and started digging. It was hard labour. For a while, Harrison could pretend he was doing something else. He was digging a foundation for a building project; he was helping one of his cousins dig a hole in the garden. His muscles ached but he kept on, even when Smith stopped for a break. The man looked at him with more respect after that.

Full night came and they continued digging, the earth piling around them. Calluses cut and bled on Harrison's hands, and he savoured them. A minor punishment for this twisted mess he found himself part of.

Once they were done, they tossed the shovels and climbed out of the hole.

"She was nobody, lad. She has no family who'll miss her. Her dad died of lung cancer a few years back. Her mum moved up north and has a second family there. She hasn't tried to contact her daughter in eight years. She spent her life addicted to drugs, stealing, selling her body. She had no friends except other junkies, and they forgot she existed the second she came with us. You hear me? She's nobody, nothing."

"Is that supposed to make me feel better, or you?"

Smith grunted as he leaned down, grabbing her shoulders. "I'm just telling you how it is."

Harrison took her feet and they threw her into the hole.

"What about you? Are you nobody too?" Harrison grabbed his shovel and started throwing dirt onto the poor woman, the corpse, the so-called nothing. "Am I?"

"You think too much." Smith picked up his shovel. "How's the hand?"

Harrison opened and closed it. "It aches a bit. But it's not too bad. I think that was an excuse, honestly, for what happened overseas."

"Reputation's everything. It affects everybody around you. And not just in the military."

As they worked to fill in the hole, Harrison didn't miss the threat. Smith knew how important his family's legacy was to him.

"Nobody will ever believe you, if you talk about this." Smith breathed heavily as he hefted more dirt; they were slowly making Rebecca disappear. "You were hired by a bloke with a fake name to help a crazy rich lady fall in love with a dog trainer. It sounds mental."

"At least we agree she's crazy."

Smith laughed grimly. "Yeah. We're not going to argue about that."

CHAPTER FIFTEEN

After the guards dragged him back to his room and locked the door behind him, there was nothing for Liam to do but replay the murder over and over. He saw the knife stabbing into Rebecca's neck, the sick look of boredom on the other woman's face; he felt her fingertips against his cheek, certain the blood was still there even if he'd washed his face several times. He'd spent most of the day locked in this memory, trying to make sense of it.

His initial feelings about Rebecca had been true, it seemed; she *was* doing an impression of a posh person. Her real voice had come out when he'd taken her hostage. And then the real lady of the house had emerged, and...

He groaned and closed his eyes tighter, rubbing his hand down his face. He wanted to sleep, to dream, to escape. He'd searched the room for weapons again upon return, but there was nothing, and he'd ruined his one good chance to get out of here. He should've kept hold of the knife, grabbed the killer before the guards had their hands on him. He'd felt rooted in place as he watched the scene, his thoughts racing to catch up to the reality, and then it had been too late.

He rolled over and pulled his knees to his chest. The bed was so much sweeter than the stone floor of the cell, and yet he found he couldn't enjoy it. Any second they could crash through the door and drag him back to the prison. Any moment that lunatic could run in here.

Shivering, he repressed a sob. He felt like a little kid; how close he was to tears. He needed to remember Emily and their child. He needed to remember Rocky, the grin on the old terrier's face every time Liam came home. He pushed the sob down. It wouldn't help anything.

The guards were going to be on high alert now; that was if they decided to go on with this twisted game. Perhaps the lady of the house had simply wanted to watch him and Rebecca, and, with Rebecca dead, she'd find another use for Liam.

Suddenly he wished he could go back to the bowling alley and hug her: fake it, do what he had to, to keep her alive. And him, because he didn't know what was going to happen next. The killer was clearly insane. She'd looked *bored* after she stabbed Rebecca.

If murder bored her, Liam had no idea how he was going to hold her interest.

The next morning, Bretherton arrived with two guards. Liam didn't recognise Smith or the lanky kid, but then he only knew Smith from his voice; he was similar height and build to the others. Their eyes gave nothing away. They stared coldly, waiting as Bretherton took a couple of cautious steps into the room. Good. Let them fear him.

"Madam requests your presence in the library."

"The dead one, or the killer?"

Bretherton frowned. "It would be prudent to refrain from comments like that."

"Or she'll take a steak knife to my throat." Liam's voice quivered, and he cursed himself. It was bad enough he'd almost cried when he was on his own; he couldn't show weakness in front of them. "Who was she?"

Bretherton tilted his head. "Who?"

"Rebecca. The dead girl. Who was she? Did she have a family? A husband? Kids? Pets?"

The butler stepped aside, gesturing at the door. "Shall we?"

Liam studied the guards. They looked all too ready to pounce if he said no. He sighed. "Sure."

"You understand we'll need to be discreet."

"Ah, the black bag again. Lucky me."

One of the guards motioned for Liam to turn around. He was familiar with the gesture from his time in the cell. He faced the wall and put his hands behind his back, and they went about their business efficiently.

Soon they were frogmarching him through the house. It was the same routine: in and out of rooms, up and down stairs, until he'd lost all sense of direction.

They pulled the black bag away to reveal a vast library, covering two floors, with bookshelves reaching from the floor to the ceiling. There was a skylight, and it had started to softly rain, tapping against the dim glass. Sconces shone brightly on the old books, and the room smelled of paper.

"You'd think you'd never seen a library before."

Liam turned at the voice. It was the killer. Her black hair was loose and she was wearing trousers, boots, and a baggy knitted sweater, pulling the sleeves up around her hands. Liam ached; he always thought it was cute when Emily did that, fingers poking out to wrap around a steaming mug of hot chocolate.

The woman stood at the bottom of the spiral staircase which led to the second floor. Liam's hands were still handcuffed, and he felt the guards standing close to him, far closer than they had with Rebecca.

"I should probably apologise." She approached, stopping just short. "I didn't intend for things to get so lively yesterday, but you'll admit you forced my hand. It was quite the shock, seeing you standing there like a beast. Do you think you would've done it, if you had to? Do you think you could've killed her?"

"No."

"I thought you might say that. You're a good man."

He laughed humourlessly. "Thank you."

"Sarcasm, how sweet. Do you use it as a shield, to pretend you're above sadness, fear, pain?"

"I don't know."

She moved even closer. Liam's fingers twitched, his body urging him to action, but he couldn't do anything. The guards; the handcuffs. "I suppose you're ready to put all that nasty business behind us. I suppose you want to learn a little about me."

There was an edge to her voice. It wasn't a suggestion.

Liam swallowed, nodded.

"Pardon?"

"Tell me about yourself."

She tittered, glancing at the guards. "It's a wonder, isn't it, what a drop of blood will do to a man's resolve?"

He almost snapped. He hadn't lost his resolve. He was waiting for his chance. And when it came, he'd be ruthless. He wouldn't hesitate this time.

"My name is Madeline Pemberton. Have you heard of the Pembertons?"

"Can't say I have. No offence."

She laughed in that annoying superior way; that was one trait she and Rebecca shared. "I don't suppose you've had cause to. But we're quite a significant family, going back many, many generations. We made our fortune in trade, plantations, manufacturing, property development. The old ways, Father says, before the world became so messy and modern. Father likes to say we own half the land in England, but he does love to exaggerate. You can call me Maddie, if you like. *Would* you like that?"

The answer was obviously no. But he'd tried that path and it hadn't worked. "Yes, I would. Thank you, Maddie."

"Oh, that's delightful. It makes me sound so wonderfully regular, hearing my name spoken in your gorgeously workaday voice."

He waited, heart pounding in his chest. In his mind, he saw Rebecca's skin tearing apart, the gushing stream of blood. His throat itched.

"I'm sure you're more interested in me than my family's history."

"Yes," Liam said.

She waved a hand, behaving as though she was in a play. She was so full of herself. "I haven't had a terribly interesting time of it. I was something of a wild child growing up, always getting into trouble here and there, drinking with the common boys, bringing disgrace on our family's name. Father is ever so forgiving, however. And then it was time for university. Ah! What a time, what an adventure. I read English Literature at Oxford. I'm sure that's quite impressive to you."

"Yes."

She pursed her lips. "You have heard of Oxford, haven't you?"

"Yes."

"In any case." She took another step, her body almost

grazing his. Something rustled behind him; the guards were getting ready for a fight. "My main passion in life, ever since I was old enough to know what passion is, is to find love. The search for love has been my great quest. I am not an old woman, by any means, at twenty-eight. But I do feel as though my time is running out. Sometimes I hear a clock ticking in my dreams."

She stared expectantly. There was something petulant about her eyes, as though her latest toy wasn't working properly.

An unpleasant shiver moved across Liam's shoulders, down his spine, as though warning him to impress her.

"That must be very worrying for you. But like you said, you're young. You've got time."

"Silly." Her hands were on his face, her touch repulsive. He almost cringed. Remembering the guards, he stood still as she softly caressed his cheek. "*We've* got time. I truly am sorry for that bother with Rebecca, but I had to know you were willing to engage in the process."

"The process," he repeated.

She applied pressure with her fingernails. It wasn't hard enough to break skin yet. But it hurt. "The game. The romance. Our great adventure. Whatever you would like to call it. I believe we've got a wonderful journey ahead of us. I believe we're going to look fondly back on these days. Does that make me mad?"

He winced. She was digging her nails in harder. "No, I don't think you're mad."

She let her hand drop with a snigger. "I'm not sure I believe you, but you'll soon see things my way. Would you agree that men, in general, don't deliver on what they promise us?"

"Us?"

"Women, silly. You promise us the world. You tell us you'll be with us forever. You'll never cheat on us. Your love for us will never wane, and every day will be like Valentine's. But then you become cold, distant, forget your duty. Would you agree with that?"

Every day like Valentine's? This woman had clearly never been in a real relationship if she thought that would ever happen. He and Emily were more in love than he could fathom, and yet they had their good and bad times; there were moods, arguments, life. It was impossible to be romantic every second of the day, every day.

"Liam, I asked you a question."

"Yes, I agree."

"But you're not like other men. I knew that the first time I saw you."

"When was that?" he asked. It might give him a clue about his connection to her. Right now he had nothing. He'd never met a Pemberton, and no matter how much he searched his memory, he was certain he'd never seen this woman before.

She ignored his question, gesturing at the room in general. "This has been rather lovely. As a special treat, I'm going to let you select a book to take back to your room. I know you must be getting terribly bored. I'll also have them bring you some food... something to eat with your hands. I know how excitable you can get when cutlery is involved."

Liam walked around the library, the guards close behind him. Bretherton had disappeared at some point during the walk here. Without his hands to take the books down, he studied the spines and the titles. One had a dog on it. *The Call of the Wild*.

"I'll take this one."

Madeline reached past him, purposefully getting close. "Ah, a fitting choice. Have you read it before?"

"No."

"It's about a dog who struggles to become free, like his wolf cousins. Don't let it give you any ideas."

"I won't."

"Excellent. Then I think we're done."

She handed the book to one of the guards and strode from the room.

Soon the black bag was over his head, and they were leading him through the house.

CHAPTER SIXTEEN

I'm not a fool. I understood Liam had been playacting in the library: saying and doing what I wanted him to, an obedience borne from fear of the guards. But I also knew I had spoken truly.

He and I had all the time in the world to move past the constraints of our meeting and fall into a true romance. It had all been there the first time I saw him: the sparkle in his eyes, the way he'd softly smiled, the sense he'd given me that he wanted me, only me, and had no interest in the whore to whom he'd idiotically tied himself.

There was only one part about our first official meeting which disappointed me. He hadn't mentioned the first time we saw each other. Perhaps he was holding it back as a final effort to retain some semblance of control. Or perhaps he was saving it for an important time, like after our first kiss. I didn't know, but it bothered me.

He *must* remember; he'd smiled so captivatingly, looking at me as though I was the only woman who existed, the only person who mattered.

But the slut and her bastard had complicated matters. Liam

was a loyal man, and he'd stand by the bitch. She'd undoubtably pricked his condom or lied about being on birth control to ensnare him. I refused to believe Liam would willingly impregnate a woman in those circumstances: he was with a person he didn't truly love, they lived in a dank depressing flat, and to top it all off they weren't even married.

I wasn't as old-fashioned as Father, who still believed sex before marriage was a taboo subject. I knew he'd had sex outside of wedlock; I'd seen the looks some of the servants had given him when I was growing up. And he'd been a widower for more than a decade. He wasn't a monk. He must've done it. But he certainly believed that a child born out of wedlock was a cause for shame, and I was inclined to agree with him.

When Liam and I had our first child, we would be married. Perhaps the marriage would come a few days after I realised I was with child, or perhaps it would come long before we conceived. But it *would* come, and I'd make that clear to Liam at some later date.

It was humiliating for a woman and shameful for a man, to bring a bastard into the world, a child who'd always know their parents didn't care enough to make it official.

Smith had brought me some interesting news after the meeting with Liam. He and Harrison – the tall boy who'd made the mistake of covering his eyes when I slit the druggie's throat – had gone on an excursion to the outside world. Upon returning, Smith had found me in the library, where I was attempting to disappear into the world of Jane Austen. I adored her romances, rereading them yearly.

Smith had taken off his mask when he entered. He's been with my family for years, arranging games, cleaning up any messes that arise as a result. He is a resourceful and loyal man.

"So?" I asked.

He nodded as he crossed the room. "It's done."

"No photos?"

"We thought it better to stay outside."

"So then how do you know it's done?"

He told me, and I accepted his reasoning. He knew what he was doing. So the baby had been born, Liam's bastard in the world. I didn't like to think about his former life, and especially not his child. I didn't have the resolve to cause harm to a baby – or to order harm caused – but admittedly the thought occurred to me.

It would be a dreadful situation if, when Liam had grown into his true self, and our life was filled with laughter and holidays and happiness, some sad wretch appeared at our doorstep claiming to be related to my husband. "Smith."

"Yes?"

"If I were a stressed new mother and I decided to go for a drive, it's possible my reactions would be slower, my attention elsewhere."

He narrowed his eyes. "That's possible."

"And, as a result of my lack of attention, it's possible I might lose control of the car with my child in it. We'd spin off the road and crash, and die, especially if the brakes had failed us and it was a rainy day."

Smith rarely looked shocked, but he did then.

"What?" I snapped.

"I'd need permission from your father to carry out something like that."

"Why?"

"It could cause problems. My job is to keep this contained."

"Are you saying I have become too elaborate?"

"I don't mean to criticise. But I've never seen you or your father kill anybody before. We were able to get rid of Rebecca because nobody was looking for her. Emily Taylor has family, friends, colleagues."

"Yes, yes, all of whom would be dreadfully sad when they learned of the tragic accident. I fail to see your point. We wouldn't have to get rid of anything. The road would do that for us."

"Just to be clear, you're suggesting I cut her brakes on a rainy day, and hope she spins off the road and dies?"

I stood quickly, gratified to see he took a step away. He knew his place. It was one of the reasons we valued him so much. "I was speaking hypothetically."

"Hypothetically – and with respect – I would need to speak to your father about that."

"Father enjoys this game as much as me. You can see that for yourself."

Smith nodded.

"So he'll want to protect it."

"He might, yes."

"But you'll have to talk to him. Fine. Let's hold off on that for now then."

Smith left me, and I returned to my reading. There were other options. Once Liam had realised how much he preferred me to Miss Taylor, we could choose a paradise abroad; we could change our names and live happily and privately for the rest of our lives.

CHAPTER SEVENTEEN

Harrison sprinted on the running machine, head down, trying to focus on the slapping sound of his trainers and his breath in his ears.

The guards' barracks were situated to the west of the main property, eight single rooms with a small en suite bathroom... if the other guards' rooms were the same as his, anyway. There were cameras everywhere and Smith had warned them the consequences would be severe if any of them removed their masks or struck up a friendship.

Even the gym was a private place, with only one guard being able to use it at a time. Harrison's legs began to burn and his heels were throbbing, but he kept running.

It was easier than thinking about Patty roaring, "*Contact! He's been fucking hit!*"

It was easier than thinking about the sandy smoke drifting through the blisteringly bright air, and the crack of gunshots all around them as they tried to regroup their position. It was easier than thinking about how hot his best friend's blood had been; that would always stay with him, how the wound had been spewing boiling blood, his belly exposed and guts spilling out as Harrison tried to apply pressure.

How had the blood been so hot? It was like the bullets had cooked him from the inside.

And then a hand had slammed down on his shoulder. It was the man they all called Chewie, on account of him being so hairy. The older man was yelling something, but Harrison suddenly realised there was no sound, like the world was on mute. Finally Harrison got the point. His best friend was dead, and Harrison was kneeling in the sand messing with the wound for no reason.

He'd got his act together, raised his rifle. They were in a terrible position, in a small town with clear ground all around them. The radios were their only hope, but they'd been playing up all operation and now it was no different.

Harrison and his friends had fought, and more of them had bled, and at some point a piece of shrapnel had stabbed into the back of Harrison's hand. But he never dropped his rifle; he kept fighting.

Eventually, he was forced to hole up in a crawlspace, gun aimed at the trapdoor, waiting for what surely was going to be his death. But the family had saved him, Abdul and his wife, Ferhana: they'd lied to the enemy, said he wasn't there, and then quickly showed him a place he could hide beneath the floorboards.

When the enemy invariably returned, Harrison huddled in the dimness, wondering why the couple were helping him. He'd barged into their home. They didn't owe him anything. But before Harrison was airlifted out, Abdul told him – through a translator – that he was simply tired of the killing. Harrison hoped they were living happier lives, though he knew the truth was probably grimmer.

The harsh buzzer cut through his thoughts, jolting him to the present.

Another guard was waiting to make use of the gym. That was how it worked: they had an allotted time, and then another guard was free to press the buzzer for their turn. Harrison hopped off the running machine and grabbed his balaclava. It was itchy and uncomfortable with his face drenched in sweat.

He left the windowless room. The other guard said nothing, pushing past him and slamming the door. Harrison walked down the nondescript corridor to his room, the second on the left. Unlocking it with his key, he dropped onto the end of the bed and tore the mask off.

This place was starting to get to him. Yesterday, Smith had visited him with a flinty look in his eyes. He had keys to all their rooms; he'd simply unlocked it and strode in. "You're an idiot, lad. What were you thinking?"

"What?" Harrison had backed against the wall of his bedroom, the older man crowding him.

"You covered your eyes. You screamed like a little girl."

"She killed someone in cold blood. What was I supposed to do?"

Smith glanced at the door. "For all you know, there are microphones in the rooms. You need to be more careful."

"I didn't react that way on purpose. It's just... I've never seen anybody killed like that. It was a murder."

"I know. But I managed to keep it together. So did the other men. You need to prove your loyalty."

Harrison swallowed. "I don't like the sound of that."

"It's not a big deal. We're just going on a little road trip. Don't do anything stupid."

They'd driven three and a half hours, from the manor in Lincolnshire, southwest to the city of Bristol where Liam had lived before his kidnapping. Smith and Harrison were on the lookout for Liam's girlfriend. They'd arrived outside her flat and sat at the end of the road for a long time, saying nothing.

Whenever Harrison tried to ask Smith about his life, the older man simply looked at him, and then turned his gaze back to the flat.

The outside world seemed busier, louder, more hectic than Harrison remembered. It hadn't been long since he'd started work at the manor – a week and a half, by his count – and yet he was already accustomed to the silence of the countryside.

Finally, Smith had said, "Let's try her parents' place."

Harrison hadn't bothered asking how Smith knew where her parents lived. The lady of the house had presumably paid for some private detectives to dig into their situation, the same way they had with him. As they arrived at her parents' house, Emily's dad had been rushing into the car. He had a duffle bag over his shoulder.

"It looks like he's running," Harrison muttered.

"Yeah, but not away from something. Towards something."

"What do you mean?"

"You'll see. I'm not sure if this is good or bad news."

They'd followed at a careful distance, all the way to the hospital. Harrison and Smith had watched the parents rushing in. Harrison guessed he'd taken his daughter there and then gone home for an overnight bag. The man looked proud as he walked into the hospital, a typical expectant grandfather. It was in the way he walked: head held high, slightly swinging the bag. But there was something else too. He looked a little guilty for his happiness, probably because of Liam being missing.

Or was Harrison reading too much into it? Smith had said he thought too much; maybe he was right.

"What do we do?" Harrison asked.

"Nothing we can do now. The baby's been born."

"We don't know that. There could be complications."

Smith groaned. "Lad, I'm not sitting here for the next couple of days, waiting for her to come out. What's the infant mortality rate in this country–"

"Four in every thousand. Last time I heard." Smith stared at him. Harrison shrugged. "I had a little brother once. But only for a couple of minutes."

"The point is," Smith went on gruffly. "It's incredibly low. Which means we can be ninety-nine per cent sure that baby's going to be okay. So we'll go back and that's what I'll tell her."

"But–"

"I'm not sitting in this car for a minute longer than I have to, especially when you've got that puppy dog look on your face. Has anybody ever told you you're a depressing bastard? And anyway, we might arouse suspicion if we hang around. We're going."

Harrison had driven on the way home. Smith slept with his head back, his eyes closed, breathing calmly.

It was a perfect opportunity for Harrison to do the right thing. He could pull over and wrestle the man out of the car, tie him up someplace, make him tell him where the blackmail recording was; once that was sorted, he'd be able to tell the world what was going on at the fancy Lincolnshire estate.

But he didn't. He just drove.

Whenever he'd acted violently, it was always in the heat of battle, when he didn't have time to think about it beforehand. They trained; they were ready. But Harrison never dwelled on what was to come, because he sensed something in himself, like a blockage. If he thought about it too much, he might become paralysed when the moment came.

It was the same now. He couldn't pull over and hurt Smith, a man he knew, a man he was friendly with even if Smith was a grumpy prick.

When Smith awoke, a question occurred to Harrison.

"What did you mean when you said you weren't sure if it was good or bad news?"

Smith rubbed his eyes. "Can't even give a man two seconds to wake up, can you?" He sighed. "I'm not sure how the lady of the house is going to react. She seems..."

"What?" Harrison urged. Any information was better than what he had. Nothing.

But something in Harrison's tone had apparently bothered Smith. He closed his eyes again. "Wake me when we're there."

Now, in his small bedroom, Harrison switched on the electric radiator and walked into the en suite. He stripped naked and put his clothes in the laundry basket. Somebody came into their rooms when they were out and hung fresh clothes in their wardrobe. Maybe it was Smith, or that butler, Bretherton. Maybe it was the lady of the house herself. That mad bitch would enjoy snooping around.

He stared at himself in the mirror. He looked far younger than twenty-five. His body was all sinew, his skin pale and veiny. He looked pathetic, a chicken who'd rather go along with the status quo than make a fuss.

Standing in the shower, he turned the water up hot. He kept seeing Becky's face, staring at him from under the tarpaulin. But sometimes the image would flicker and there would be a young girl there instead, her skin turned mostly red, her flesh in tatters, one eye distended as she gazed up at him.

Turning the water up even higher, he closed his eyes as it burned his skin: hotter than his best friend's blood, hotter than his thoughts. He focused on the pain and nothing else.

It would be over soon. It had to be.

CHAPTER EIGHTEEN

Liam had hated school in general, but especially reading. It was an effort to focus for long enough to get to the end of a page and, when he finally did, he'd always forgotten what he'd just read. It had made him feel trapped, his legs twitching under the table, as he thought about playing rugby or riding his bike or anything other than the words in front of him.

That had changed a little as he'd grown older; he'd read plenty of books on dog training, and he'd even read a few autobiographies here and there. But Emily was the real reader in the relationship.

As Liam sat at the window, the book in his lap, he thought about Emily tucked up on the sofa. She'd wrap her favourite blanket around her knees with her Kindle in her hand, sometimes gripping it so hard her knuckles turned white.

"Relax, you're going to break it."

She'd glare, or try to. She could never stop herself smiling. "You wouldn't be saying that if you knew what was happening."

He peered through the window, judging the drop. Surely he'd break something. That was a last resort, for when things got really bad. He almost laughed. As if things weren't really bad already.

With nothing else to do, he started the book. It was written in an old-fashioned style, forcing Liam to concentrate. The story was about a dog called Buck, a giant St Bernard cross, who is kidnapped from his home in California and taken to Seattle.

Liam winced when the captors beat Buck, viciously, in no way a person should ever touch a dog. He squeezed the pages hard, wringing them, and suddenly there were tears in his eyes. He was weeping over the dog: the beating. The poor bastard. No dog deserved that.

He placed the book down and went into the bathroom, splashing cold water on his face. He needed to get his act together.

Returning to the bedroom, he realised a few hours had passed. It was growing dark. They hadn't brought his food yet. His belly grumbled as he sat down and picked up the book.

He read quickly through all the beating sections, following Buck as he became part of a team of sled dogs.

It had been a funny quirk of fate that he'd chosen this book. There were too many similarities. He'd been kidnapped and beaten and he was being trained for something.

As Liam contemplated the end of this road – the things he would have to do to fulfil her sick desire – he wished he was the dog, pulling the sled, with the cold and the beatings and the endless threats. At least then all he'd have to do was put his nose down and run, keep running until he could collapse exhausted into Emily's arms.

He stood and stretched. The autumn day had become evening without him noticing. There was a slight chill in the room, but it was nothing compared to the bone-deep cold of the cell. His injuries still ached, but they had receded to the background, part of his everyday existence. He could handle them.

A few minutes later, a knock came at the door. Liam recognised it for Bretherton. That was a worrying sign, identifying people by their knocks.

"Sir, I have brought you supper. I'm opening the door."

"You say that like I'm a feral animal. Like I'm going to attack you."

He thought of Buck, when he'd attacked the man in the red sweater. It had been a vicious assault. But what did he get for his efforts? More beatings, harsher punishment. Liam stood back as the door opened. Bretherton held a paper bag, and there were no guards behind him.

"Feeling brave?" Liam said.

"I assured the lady of the house that, if you intended to attack me, you would have done so already."

"You're expendable. She doesn't care if I hurt you."

"There is no benefit for you, then, proving my original point."

Liam took the bag. There was a haunch of meat inside and some green veg, juices swilling around at the bottom. He turned, intending to sit in the chair by the window.

"Sir, there is something else."

"What?" Liam faced the butler again.

"Your wife–"

"Emily and I aren't married. Not yet. In fact, Mad Maddie's goons picked me up the night I proposed to her. How's that for timing?"

"I would advise against using that moniker in her presence."

"That what?"

"Nickname, sir. It means nickname."

"Then you could've just said nickname." Liam clenched his

fist around the top of the bag. "So what were you going to tell me?"

"Your wife... excuse me, girlfriend." There was some judgement in the butler's tone, as though Liam deserved everything that had happened because he hadn't proposed to Emily sooner. And maybe he did. He regretted that as much as anything. "She has given birth."

"Really?" Liam gasped, his smile taking shape despite everything. "And the baby's healthy?"

"As far as we know, yes."

"I don't like the sound of that."

Bretherton shrugged. "That is all the information I have. Our men did some reconnaissance in the outside world."

Liam was suddenly full of energy. He paced the room, a stupid grin on his face. He couldn't stop smiling. His heart was pumping crazily fast, as he thought of Emily and the child, their sweet precious healthy baby.

He almost hugged Bretherton, just to share the moment with another person. And then the smile dropped.

He'd missed his child's birth, despite promising himself he wouldn't. He'd never be able to reclaim that.

"Thanks for telling me." He sat in the chair. "Is that all?"

"No." Bretherton lingered at the edge of the bed. "I am not here merely to deliver the food and good news. I come with a... a suggestion."

Liam stared.

"What I mean to say is, I am here to tell you that it is incredibly important you do everything in your power to satisfy Miss Pemberton. Because the men, you see, they know where your fiancée is, at all times. They know where you live. They know where her parents live. They know where all her friends live. Anywhere she goes – anywhere your child goes – we'll be able to find her."

Liam placed the bag on the windowsill and strode over to Bretherton. The butler flinched, but gave no ground. Liam glared. "Don't touch Emily. Don't even think about touching my child. I swear to God, I'll kill everybody in this hellhole if you do that."

"I'm merely the messenger."

"Maybe I feel like taking out my anger on somebody."

The butler was infuriatingly calm. "I understand. But it will make no difference. In fact, it might produce the exact opposite of your intended effect."

"Speak. Plainly."

"What I mean to say is that in harming me you will only be harming yourself. The lady of the house may wish to punish you for your insubordination."

"She'd hurt a child?"

Bretherton's eyes flickered. Something like humanity entered them, and left just as quickly. "I'm not sure. I wish I could say no. But she has been acting..."

"What?"

"She's always had a little fire in her, but of late it has become an inferno. Her quest for true love, it is burning inside of her, bursting out of her. Be what she needs you to be. That is the only advice I can give you."

Liam was throttling the bastard; he was on top of him, headbutting his nose until it shattered, gnawing chunks out of his cheek and spitting them in his face. He brought his thumbs to his eyes and drove them in, until something popped, and then he kept pushing until he felt brain and mulch.

In his mind, he was hurting him. Badly. But in reality he only returned to his chair, saying nothing.

Bretherton hovered. Liam looked at him.

"I'm sorry, sir, but the lady requests your presence. I am to let you eat your meal and then you are to come with me."

"Threatening a child, a newborn baby. And you want me to be her lover boy."

As Liam ate, he wondered how close the guards had come to Emily. Had they seen the baby through a hospital window? Or perhaps Emily and his child had taken a walk around the hospital. Her mum and dad would be taking good care of her, and Liam hoped she'd be able to enjoy this moment despite his disappearance. It wouldn't be the day they'd dreamed of, he knew that, but some happiness, a little joy to mark the occasion.

"Can you tell me if it was a boy or a girl?" Liam wiped his hands on the paper bag and walked into the en suite to wash his hands.

"I'm afraid not, sir."

"I'm guessing if your men were able to get close, Emily isn't surrounded by police cars. Which means my disappearance hasn't been marked as suspicious."

"Apologies, sir. I didn't realise you were an expert in the law."

Liam stood in the bathroom doorway, his hands drip-drying at his sides. "I didn't know you could be sarcastic, Bretherton, but I guess we learn something new every day."

"I have no knowledge of how the police are handling your disappearance."

In his early twenties, one of Liam's mates had gone missing. His girlfriend had gone to the police but they hadn't taken it seriously. He was a young man and he would come back in his own time; he probably needed space.

Liam's mate had returned, grinning, eyes bloodshot from two days of partying.

Liam prayed the police guessed something was amiss in his case; maybe they'd left a sign of a fight in the alleyway. Maybe the homeless man had heard something.

"She's going to go crazy, not knowing where I am."

"Yes, I'm sure your girlfriend will be very worried. Now, shall we?"

"You don't have to sound like such a stuck-up prick when you say girlfriend."

Bretherton shrugged, a soft smirk on his lips. Was he mocking Liam? "Apologies if that's how it came across. That was not my intention. But you must admit, it is rather less serious."

"What is?"

"Your situation. Missing boyfriend. It doesn't have quite the same ring as *missing husband*, does it?"

"We've lived together for years. I love her. We have a child together. We're engaged to be married." Liam shook his head. "I don't need to defend myself to you."

"As you say."

"You lot are out of the fucking Middle Ages, making comments like that. She's the love of my life. I'd die for her. I'd kill for her. And you think the lack of a ring and a piece of paper devalues that."

Bretherton stepped aside, gesturing at the door. "If you will. The lady is waiting."

Liam barged past the butler, not caring when his shoulder almost caused the older man to lose his footing.

At least he knew his child had been born. He was a father. It was even more reason to keep fighting. Unless Bretherton had lied to him. Liam had no way to be sure.

Two guards appeared at the top of the stairs. One of them was the tall one, the one who'd yelled and covered his eyes when Madeline killed Rebecca.

"Nice to see you again," Liam said, as he turned and faced the wall.

They bagged him, cuffed him, and went on their way.

CHAPTER NINETEEN

They pulled the bag off to reveal a large indoor swimming pool. The lights were electric and bright. There were no windows, and there were two doors off to the side: one for the sauna and the other for a steam room. A fan hummed in the corner, and Madeline was lying face down on a massage table.

Liam assessed the room. There were no weapons that he could see. He might be able to snap the legs on one of the poolside chairs, use that somehow, but he doubted it. The guard nudged him. Liam turned sharply; it wasn't the lanky kid, but the other one. Liam didn't recognise him.

"Do that again," Liam snapped, under his breath, not loud enough for Madeline to hear.

The man reached for his pocket. The taller one placed a hand on the other guard's arm. He gave a shake of his head and then nodded firmly at Liam. Liam stared into his eyes, and he was certain he saw something there: pity, regret, something human. Something more than the others.

"Liam, baby, are you going to keep me waiting?"

Liam approached the massage table. There was a smaller

table nearby, with oils and a towel on it. The guards were never far behind, sticking far closer than they had with Rebecca. But then, Rebecca had been as disposable as him.

Madeline was only wearing a pair of knickers, tucked right up into her arse. Countless scars criss-crossed from her shoulders down to the base of her spine, faded but deep and ridged, some of them raising the skin.

"Is something the matter?" she said.

"No, I'm just... What do you need, Madeline?"

She tutted, propping up on her elbows and facing him. Her hair was down, spilling over the head-hole of the table. "What did I say, hmm?"

"Maddie."

"Much better. And what does it look like I need? I've been ever so tense lately. I'm sure your strong capable hands will be able to find all my sore points. Won't they, Liam?"

The tall kid stood on the other side of the table, the other guard behind Liam. It was the same as in the bowling alley, when he'd refused to hug Rebecca. Only this time, he'd be offending the real lady of the house if he said no.

Praying Emily would forgive him, he forced himself to smile. "I'll do everything I can."

"How *lovely*. Why don't you put on some music to get me in the mood, and then get your hands nice and oily?"

Liam looked around, spotted the Bluetooth speakers on the floor next to the table. He leaned down and pressed play on the chunky unit. Classical music filled the room, a song he vaguely knew, though he couldn't have said who it was or what the track was called.

Returning to the table, he picked up the massage oil and squirted some into his hand.

The scars on her back sent his mind to silly places, like

imagining how she'd got them, like maybe there was an excuse for everything she'd done. But no matter what had happened, Liam wouldn't let himself feel sorry for her.

He lowered his hands, paused. He couldn't make himself go the last inch. He hadn't touched another woman in years, except for his mum and Emily's mum, and it wasn't like he'd given them near-naked massages.

"Is something wrong?"

"No. I just..."

"Is it my back? Am I ugly?"

Her voice became petulant. She sounded dangerously close to throwing a tantrum.

"No, you're not ugly."

He pressed his palms into her flesh, telling himself it was Emily he was touching. He rubbed as lightly as he could, but then Maddie huffed. "If you're not going to do it properly, what's the point?"

Swallowing his disgust, he got on with it. And then she started to moan. It was like a scene out of a comedy. She was making the most over the top sex noises, whining and squeaking every time he so much as brushed against her.

"Oh, that's it, oh, baby, oh."

Liam glanced across the table, at the tall guard. His eyes were shining and the fabric of the balaclava had changed shape, as though he was grinning.

Liam almost laughed when her whole body began to shake. It was absurd. He was barely touching her. And he could tell it was fake; it was so theatrical, especially when she began to scream. Her cries of forced pleasure bounced around the room.

They went on like this for a ridiculously long time, until finally she stopped moaning.

"I just came," she said.

That was almost it for Liam. This was too surreal. It was like he was on a gameshow. Despite all that had happened – despite the beatings and the threats to his family – he had to turn away to stifle a laugh. The other guard glared at him, and Liam quickly fixed his expression, walking over to the table and wiping his hands on the towel.

Madeline had rolled over in the meantime. She was on her back, legs crossed, one finger idly moving between her bare breasts. Liam looked at her face, into her eyes.

"I bet it's horribly difficult to resist me."

She wasn't Emily. She was his captor. She was a killer. And she was clearly living in a dreamland.

"Well?"

"Yes," he said.

"What if I did this, hmm?"

Her hands glided up to her breasts, and she pushed them together. Liam felt nothing. In fact, he felt a tiny bit sorry for her, of how clearly desperate she was to illicit a reaction.

"Or this..."

Her hand snaked down her belly, inching closer to her knickers. The lanky kid turned away, as though out of respect.

"It *is* hard to resist you." Liam spoke quickly. He had to end this. "But I wouldn't disrespect you by doing anything when we have company."

"The help?" She giggled. "Who cares about that?"

Her fingertips were probing at the edge of her knickers. Her eyes were glassy. Was she on drugs?

"I do," Liam said. "I want you. You have no idea how much. But you have to understand, I wasn't..."

He trailed off. He hardly knew what he was saying. Anything so she didn't start touching herself, and then tell *him* to touch her. He wouldn't be able to cross that line.

"I wasn't raised like you," he went on. "I know you've

probably lived with servants most of your life. And so maybe they've become, sort of, invisible to you. But it isn't like that with me. I wouldn't feel comfortable. I don't want them looking at you either."

He didn't care if the guards wanted to take turns massaging her while she moaned like a bad actress in a porn flick, as long as he didn't have to do anything sexual with her.

"That's so considerate," she said after a pause. "I'm almost tempted to ask them to wait outside."

Yes. That would be good. Then he could get his hands on her and figure a way out. There was no way *she* was fake too, was there?

He looked at her hungrily; he deserved a bloody Oscar. "I think that's a great idea."

She sat up, appraising him. "I wish I could believe you. But after what you did to poor Rebecca, I'm not sure I can. Not yet, anyway. I know your heart is in the right place. But it's going to take some time."

What *he'd* done to Rebecca.

"But thank you. That's so sweet. Guards, please take Liam back to his room."

And then it was the same old routine. Black bag. Handcuffs. A frogmarch in circles until he was back in his room.

Later, Liam thought about her scars, how deep they were. They followed him into his dreams. Only now they were weeping blood, pushing through the creases of her lacerated flesh.

She grinned, more red leaking from between her teeth. "You know you want to fuck me, you bad boy. You've always been naughty. Do you remember how wild you used to be? I know what the *old* Liam would've done. He would've bent me over and fucked me ragged. You wanted to, baby. You wanted to. I could see it. Baby, baby, baby."

Everything shifted, and Bretherton was standing with a newborn child in his hands, holding him over a bucket of water. Liam tried to scream. The dream wouldn't let him. Then Bretherton plunged the child into the water.

CHAPTER TWENTY

The massage had been a big moment for me. It wasn't just the pleasure. In truth, I'd had to fake most of it. I was too self-conscious to fully sink into it, but I felt sure Liam wouldn't notice. Men only heard and saw what they wanted to, at least when there was a naked woman moaning for them, shaking for them: making them feel like conquerors.

I'd debated holding off on revealing the scars on my back. I wasn't naïve. I knew they were ugly, the lacerations deep and unsightly. I'd spent an inordinate amount of time studying them in the mirror, looking over my shoulder.

Father said I could pay for the necessary surgeries if I wanted, but they were a part of me, a reminder of who I was: Madeline Arabella Pemberton, heir to the Pemberton fortune, a different sort to the regular folk.

When I was a girl, I'd made the mistake of sometimes viewing the servants as the same as us. Once, I'd struck up a friendship with a young woman called Paula, who was then cleaning Father's flat in the city. She was an interesting lady, with an exciting history; she'd been a sailor on a merchant vessel and used to sit me on her knee, telling me stories about her voyages.

Father spied us together one day, and Paula was dismissed. But of course I had to receive my punishment, to remind me: lashes across my back, done with mean intent, as Father ranted. "I suppose you want to crawl around on the floor too, snorting like a pig. I suppose you want to find some plumber and open your legs for him, don't you, you little slut?"

That was the first time I recalled, and it achieved its intended effect. For perhaps a year afterwards I remembered my place.

One summer, when we were staying at the Somerset estate, I'd spent my afternoons roaming with a lunch bag under one arm and a book under the other. Sitting beneath the shade of a towering Douglas fir, I'd spent a good two hours reading before I heard a laugh above me.

Looking up, I saw her. A young girl with her hair in pigtails, a year or so younger than me, with freckles across her cheeks.

"How long have you been there?" I asked.

"The whole time. Didn't you hear me?"

"I did not."

"What are you reading?"

It was an innocent enough exchange, and we struck up a friendship. Tina would climb trees as I read aloud to her, or sometimes we'd climb together. One day I fell, twisting my ankle. At first I tried not to tell Father what I'd been doing. But he always knew how to get the truth out of me, being my only family, the only person who truly understood me.

Once I'd told him about Tina and our tree-climbing forays, he beat me again. This time was far more severe than the first, and I passed out. When I awoke, he was still hitting me.

"We are not like them. You need to learn. The sooner you

accept it, the happier you'll be. We will *never* be like them. Understand?"

I managed to tell him yes, though my voice was weak. The message had been hammered into me; in time I grew to be grateful for my father's instructions.

There are people in this world who will take advantage of a wealthy lady whose head is not screwed on right, and in his own way, that was what he was trying to teach me: to be cautious, to guard our family's fortune and legacy.

I hoped Liam hadn't been too disgusted by the scars. But if he was going to love me, he was going to love the real me.

Father only condoned all of this because he saw it as me toying with the lower sorts. As far as he knew, the whole thing was a big game, nothing more, and my excuse about finding true love was just that: an excuse.

But ever since I'd laid eyes on Liam, something had ignited inside of me. I'd been so numb before that. I'd felt like I was sleepwalking through life, never fully aware, never present, and suddenly...

There he was, my dashing man with his messy black hair and his strong features and that invincible look in his eyes. Liam and I were starting our romance unconventionally, I wasn't blind to that, but in time I knew he would want me as hungrily as I wanted him.

If – when – that happened, I would have to talk to father and explain my desire to marry a dog trainer who'd never been to university. I would have to hope he could accept our love for what it was: pure, unique, beyond the confines of class or convention.

When Liam loved me as I loved him, I'd allow nothing to threaten us.

CHAPTER TWENTY-ONE

The next morning, Liam rested his forehead against the glass, thinking of better days.

Suddenly he was at a club. He was leaning against the bar, waiting for a pint of beer, when he spotted Emily on the dance floor. She was shit-faced, wearing a lacy black dress that flowed around her each time she spun and jumped up and down.

Immediately Liam felt something, a twitch of rage, as he saw a couple of drunk lads moving over to her. Liam had no right to feel protective. And yet he did. He wanted to keep her safe so badly. He didn't understand it, but he didn't question it.

Striding onto the dance floor, he offered her a big cheesy grin. "I've been looking for you everywhere."

She was so drunk, she actually looked confused for a second, like she believed him. "You have?"

"Yeah." He glared at the lads. "Come on. Let's get you some chips."

His pint forgotten, Liam took her arm and softly led her from the club. He didn't even think about what he was doing until they were outside. Then he turned to her and laughed, and she laughed, and they kept laughing until Liam was sure they were going crazy. It was raining and, without any fuss, Liam took off his jacket and draped it over her shoulders.

"Have we met?" she asked, brushing hair from her face.

Liam chuckled. "No. I just felt like saving you."

She made to playfully thump him, but she missed, and almost ended up in the gutter. He scooped his arm around her, pressed their bodies close. Then she leaned up for a kiss. Liam stepped away.

"What? You don't think I'm pretty?"

She was beautiful, with her hair messy and spiralling in the rain, with her bare legs poking out of the bottom of her dress, with that look in her eyes; it was a look that said, *I might be a fuck-up right now, but we can go places together. We can do anything together.* Liam was intoxicated with her. He'd tried explaining it to her later, and she'd laughed. "You were drunk."

But it was more than that. He'd never believed in love at first sight, but he wasn't sure how else to describe it.

"I'm Liam, by the way."

She smiled. "I'm Emily."

"Do you have a boyfriend?"

"Wow, somebody gets right to the point."

"Says the girl who just tried to kiss me."

"Fair. But why are you so interested?"

"I'm only asking. But I will cry if you say yes."

He loved making her laugh. It sounded like music to him. "No, I don't. I'm single and alone. A proper disgrace. I was in university, studying business, but I hated it. Hated the whole thing. So I dropped out and now I've got some lovely debt to pay off and my dad looks at me like I'm a failure and..."

Suddenly she was crying. Liam wrapped his arms around her, stroked his fingers through her hair, whispering it would all be okay. Emily would always say how shocked she was that Liam hadn't run for the hills the moment she started to cry, but it was the opposite. He wanted to make her feel better. He wanted to heal her, or for her to heal him.

He took her to the chippy around the corner and they scrounged together one pound between them, sharing the bag as they walked through the city centre. She asked about his job and he told her it was boring. He asked about her dreams and she said she didn't know what she wanted to do, and that was part of the problem.

They spent a lot of time talking about Rocky, Emily laughing at all the stories from Liam's childhood, and then, before they knew it, they were standing outside her parents' house.

She thrust her phone at him in the cutest way. Liam would never forget that. It was part shy and part confident and part uniquely Emily. "You can put your number in there. If you want."

Of course he bloody wanted to.

It was nothing anybody would ever make films about. There had been no grand romantic gestures that night, just two young people sharing a bag of chips, the paper wet with the rain. They hadn't kissed; Liam felt adamant she was too drunk. But something magical had happened, something difficult to explain to anybody who hadn't experienced it. From that day on, he thought only of Emily, dreamed only of Emily.

He read his book for a while, and then Bretherton's knock came.

"Sir." He pushed the door open. "I have brought your breakfast. And good news. Miss Pemberton is very pleased with you. She wants to share lunch in the library. I'm sure you're as excited as she is."

Liam eyed the paper bag in the butler's hand. It smelled like bacon. "Yeah, I'm as excited as a man can get." He stood and took the bag, returning to his chair. "Anything else?"

"Yes, she has a small request. Rather, it's not a request, more of a..."

"A command? Come on, I'm a dog, and I need to be told what tricks to do."

"She would like you to write her a poem."

"Is this a joke?" Bretherton shook his head, and Liam groaned. "I don't know how to write a goddamn poem."

"It doesn't have to be anything of literary merit. Just... just speak from the heart."

"I don't think she really wants me to speak from the heart."

"Then speak from the heart she wishes you had. Enjoy your breakfast."

Bretherton left, locking the door behind him. Liam munched on his bacon rashers and tried to work out how to handle this. If he came on too heavily, she might guess he was faking. Or she might believe him and take it as a sign he wanted to be with her... which could work in his favour, now he thought about it. Maybe this was a chance, one step closer to grabbing her, using her as leverage. Like he had with Rebecca, only this time nobody would die.

He finished his bacon, crumpling up the bag. A guard was patrolling the grounds, walking past the trees. Liam watched until he was out of sight.

And then he realised something.

He hammered on the door.

"What?" a guard grunted.

"I don't have a bloody pen."

"Yeah."

"How am I supposed to write a poem without a pen?"

"Memorise it. No sharp objects."

He sat on the end of the bed, feeling like a stupid kid in

English class all over again. His mind was empty. But he had to think.

If he didn't get this right, she might snap. It wouldn't be the cell. It wouldn't be beatings from the guards. It would be Madeline standing over his child, a blade in her hand, ready to end little Jamie or Hazel's life before it began.

CHAPTER TWENTY-TWO

B ag, cuffs, frogmarch.

And then Liam was back in the library, two guards flanking him.

Madeline stood at the top of the staircase. Liam felt like a peasant coming to pay homage to a princess. It was the way she was looking at him, properly dramatic, with her hands clasped in front of her and an expectant look on her face.

"I'm so glad you came," she said.

Liam rubbed his wrists, sore from the cuffs. Some of the guards enjoyed tightening them more than others; the lanky kid never tightened them all the way. Liam assumed it was the guards he'd hurt during the fighting.

"Have you gone deaf, silly?"

Liam gazed up at her. The skylight let in the bright sun, catching motes of dust. "No."

"I suppose you've simply forgotten your manners. It's rude not to reply when somebody speaks to you. I said I was glad you came."

"I'm glad I'm here."

This was better than the massage, at least. There was plenty of space between them. She was wearing a sweater, trying to look cute as she adjusted her sleeves.

"I believe you've prepared something for me?"

Liam nodded. "I, uh, yes. I have. I've written you a poem. Not written. But..."

He spread his hands. This was a joke. But Bretherton's threat was still fresh in his mind: Emily, his child. They were all that mattered.

"Awh, Liam, are you *nervous?* Don't worry. I'm sure it's excellent."

Liam could almost guarantee it wasn't. He hadn't been able to think of anything. He cleared his throat. She was staring at him with a manic glint in her eyes, the same way she'd looked in the dining room before she slit Rebecca's throat. She was looking for an excuse to hurt somebody.

"I'm not much of a poet–"

She tutted. "Don't start with excuses."

The guards shifted behind him. Liam glanced over his shoulder. They were standing a few feet away, close enough to spring into action if he made a run for the staircase.

"Why are you looking at them? They can't help you. Surely if you're serious about developing a romance with me, you should be able to recite a simple poem."

Liam scratched his throat. He felt like such a dick. "When I look into your eyes, I, uh, I see heaven. It makes me want to go on a holiday with you... maybe to Devon." He was making this up as he went along. And it was bad. But he couldn't stop now. "There are so many reasons I love you, way more than seven. I... I would do anything for you, even, uh, even change my name to Evan."

What was he babbling about?

He sensed the guards trying to hold back their laughter. Or maybe he was being paranoid.

Madeline wasn't remotely pleased. She gripped the railing and her eyes widened to saucers, her features twitching.

"Am I a joke to you?" She began to descend the stairs slowly, her heels clicking against the wood. "Is that what you think this is? A big joke?"

"No." Liam took a step back; the guards moved up behind him. "I did my best, Maddie. Really."

"You did not do your best," she stated flatly. "You're trying to humiliate me. I thought we'd made some progress yesterday. I thought you were ready to take this seriously."

"I am."

He was pathetic; his voice was quivering. The closer she got, the harder his heart thumped. They had so many resources. They could kidnap Emily, the same way they'd kidnapped him, and who knew what horrors Madeline would inflict on his fiancée?

She stopped just short of him. "Shall we try again?"

His cheeks were burning. He hadn't felt like this in years. "I..."

"If you care about me, you should be able to come up with something better than that. You want to change your name to Evan? How is that even slightly romantic?"

The guards were standing so close he could feel the heat of their bodies. Madeline glanced at them, as though deciding whether to give the command. A nod and they'd be on him; a nod and they'd be driving out of the estate, on the hunt for Emily and his child.

"*Liam.*"

He had an idea. Pretend she was Emily. Imagine he was standing at the altar on their wedding day and they'd written their own vows. He looked down at Madeline, imagining her black hair was Emily's brown, her judgemental eyes were

Emily's understanding gaze, her pursed lips were Emily's soft smile.

"All my life, I feel like I've been searching for something." In his mind, Emily was smiling up at him encouragingly, knowing how difficult it was for him to talk about his feelings: ready to give him leeway if the words didn't come out perfectly. "But the second I saw you, I knew I was done searching. I knew I could finally begin my life."

He saw Emily on the dance floor, spinning wildly around, so drunk she could barely stand. He saw her with that cute grin on her face as she thrust her phone into his hands. He saw her the next day, when they'd met in a café and she laughingly told him she remembered very little from the night before... but she'd like to get to know him, if she hadn't scared him away.

"I don't need money, or fame, or glory, or any of that. I only need you. I only want you. Forever."

He swallowed, wondering if he would ever see Emily again, if he'd ever hold her as Rocky got jealous and tried to wriggle between them.

Madeline looked at him for several seconds, then almost a minute. Liam's body tensed. She was studying him as though trying to read his mind, as though she could somehow tell those words hadn't been meant for her. But then she finally clapped her hands together.

"Oh, how wonderfully direct!" she squealed. "Away with your fancy similes, your clumsy metaphors. Give me the straightforward truth of the matter. Yes, Liam, delightful. Absolutely delightful."

She wrapped her arms around his shoulders and squeezed close. Her body felt so wrong against his. She moaned and squeezed tighter, urging him to return her embrace. What choice did he have?

He held her, inhaling the stink of her perfume, hating the

warmth of her body pushing through the fabric of their clothes.

"This is lovely. I feel so safe in your arms. You'd never let anything happen to me, would you?"

"Never."

All it would take was a spin: tighten his grip on her, turn so that she was between him and the guards. But there were risks.

What if Madeline was a fake, just like Rebecca had been? Liam didn't believe that. It seemed too elaborate. How many women were they going to kidnap and force to play this twisted game?

It wasn't only that. Liam didn't know his way out of this part of the house. There were too many chances for the guards to intercept him. And the guards were standing close, ready to leap on him if he tried anything.

Maybe this was cowardice. He didn't know. He kept hugging her, willing himself to do something. What if they had people watching Emily right this moment, ready to grab her?

He tightened his grip on her slightly. She made a sickening purring sound. "It's been so long since somebody held me like this."

This was it. He had to do it. He couldn't act based on *what ifs*. Once he had her as a hostage, he'd figure out what to do. The guards wouldn't risk letting her get hurt. Did he have it in him to hurt her, really, when it came right down to it? The answer was no, no way. He wished Madeline was a man.

Then she stepped away. He'd missed his opportunity. Again.

"I have to leave you for a little while. Perhaps a week." Madeline sighed. "Of course, I'd rather stay here, but certain things are expected of me. Father says it's paramount the Pembertons keep up their public appearances, at the most boring affairs: charity functions, parties, that sort of thing. It's so horribly dull."

"You can't tell your Father no?" Liam probed.

Perhaps there was a way for him to learn more about her family and use it against her.

"Francis Pemberton is not a man to whom one says *no*, I'm afraid. But I'll only be a week. We're heading down to London and then flitting to Paris, but you'll be here waiting for me when I get back, won't you?"

Liam suppressed a dark laugh. As if he had any choice. "Yeah, I'll be here. Waiting for you."

She bit her lip, trying to look shy and flirty. Everything she did was so forced. It was like she'd watched a few romantic comedy films and was trying her hardest to do what those women did, to feel what they supposedly felt. Walking past him, she brushed her hand along his belly.

Liam tried to see into the hallway as she left the room, but she closed the door too quickly. Then it was just him and the guards.

One of them gestured at him to turn around.

"What if I don't feel like it?"

"I don't know, Evan. I guess we'll have to figure it out."

The other guard sniggered.

Liam stepped forwards, fists clenched, and the guards quickly backed up.

"Or we could pay your lovely lady a visit. Don't be a dick, mate. You tried fighting. Look where it got you."

At the mention of Emily, Liam almost erupted. But he knew they were right. There was no point beating up these guards or giving them reason to beat him up. He had to play the game... until when, though? He'd just had a chance, better than any he was going to get, and he'd done nothing.

He told himself it was to keep Emily safe. But the truth was far sadder. The truth was he was scared.

He turned, putting his arms behind his back.

CHAPTER TWENTY-THREE

They locked Liam in his room all week.

He finished *The Call of the Wild* and then started it again. The violence against the animals was difficult to read, but it was his only way to escape the drudgery of his everyday existence. When he was spiriting across the Yukon territory in search of gold, he didn't have to think about Emily or his child or what that psychotic bitch Madeline would do when she returned.

Bretherton was gone; the guards brought Liam's breakfast and dinner, as well as a change of clothes.

Sometimes, Liam wouldn't even bother getting up. He'd lie on his back and stare up at the patterns on the four-poster bed, wondering if this was what happened when a man's spirit broke. The guards didn't care; they'd open the door a crack, throw his food or clothes in, and then quickly shut it. It was then up to him to leave the paper bags by the door. But often he ignored them, not getting changed for days in a row.

He willed himself to slip into dreams; then he could hold his baby, bring his ear down to their tiny chest and listen to – and feel – their little heart beating.

He wanted to know if it was Jamie or Hazel. Emily had chosen the names, finding them in one of her favourite books, and Liam had thought they sounded perfect. Jamie was a good strong name, and Hazel was beautiful. He would give several fingers just to see them, even through a window, even if he couldn't tell them he was there: just to see them, once, to know they were alive and safe.

Towards the end of the week, his bedroom door opened all the way.

He sat up. The lanky kid stood in the doorway, a brown paper bag in his hand. It was dinnertime already. The day had flitted by far too quickly. More and more, Liam was disappearing into himself, barely conscious of the passage of time. It was dangerous. He needed to stay sharp, alert to any chance of escape.

Maybe this was it; the guards never normally opened the door all the way.

"Hello," Liam said. The guard stared. "What, you won't speak to me?"

"We're not supposed to."

Liam hadn't realised how badly he missed talking, even to these bastards. He wasn't built to be stuck on his own.

"It's all right. I'm not going to tell on you."

Liam moved to stand. The guard shook his head. "Don't."

"Why not? I'm not a threat." Liam stood, but remained where he was. "What has the lovely chef made for me today?"

"Smells like chicken. Think there's some veg in there too."

Liam patted his belly, hoping he didn't look as beaten down as he felt. "I was hoping for a Big Mac, but I guess this will have to do."

The kid grinned. At least, his eyes shone as though he was smiling. It was difficult to tell with the mask. "The nearest McDonald's is…"

He trailed off. Liam knew why. He'd been about to reveal information which might give Liam an idea of where they were.

"You're not like the others." Liam took a cautious step. "I spotted that right away. When Madeline killed Becky, you were the only one who reacted. Why are you doing this?"

The kid stared. Liam took another step.

"Is it money?" he went on, watching him carefully. "Nah, I don't think so. You would've left by now if it was just money. What is it? Are they threatening your family?"

"Stay where you are. Please. I don't want to hurt you."

"Fancy your chances, do you?"

"Yeah, I do. All I have to do is shout and there will be five guards here in less than a minute."

"Were you one of the bastards who took me, the night I proposed to my girlfriend? In the alleyway?"

He shook his head.

"What's your name?" Liam asked.

"We're not supposed to say."

"I'm asking anyway."

"If my boss finds out..."

Liam mimed sealing his lips shut and throwing away the key. "It's just a name."

The kid sighed, glanced down the hallway. Liam wondered if he had time to rush him. But then it was too late; he'd turned back. "Harrison. Please don't tell anybody I told you that."

Liam nodded to the brown paper bag. "All right then, Harrison. I'd like to eat if that's okay with you."

Harrison slowly placed the bag on the floor then backed away from the doorway. Liam approached, noting the way Harrison tensed up, his hand near his waist.

"Is it just the needles?" Liam asked, as he picked up the bag. "Or have you got something else in there? Extendable batons, maybe? I guess you can't tell me."

Harrison just stared.

Liam took the food to the bed and dropped down. There was no point making a run for it. He knew what Harrison was saying was true; there were too many guards for him to be able to fight his way out. His injuries had started to heal, the pain lessening, but sometimes his jaws twinged and his body ached from the beatings.

Liam opened the bag. Five chicken breasts and several big chunks of broccoli.

"The lady needs to keep her sex slave well-fed, I guess," Liam mused as he took out a piece of chicken. "Do you think that's where this is heading? Do you think she's going to try to make me have sex with her? Maybe she'll get you lot to inject me with Viagra."

"I don't know. I'm as in the dark as you."

"You know, Harrison. I find that difficult to believe."

Harrison glanced up and down the hallway. "Please stop using my name."

Liam shrugged. "Fair enough."

He began to eat, but still Harrison didn't leave. Liam met his eyes and saw something like regret there. What did the kid want, forgiveness?

"As prisons go, you have to admit this isn't too bad," Harrison said.

Liam snorted. "Yeah, it's a nice house."

"All you have to do is act like you love her. Just pretend."

"And then what? Where does this end?"

"I don't know. All I'm saying is, there's no reason to make it hard on yourself. We don't like hurting you."

"I think some of the others do, actually. But you're different. If it wasn't for the fact you were part of this, I might go as far to say you seem like a decent bloke. I can't, though, can I? Because there you are."

"I didn't know it was going to be like this. I thought I'd be working security for parties, that sort of stuff."

"No judgement. We've all got to make a living." Liam tore a chunk of chicken off with his teeth, chewing loudly with his mouth open, grinning over at Harrison. "Sorry, mate. I've forgotten my manners. Shitting in a bucket will do that to you."

"It could be much worse. You're not being tortured. You're eating well. You've got more than most prisoners could wish for."

"I know. I'm a lucky man."

"You have to admit it could be worse," Harrison said, almost whining now.

"Who are you trying to convince? I just told you. I'm grateful."

"So when she comes back, you're going to do what she wants? You're going to make this easier... for everyone?"

"You sound anxious, Harrison."

"I told you not to use my name—"

"My girlfriend... no, my fiancée, Emily, she gets anxious sometimes." Liam took another bite of the chicken, chewing quicker, picturing Emily with her eyes bloodshot from crying and her nails bitten down to the stubs with worry. "It's the reason she dropped out of university. She's so clever, way smarter than me. But she used to get panic attacks. She's improved loads since I've known her. This, though... losing her fiancée, a week before she's due to give birth, I'm worried, mate. If you want the truth, I'm terrified it's going to send her over the edge."

Harrison shifted from foot to foot. "I don't know what you want me to do about it."

"Yes, you do. You're just scared. I get it."

"Helping you would ruin my life. My family's life."

"So do nothing. Don't help. But don't expect me to tell you you're a good person for it."

"I–"

"What's going on here?"

Liam recognised the voice. It was Smith, the man in charge of the guards. His footsteps pounded down the hallway and then he appeared behind Harrison. He looked at Liam and then at Harrison. "What are you doing? I told you to deliver the food. That was it."

"I..."

Smith grabbed Harrison by the shoulder and shoved him out of view. "Get back to your room. Bloody liability."

Harrison disappeared and Smith took a step into the room, hands behind his back. "What did he say?"

"Nothing useful. You're right. The kid's a liability."

"So what were you talking about?"

"I was asking him if Madeline was going to rape me."

Smith flinched.

"What? It's a fair question. I was thinking of it the other night. You know, *rape* sounds like such a strange word, at least to me, when it comes to a woman assaulting a man. Maybe that makes me a sexist prick. But what else can you call it, when somebody forces a person to have sex with them?"

"The lady of the house isn't unattractive."

"She's not my fiancée. And I don't want to fuck her. But yeah, sure, she's okay to look at. I guess that makes everything all right."

"He didn't tell you anything about the grounds, the layout of the house, anything like that?"

Liam took out another piece of chicken. "Nope."

"How can I believe you?"

"Why bother asking me if you're going to come back with that? I asked him to. He didn't."

Liam was thinking about the future: the day he might eventually get out of this hellhole. Harrison was the only guard who'd offered him any sort of humanity. Liam didn't want to get him in trouble. He might come in useful.

"They have something on him," Liam went on. "I'm not sure what. But it's obvious. Is it the same with the rest of you? Are they blackmailing you too, Smith?"

Smith grabbed the door handle, pulling it shut. "Don't use my name again."

Liam finished his meal and placed the paper bag next to the door. He was strangely tired after talking to the guards, as though even that small amount of social interaction was too much for him. He felt like he was becoming a different person, or not a person at all.

Maybe this was what going mad felt like.

CHAPTER TWENTY-FOUR

I'd known being apart from Liam would be painful. I'd grown used to seeing him regularly, either on the camera or in person. But the parties were necessary, Father said. "We have to keep up public appearances, show the world how delightfully superior we are." He said it with his typically Father-like irony, but I knew there was truth in there; he did believe it was our duty to demonstrate how much better than everybody else we were.

The usual attention was lavished on me at the parties. Men lined up to make fools of themselves as they fought for my interest. I gave them as little as I could to instil a false sense of hope. I had no desire to force myself to love a man simply because he was from the same class as me.

That was the secret I could never divulge to Father; this was not just a game. When I'd first laid eyes on Liam, it was like the heavens had collided with the earth. It was like one of those wonderful Hollywood films, a love-at-first-sight scenario; my interactions with these high-society gentleman didn't even come close. If lightning had struck me when I first saw my Liam, these men provoked not even the barest flickering candle flame.

In Paris, Father joined me on the balcony. He smoked his pipe like the old-fashioned relic he was, a soft smile on his face as smoke drifted around his face. For a minute or two we looked up at the Eiffel Tower together, the sky orange and red with the setting sun.

"You've seemed a little distracted of late, Maddie."

"I have?"

"It has been remarked upon. A little curt, not willing to fully engage. That Robinson boy is, by all accounts, a very promising young man. It's widely agreed he's handsome and charming; lots of people mention that, whenever he comes up in conversation."

"Yes, he seemed friendly enough."

He was talking about one of the high-society vultures who always circled me whenever we went to a function. Father had made no secret about wanting me to find a suitable partner, get married, and start shitting out grandchildren.

"I hope this isn't about... the game."

He spoke as though we were in a spy thriller, as though there were listening devices in the walls.

"Of course not," I said quickly. "I haven't thought about that since I left. It's only a bit of fun."

Father had an unnerving way of staring at me sometimes. He hadn't hit me since I was a child, but I always felt as if he wanted to, or perhaps he missed the days when he was able to strike me freely. "You're not getting any younger."

"Charming."

"I mean it. Your mother would have had several children if she'd..."

He trailed off, sounding almost human for a moment. He rarely mentioned Mother. It pained me. I didn't like to think about her, about the woman she'd become, about what my life might've been. She had always been the kinder of the two, if my memory was correct; she never would've let him hit me.

I didn't even think about mentioning his abuse. Father had tucked it away into an ignored corner of his mind, and I was expected to do the same. I had only mentioned it once, during an argument a few years ago. He'd looked at me like I was insane.

"I did *what*?"

We'd been fighting about Mother, the only topic of conversation which brought us to such passion. I'd been in such a state, I tore my dress and spun so he could see my back, the scars criss-crossing on my skin: the ugly scars which would make me so difficult to love.

When I turned to face him, Father had left. He hadn't even lingered long enough to take a look at his handiwork.

On the balcony in Paris, he puffed on his pipe. "You don't have as long as you think. That Robinson boy is handsome, from the right family, funny and, according to several trustworthy sources, a very interesting man. You'd be a fool not to at least entertain the notion."

"I suppose you wish we still did arranged marriages in England."

"We *can* do arranged marriages."

"Is that so?"

"It would be a simple matter. I would strip you of your trust and remove your name from my will until you'd married a man of my choosing."

"Perhaps I'm not as reliant upon your money as you like to believe."

Father waved a hand, causing the pipe smoke to shimmer around him. He was gesturing to all of Paris, to the presidential suite of the hotel, to the balcony, to the world. And then he nodded over the balcony, to the street below. "That's where you'd end up without me. Never forget that."

"I'll choose a husband soon. You don't have to make threats."

It was the truth. Things were going well with Liam. He was still requiring more encouragement than was ideal, but he was getting there.

"You never grew up, Maddie. That's the problem. All those silly novels you read. All those silly films you watch, filling your head with nonsense about love and destiny. Life doesn't work that way. Very few married people are in love."

I didn't like the sound of that one bit: a loveless marriage, bringing children into a cold and callous home. I wanted Liam to smile at me like he had the first time I saw him: the smile that told me he'd always be there, always support me, no matter what happened, no matter what I had to do to make him love me.

It was almost time to return to England, to the Lincolnshire estate. It was almost time to reunite with the man of my dreams.

CHAPTER TWENTY-FIVE

Emily Taylor stood at the window of her childhood bedroom, her arms wrapped across her middle. Even with the heating on and in two jumpers, she couldn't get warm. She kept expecting Liam to walk up the driveway any second, his signature grin on his face, looking at her sheepishly.

And then he'd tell her he was abroad sorting the honeymoon of their dreams, but he got held up doing... something regular and easily explained, something that meant she could instantly forgive him and they didn't have to argue and everything would be okay.

She walked over to Jamie's cot, reaching down and softly stroking her hand over his head. She hadn't been able to stay at the flat after Liam disappeared, but she'd felt sure that in a few days he'd return and everything would go back to normal.

But it had been three weeks: three weeks since he vanished, no witnesses, no leads, nothing.

After kissing Jamie on the top of his head – and muttering a silent thanks that he'd finally settled – she made sure the baby monitor was on and crept down the stairs. Dad was sitting in his armchair, a cup of tea in his hand, watching the news.

"Anything?" Emily asked, belly churning.

Dad frowned deeply. Emily sensed he was getting tired of that question. It wasn't as though Liam's disappearance had become a notable news story. The local paper had run a small column and the police had put out an appeal, but it hadn't rocked the world.

"No, I'm sorry, love."

Emily dropped onto the sofa. Rocky immediately untangled himself from his blankets and padded across the cushions, curling up in her lap. He hadn't been the same since Liam's disappearance. He was growing old as it was, but lately he'd been more sluggish, less inclined to eat. He spent hours sitting in the doorway, staring, exploding into barks any time the wind blew, which would set Jamie off sometimes. But Emily couldn't blame him. He'd been with Liam his whole life, pretty much. He missed him as much as Emily did.

"You should try to get some sleep," Dad said.

Emily stroked her hand over Rocky's head, flattening his ears. The dog whined. Emily was going to take him to the vet tomorrow if he gave them any more fuss when it came to his breakfast. She'd been meaning to take him for a couple of days. But he was so old. What if he had to be put down before Liam returned? What if Liam never returned?

"Emily, did you hear what I said?"

"I can't sleep."

"Maybe we should see if the doctor will give you something. You need your rest."

"How can I when Liam's out there somewhere, probably hurt, probably in danger?"

Dad took a long, slow sip of his tea.

"What?" Emily snapped.

She and Dad had always been able to read each other, ever since she was little. He didn't bother trying to make excuses.

"You need to think about Jamie."

"I *am* thinking about Jamie. He needs his dad."

"He also needs a mother who takes care of herself." Dad stood and walked around the coffee table, placing his mug down and sitting beside her. Looping his arm over her shoulder, he pulled her to him. "I don't mean to sound like I'm criticising you. I hope it didn't come across that way. But we don't know how long it's going to be until Liam comes back."

"What do you mean, *comes back*?"

"Until they find him," Dad said quickly.

This was the exact reason she'd stopped checking her phone. The flood of supportive texts and emails and social media notifications had been overwhelming enough, but then there had been the snide messages, little hints dropped here and there. One woman, who Emily had known in secondary school but hadn't spoken to since, had even messaged her with a story about how her boyfriend had run away and was refusing to pay child support.

That was just one example of the theory a lot of people seemed to believe: Liam had walked out. The pressure of a marriage and a baby had been too much for him, and so he'd left, ready to start a new life.

Emily didn't believe that. She'd been with Liam for too long, had spent too much time with him, loved him too deeply to entertain the notion even for a second. She remembered lying in bed with him a few weeks after they'd met, his fingertips moving tantalisingly across the back of her neck.

"Emily, I love you."

She'd propped up on his chest, looking into his boyish face and his bright eyes and not doubting it for a second. "I love you too."

She always thought of that as the point where their relationship truly began. She'd been so embarrassed by how they'd met; she'd told her friends she was going home, but had returned to the club to get as many drinks down her as possible, to drown the shame of dropping out of university. She'd always wished she could've been more elegant, more composed that night.

But that moment, when they said *I love you* for the first time – with a light snow falling outside – it was so romantic. It was so real. That was the moment she knew they were in it for the long haul.

Why did she have to send him for beers? He'd just proposed and her first thought was for him to go and get some alcohol. But she knew Liam; she knew he'd enjoy the evening more after a couple of drinks. But she still hated herself. She should've held him, held tight, never let him go.

"He was so excited to be a dad," Emily said. "Why would he bother proposing if he was going to walk out? Liam isn't cruel. If he was planning on leaving, he wouldn't have done it like that."

"I'm sure you're right." Dad gave her shoulder a squeeze. "But all you can focus on is the day-to-day. Can you do that? Please? For your silly old dad?"

"I just wish the police would do more."

"I'm sure they're doing everything they can."

"I know. I get that. But there's nothing, is there? No CCTV. No eyewitnesses. No evidence of any kind. It doesn't look good."

"You can't lose hope."

Emily sighed. "I know. But let's say we were talking about somebody else, not Liam. Let's say we weren't emotionally invested in it. What would we say? We'd say there's not much chance of this having a happy ending."

"I don't think that sort of thinking is helpful."

"Tell me the truth. Do you think Liam ran out on us?"

Dad kissed the top of her head, the same way he had when

she was a kid. Emily couldn't help but think about what should be happening right now, with the four of them – Mum, Dad, Emily, Liam – in their flat, quietly drinking tea in the living room as Rocky sprawled on the floor and Jamie slept in the next room.

"I don't know," Dad said after a pause. "That's the truth."

Emily nodded. She understood why he was doubting. It wasn't that Liam had ever given them cause for concern – he and Dad got on well – but what else was everybody supposed to think? Liam had no enemies. He hadn't been mugged or killed; surely there would be evidence somewhere. There was no explanation. It was random and horrible and that, it seemed, was that.

It didn't mean Emily had to like it. Scooping Rocky up, she cradled him to her chest and made for the door.

"Love you, Dad."

"I love you too."

She carried Rocky upstairs, into the bedroom. Rocky squirmed until Emily put him down, then he padded over to the cot and lay beneath it, grey beard resting on his paws as he stared at the door. He was guarding Jamie until Liam got home.

CHAPTER TWENTY-SIX

"Get up. We're taking you to the pool."

Liam blinked his eyes open. Two guards stood at the edge of his bed. One was holding a pair of handcuffs, the other a black bag.

"Where's Bretherton?" Liam asked. The butler was usually the one who told him where he was going, what was expected of him.

The guards exchanged a look. And then the one holding the handcuffs stepped forwards. "The lady of the house has decided Bretherton has outlived his usefulness. He's been discharged from service."

Liam swallowed, thinking about the old man. They hadn't been friendly by any means, but he was still preferable to these faceless bastards. "So he did something that crazy bitch didn't like, and she killed him for it? Am I getting the gist of it here?"

"Are you going to make this hard?" the other guard grunted.

Liam shook his head, standing and putting his hands behind his back. It all felt so pathetically natural. But still, if they were taking him to the pool, that meant Madeline had returned. He'd have another chance to get his hands on her, to use her as a hostage... but as the days passed, he was beginning to wonder if this was a lie he was telling himself, a way to justify his lack of action.

He'd acted before, and the result had been the cell, the darkness, the bucket, the stink of shit. He couldn't go back there.

As they did their frogmarching routine, he thought of the old man. Liam had warned him that they were both expendable. Did he have any family? Liam guessed not; Madeline clearly selected people she knew she could get away with murdering. But she wouldn't be able to kill Liam without any consequences, would she?

He had Emily, his friends, his parents, *her* parents. Too many people would miss him.

They uncuffed him and pulled off the black bag. They were at the interior swimming pool again, but thankfully Madeline wasn't half naked this time. She wore a one-piece swimsuit with her hair piled atop her head in an intricate weave. Liam wondered if the one-piece was to hide her scars.

There were four guards dotted around the room, as well as the two behind him. Liam saw Harrison in the far corner. All the guards stood like statues with their hands behind their backs and their balaclava-covered faces aimed stubbornly ahead. Liam guessed they'd been given instructions not to move or draw attention to themselves.

Madeline smiled in her typically dramatic way as she walked over to Liam. "It feels like it's been years since I've seen you." She paused, narrowing her eyes. "Have you been eating? You look pale."

"Bretherton promised he'd take me on walks around the grounds while you were away, but he's disappeared."

Maybe that would get some information about the old man.

Madeline frowned. "Bretherton really said that?"

"But he's gone. Just like that."

"He was behaving in a very silly way, and so I had to let him go. Don't give him another thought. I'm certainly not going to." She leaned close, lowering her voice. "Think of it like this. Things are expected of you. If you don't fulfil your responsibilities, there are consequences. See? It's simple. Shall we go for a swim?"

Her message was clear. She'd killed Bretherton the same way she'd killed Rebecca, and neither murder meant anything to her. She'd kill every guard in this room without a second thought, but still they stood there, loyal brain-dead idiots, all because of blackmail or money or whatever it was. Liam didn't care. There was no excuse.

But maybe he was as bad as the rest of them, because he smiled. He nodded. "Sure, a swim sounds nice. But I don't have any trunks."

Madeline gestured to the poolside chair. A pair of trunks and a towel were draped over the back. "There you go. Don't keep me waiting."

He picked them up and looked around. "Where do I get changed?"

Madeline giggled. "Silly. Right here. Don't worry. I won't judge."

Liam glanced at Harrison. The kid was the only guard with his fists clenched. The others stood completely still, not reacting at all. The only outliers were the two who'd brought him there; they followed him wherever he went, always a few paces behind, ready if Liam tried anything.

Liam took off his clothes, figuring there was no point messing about. She was going to make him do it anyway. Madeline ogled him openly, her eyes moving up and down his body. He tried to turn away as he reached for his trousers, but she tutted. Just that. A tut. And Liam turned back to face her. He was learning to read her moods.

He pulled down his trousers and his boxers quickly. His prick flopped and Madeline stared at it, running her tongue over her lips. She looked deranged.

Liam quickly pulled the trunks on, returning to her.

"You really are all man. What a big boy."

He didn't know what to say. He felt like meat.

She moved to the end of the pool and sat down, softly moving her legs back and forth through the water. Liam followed suit and, when she hopped in, he did the same. She grinned at him like he was her prize poodle, finally learning to follow her commands, even her unspoken ones.

As they swam, the guards moved to the very edge of the pool. They'd clearly planned this beforehand. They were going to drag him from the water if he did what a dark part of him wanted to: grab a big bunch of the bitch's hair, twist it in his hand, and push her under the water, keep pushing until her body stopped thrashing and there were no more bubbles.

The water was cool and refreshing, and it felt good to use his body. He felt far weaker than when he arrived, having to will his muscles into action. He'd spent the last week doing little but lying around in bed, so it wasn't surprising. He promised himself he'd start doing some push-ups and squats. He needed to be ready when the time came. If it ever did.

"I have a fun game," Madeline announced, standing up to her hips in the water. "Let's see who can hold their breath the longest."

Liam shrugged. He didn't care what they did. He just wished the guards would back up a little bit. But even if they did, what could he do? Grab her when they were both soaking wet; she'd be difficult to hold on to. And then, once he had her, he'd have to somehow drag her from the water without the guards getting hold of him.

"What's the matter?" She pouted. "You don't want to play the game?"

"No, I do," he said quickly. What a good boy he was. "Let's do it."

"Excellent! No cheating, okay? On the count of three. Three, two, one..."

Liam plunged beneath the water, eyes closed, all sound blocked off except for that eerie watery echo. His mind flitted with vignettes, with Buck from *Call of the Wild*, the dog who went to join the wolves, and then Rocky was there, and Emily was smiling down at him, her hand on the Jack Russell's head, and he saw his father: he was holding a suitcase, frowning at Liam, telling him he was sorry; he had never been cut out for marriage.

Liam liked to think, later, that was why he'd felt so certain about him and Emily; he wouldn't be like his father.

He was running out of air, but he remained under a little longer; it was better than up there, with the guards and the psychopath.

Finally, he burst up. He had no idea how long he'd been under, but Harrison was looking down at him, concern in his eyes. No... not him: at Madeline. She was still in the water, black-haired head bobbing up and down. Her arms and legs were splayed.

A long time passed, too long.

"What happens to us if she drowns?" Liam said. When nobody answered, he spoke louder, almost shouted. "If she dies, what happens to us? Answer me, you stupid motherfuckers."

Harrison was shaking his head.

Liam groaned and moved through the water. Fighting every instinct in his body, he forced his hands to grab her shoulders and haul her upright. He almost expected her to be unconscious. She'd been in the water twice as long as him. She sputtered and coughed, throwing her arms around Liam, saying something about how he was her saviour, and then she made to kiss him.

Liam pushed her.

It was a reflex, but it didn't matter. She fell back a few steps and then caught herself, staring at him as her jaws tensed and her nostrils flared.

"You... you hit me."

"I'm sorry," he whined, sounding pathetic and not caring. She looked even more unhinged than when she'd killed Rebecca.

"I was just trying to kiss you, and you, you... Guards." Soft at first, and then her voice rose. "Guards, get him! Get him!"

Liam tried to put up a fight. But his body was weak and there were six of them, removing their walkies and leaping into the water. He caught one under the chin and elbowed another across the mouth, but then there was an arm around his throat.

Harrison's voice was in his ear as Liam's legs thrashed wildly. "Stop fighting. You can't win. Just bloody stop it."

They hauled him from the water, as Madeline's voice got even shriller, even louder, until Liam felt like it was bouncing around his skull. "Darkroom," she kept saying. "Take him to the darkroom!"

CHAPTER TWENTY-SEVEN

H arrison wrestled the black bag over Liam's head as Smith cuffed him. Their clothes were soaked, sticking to their bodies, as the lady of the house kept screaming at them. Harrison didn't know where the darkroom was, but Smith led the way. The other guards followed close behind as they dragged Liam through the door.

Normally, whenever they moved Liam, they took him on a winding tour of the house, walking in and out of rooms to disorient him. It even disoriented Harrison sometimes, as they entered bedroom after bedroom, a giant room with a piano in it, a library, a second library... this place was insanely massive, big enough to house several families, but most of the furniture was covered in sheets to protect from dust, only removed if Madeline requested it.

This time Smith led them on a straight path, with a clear destination in mind.

The balaclava itched more than usual as it stuck to Harrison's face. Smith led them down a long corridor and to a small room on the right. There were more mounted animal heads in there, things Harrison was surprised to see: a lion, a wolf, what looked like a stuffed eagle. It was like the owners of the house wanted everybody to know how powerful they were. They could even conquer nature.

Liam didn't fight. They'd beaten him too badly. Harrison ignored the voice at the back of his head, whispering that they needed to stop. He tried not to think about what his dad would say, or his granddad, or his old Army buddies.

Finally they came to the darkroom. The light was turned low, an eerie mixture of yellow and red, and dozens of photos hung from wires criss-crossing from wall to wall.

They were of Liam. He was standing in a park, a wide grin on his face, as a German Shepherd sat obediently at his feet. He was walking out of the gym, a towel draped over his shoulders. He was sitting in a pub. He was standing at his bedroom window in his boxer shorts.

Harrison looked at Smith, but the man just shook his head. Then Madeline burst in behind them and Harrison stood up straight, pretending the photos didn't bother him: that they weren't yet another sign of how wrong this was.

Madeline was still in her swimming costume, and she held a short stick in her hand. She walked around to the front of Liam as she swatted it against her palm. "Remove the hood."

Smith pulled it away. Liam stared at Madeline for a moment, and then noticed the photos. "What is this?"

"Research, silly," Madeline said, giggling in that off-putting way of hers. She reminded Harrison of a girl he'd known at school, who'd once bullied one of the other girls so severely she'd had to move. "Well, that and I needed something to keep me going until the time was right."

"The time..." Liam trailed off. "Until Emily was due to give birth. Until you knew you could use that to blackmail me."

Madeline shrugged. "I couldn't possibly comment."

Liam sagged in Harrison's arms. Harrison gripped him

tighter, hauling him up. He'd made sure he was the one who got to Liam first. The other guards weren't above getting a few extra digs in, and Liam didn't deserve that. Not that he deserved any of this.

Liam groaned. "Why me? I don't understand. Why did you have to pick me?"

She pursed her lips, whistling softly, swatting the stick against her hand.

"Somebody hurt you," Liam went on. "Didn't they? Maybe when you were a kid. I don't know. But something happened to you. This isn't normal. You have to see that."

"Who would want to be normal? And yes, I was hurt repeatedly as a child. My father beat me relentlessly. You've seen the scars. But that's not why I chose you. That's not why I'm doing this."

"Then why?"

"You hit me, Liam."

"I pushed you."

"Pushing is hitting, silly. You understand I can't let you get away with that. I thought things were going so well. I thought you were learning."

Harrison cringed at Liam's next words. He sounded like a little kid. "I am. I will. I didn't mean it."

"And?"

"And I'm sorry."

"Hmm, I'm in a bit of a quandary here, because I want to believe you. But I think you need to be taught a lesson." She glanced at Smith. "Hold him still."

"Please, Maddie. Please."

Harrison thought about the video confession he'd made: how the families of his dead friends would react, how his own family would react. But was it worth all this?

"Bretherton begged too. Do you want to know why I killed

him? I asked for soft-boiled eggs. I do love dipping the soldiers in. I like to imagine they're drowning. But when I cracked the egg open, what did I find? It was solid. So I stabbed him, and I kept stabbing until my arm hurt. I had him fed to the pigs."

Liam shivered. Harrison repressed a gasp. He had no way of knowing if this was true, but he didn't doubt it. He'd seen what she'd done to Becky. And the butler had mysteriously vanished.

Madeline moved behind Liam. "My father beat me with this same riding crop."

She started hitting Liam. Harrison winced with each strike, the riding crop slapping against Liam's bare back. Liam breathed heavily, but he didn't make any noise otherwise. Harrison's instincts told him to make it stop. But he didn't; he held onto Liam tightly, squeezing onto his arm, so that he could feel each strike reverberating through his body.

"How does it feel, huh?" Madeline struck him again and again. "That'll teach you, you naughty boy. That'll show you what happens when you hit a woman."

Harrison glanced at Smith, but the commander was staring straight ahead, as though this didn't bother him. The other guards watched impartially.

Cuts opened on Liam's back, blood sliding down his skin. Harrison almost yelled at her. Surely this was enough. But she kept going.

Eventually, she let her arm drop, breathing shakily. "This isn't working. Look. He's not even hurt."

Harrison turned when she tapped him on the shoulder. She stared up at him, her eyes glinting in that sick way. Harrison wondered if she was on drugs. Or if hurting Liam was enough of a high.

She offered him the riding crop. "Do me a favour, soldier boy."

Harrison's body tensed. It was one thing to wrestle Liam

into submission, but hitting him when he couldn't defend himself... He couldn't do it.

"Don't think I've forgotten how melodramatic you were about that junkie slut." Madeline waved the riding crop. "You need to prove your loyalty. Or maybe I'll have Smith release that video of you. I watched it, you know. I think you did a fine job. Very convincing. Or, if that's not enough motivation, there are always other avenues we can explore."

Harrison sensed everything had been leading up to this. This was the moment where he had to make a choice. What sort of person was he? Was he really going to let her threaten him into doing this disgusting thing?

The answer was yes.

He blamed it on the video, the threats, the presence of the other guards. He blamed it on the fear twisting in his gut and the image of his mother's face crumpled in shame if she ever learned he'd been involved in this.

The only way to survive was to comply.

One of the other guards replaced him, grabbing onto Liam's arm. Harrison took the riding crop and moved behind Liam, staring at the light cuts on his back.

"Go on." Madeline stood on her tiptoes, whispering close to Harrison's ear. "He's a woman beater. You saw it. He hit me."

Liam hadn't hit her. He'd pushed her as a reflex, hardly touched her, and she'd theatrically thrown herself back. It was like she'd wanted this to happen.

"We haven't got all day," she snapped, when Harrison only stared.

"I..."

"You *what*?"

He didn't want to do this, he was going to say.

Betraying every lesson his parents and military mentors had taught him, Harrison began to strike Liam. He did it softly, hoping he could get away with it. But then Madeline screamed at him to do it harder; she kept screaming.

Tears rose in Harrison's eyes as he applied more force. Liam croaked and gasped, and this seemed to excite Madeline. She kept yelling.

Harrison hit Liam over and over. He opened fresh cuts, deeper this time, until his back was slick with blood.

"Harder," Madeline cried. "Harder, harder, harder!"

Harrison yelled as he put his whole body into the next strike. With a loud *snap*, the riding crop broke. Harrison let it drop, taking a few stumbling steps away, certain he was going to fall. There was a sick taste in his mouth. He couldn't look at what he'd done.

Madeline placed her hand on his arm. "Very good. If I wasn't so in love with my Liam, I might give you a special prize. But your life, hmm, isn't that a lovely prize?"

She walked around to the front of Liam, touching his chin and guiding his gaze to hers.

"I'm sorry you made me do that," she said, and then she kissed him.

Unlike in the pool, Liam kissed her back. Their mouths glued together as Madeline started to moan. She clawed her hands around him, dragging her fingernails over the freshly opened cuts. Liam shuddered but he kept kissing her.

Minutes passed like this, with Madeline grinding her body against Liam's. Harrison wished he was back overseas. Anywhere but here.

And then Madeline stopped. "I hope you enjoyed that as much as me."

"I did," Liam said quickly.

"Excellent. I think you've earned a rest. I might treat you to a walk later, seeing as my dead butler promised..."

She left the room and Harrison leaned down, gripping onto

his knees. He was a coward. That was the truth. He'd secretly smiled when he learned he was going to be discharged from the Army. Because he was a wimp. A spineless nothing. A loser who beat a defenceless man.

He almost told Liam he was sorry. But what good would it do? Harrison had to stop seeing Liam as a human being. It was the only way he was going to get through this.

Liam didn't fight when they pulled the bag over his head and handcuffed him. He hardly walked as they led him back to his room; they supported his weight between them. It was like all the strength had faded from his body.

Once they'd locked the door behind him, Harrison opened and closed his injured hand. It didn't hurt at all.

CHAPTER TWENTY-EIGHT

I t was unfortunate that Liam had needed the extra encouragement to kiss me.

Of course, it wasn't what any girl dreamed about: coaxing their lover into wanting them. But that wasn't exactly what had happened. I'd had to persuade him to kiss me, fine, but he'd wanted me all along; I'd felt it the moment our lips met. Once the kiss began, he'd started to get into it, his tongue eagerly seeking mine out. His body couldn't lie, even if he wanted to lie to himself.

I felt giddy all day, thinking about the way he'd sunk into the kissing. My moans had spurred him on. Liam had groaned and trembled, his pleasure hardly containable, and I just knew he was beginning to see things my way.

He could tell himself he was loyal to the slut who'd shit out his bastard, but it was nonsense, and he knew it.

I knew how to read men. I would never publicly brand myself a whore, like Emily did in her Facebook photos, but it wasn't like I was a virgin either. I'd had my fair share of lovers in my time, and I always knew if their passion was faked or real. Liam's had been real. When he'd pushed against me, I knew he wanted it; I knew the only reason he wasn't getting hard was because of the presence of the guards, and maybe he was a little distracted from his punishment.

Next time, it would be so romantic. He'd do exactly as I wished.

But he needed to be careful. The way he'd pushed me in the swimming pool had been completely unacceptable. There was no excuse, especially when he knew how much I cared about him. He should've known better than to toy with my affection. It took a lot for a woman to be vulnerable, and all too often men took that for granted.

Men were always that way, so take-take-take. It was like they thought they were owed a woman's affection, and so they didn't treat it as the special and wonderful thing it was.

He'd done so well, passing the drowning test. As my vision had clouded under the water, darkness enveloping me, my man had wrapped his strong arms around me and hauled me up. He'd known he couldn't live without me, on a primal level, before his pesky guilt and nonsense reasoning got in the way.

When it came right down to it, he'd saved me. He'd been the man I needed him to be.

CHAPTER TWENTY-NINE

After the beating, Liam had been left in his room for hours. At first he'd sat on the floor, head bowed, telling himself he was going to tear Harrison to pieces the first chance he got. But if it hadn't been Harrison, it would've been another of the guards. He wasn't to blame. Mad Maddie was.

Finally, he'd forced himself to take a shower, wincing as the warm water sluiced over his cuts. He made himself rub shower gel into them, tears stinging his eyes as the chemicals stung his skin.

But it was better than thinking about the kiss: the way he'd returned her pressure, the way their tongues had sought each other out. There had been a sick moment – a truly sick moment – when he was grateful for the kiss. It was better than the alternative. It meant he didn't have to feel that riding crop against his back.

The guards had collected him as the sun was setting, and now he and Madeline were walking down the gravel driveway.

Madeline stood a few feet from him, and four guards followed a few feet to the rear. The implication was obvious. If Liam made a dash for Madeline, the guards would swiftly intervene. Maybe it would be the needle; maybe it would be something worse. His shirt rubbed against his raw skin with each step.

Liam promised himself he'd make use of this rare trip. He'd scan the grounds, try to see if there was a wall surrounding the property.

"It's a lovely evening, isn't it?" Madeline said.

Liam looked past the driveway and the fountain to the trees, the air turned a dusky red with the setting sun. A light fog had moved over the grounds.

"Yes, it's lovely."

They walked in silence for a time, heading for the trees. They left the gravel path and walked on the dew-wet grass.

Liam looked left and right, trying to see into the distance, but there were too many trees dotted here and there. It was as though they'd been tactically placed so he couldn't get a sense of how big the property was.

"What are you thinking about?" Madeline asked. "I feel like you're not even here with me."

Liam's spine tingled. The cuts on his back pulsed. He felt like he might let out a boyish sob. "I was thinking about our future together. Looking over these grounds, I can see they'd be a great place to raise a family."

"Really? I've always thought this one was rather boring."

This one. Liam resisted the urge to call her a stuck-up spoilt brat. This was the sort of estate most people could never imagine owning, let alone looking down on. It was the sort of place people fantasised about living, but deep down knew they never could.

"Boring?" he said.

"I suppose because it's in the middle of nowhere. I much prefer my place in the city. There's always something to do. But, of course, I wouldn't be able to see you in the city."

Because he was her prisoner. Because she was a sick deranged fuck. He didn't think about saying any of this. He was too beaten down for that. The thought saddened him.

"What do you do in the city?" He had to ask something, as his gaze scanned back and forth, searching for a wall or a way out. If he was going to make a run for it, he needed to know where and how far he'd have to go.

"This and that. Shopping. Parties. Plays. Sometimes I even find a nice young man to take home with me..."

She trailed off, looking at him closely. Liam realised she wanted him to act jealous.

"Maddie, please don't talk about that. I can't think about you with another man."

How did she not know he was acting? He didn't sound remotely convincing, even to himself.

"I'm sorry," she said seriously. "How silly of me. You're right. So you want us to have a family together?"

"One day." Liam nodded, temples pulsing.

"Tell me about it, Liam. Don't just leave it at that."

They were walking beneath the shadow of the trees, their shoes crunching over twigs and brown leaves. Looking to the left – away from the house – Liam saw that the terrain rose into a slight hill. They were sitting in a bowl. He felt sure it was another intentional design.

"Liam."

He cleared his throat. "I see us with two children, a boy and a girl. And we'll always dote on them. We'll make sure they never want for anything. We'll always be there for them, no matter what happens. We'll do our best to raise them well, and we'll have so many good times. We'll get a dog and–"

"Ew, no thank you."

Liam flinched. "No?"

She stared at him like he was stupid. "Why on earth would

we want some mangy mutt getting in the way of things? I know you had to do certain things in your old life to make ends meet, but you must be able to see how downright disgusting dogs are. Once you remove your financial incentive to pretend otherwise."

"Hmm." It was all he could say.

Luckily she didn't notice as she went on, waving her hands. "Dogs have caused me trouble in the past."

"What do you mean?" Liam asked, even if he didn't want to know.

"Oh, it was nothing. We were staying in France and there was this farm nearby. One of the dogs had a bunch of pups, and I begged Father for one, begged him until I was crying. I wanted it so badly."

Liam's blood was turning cold.

"Finally, he said yes. It was *my* dog, you understand, to do with as *I* wished. So I invented some games for it. I've always loved games, even as a girl."

"What sort of games?"

His fists were clenched. He quickly unclenched them, but he couldn't stop the pounding in his skull. He'd grown up with Rocky, and he'd always been close to dogs. As a teenager he'd often walked his neighbours' dogs just so he could be around them. They were innocent and loyal and they didn't deserve to be hurt.

"Are you judging me?" She paused, staring at him across the semi-darkness. Soon it would be total. "Because it sounds like you are."

"No, I'm just curious. If we're going to be together, I want to learn as much about you as possible."

She smiled in that ugly way of hers. She was attractive on a surface level, in her stylish jacket, her hair in a bob, her features sharp and seemingly charismatic. But she was also repulsive.

"Nothing too extreme. I wanted to see how resourceful the little thing was, and I also wanted to teach it to swim. I would take it to the river and toss it in, you know, to teach it strength, to teach it to be able to rely on itself. But apparently somebody saw me and they made such a fuss. Father forced me to give it away to avoid the drama. I think it was for the best. It always smelled awful when it emerged from the water."

Liam struggled to keep the smile fixed to his face. His heart was thumping so hard. He'd never wanted to hurt anybody more than right then.

If she was telling the truth, she was a monster, the lowest of the low. He couldn't imagine doing something like that to an innocent animal, to a dog, to man's best friend.

To Rocky. Fucking bitch. Fucking psycho *bitch*.

She walked towards him. The guards moved at the same pace, always keeping the same distance as Madeline. They paused when she stood right in front of Liam, just out of reach, their hands near their hips.

"I know I'm not perfect," Madeline said. "But you can still love me, can't you?"

"Yes."

"Say it." She looped her arms around his shoulders, her touch tickling disgustingly.

"I could love you."

She stood on her tiptoes, looking into his eyes like they were in a romantic film. It was so bloody theatrical, all the bloody time. She was full of herself. "Show me, Liam."

He did what he had to do. Grabbing onto her hips, he pulled her close, feigning passion as they kissed. She moaned and whimpered and rubbed her body against him, the same way she had in the darkroom.

"Easy tiger." She giggled, breaking it off. Liam was glad

when she stepped away. "Maybe if you're lucky, we can pick up where we left off after the dinner."

"The dinner?"

"Didn't I mention? My father is visiting next week. He's excited to meet you." Liam was sure she was mocking him somehow. She could barely hold back her smirk. "Won't that be fun?"

"Yes."

"And after..."

She darted her hand out and grabbed onto his cock. Liam cringed. He thought about Emily's face the one time he'd made a mistake: the one time he'd risked everything.

"Maybe I'll give you a little treat," Maddie tittered, removing her hand. "I know you find it difficult with the help watching, but I'm beginning to trust you. I really am. I think soon, we'll be able to be alone."

This was it. This was a way out. If they left them alone together, he'd have a chance.

He smoothed her hair from her cheek. "I'd love that, Maddie."

CHAPTER THIRTY

The sky was clear. Thousands of stars glittered down at Liam as he stood at his bedroom window.

The night shimmered and he saw Emily a few months into her pregnancy, sitting on the toilet seat with her head buried in her hands. He'd heard her crying through the door and quickly pushed it open, wondering if it was something to do with the baby.

"I'm going to be a terrible mother." She'd leaned against him. "I don't think I'm ready. It's too much. I can't do this. What if I'm not good enough?"

"I'll always be here for you," he'd told her. "We'll face it together. And, for the record, I already know you're going to be an incredible mother. I love you."

Emily stood at the window, ignoring Jamie's wailing as she stared down at the street.

A father and his son were kicking a football against the wall, laughing together when it bounced away and the son had to sprint to catch it. It was the sort of thing Liam would've been amazing at; bonding with their son, laughing and joking with him. She'd always counted on Liam being the dominant parent. She didn't like to think of herself in this way, but sometimes she felt weak. Sometimes she felt like she couldn't handle life.

But no. She had to pull herself together.

Rocky watched from the bed as she walked to Jamie's crib. She picked up her baby, checking his nappy. He was clean, and he'd recently been fed.

He was crying because he knew he was never going to meet his father: that his father had either been taken or walked out. Emily didn't know which would be worse.

"Please, sweetness," Emily whispered in her son's ear. "It's okay. It's all going to be okay."

Rocky tilted his head and tracked her movements as she paced the room. But that was as much as he was able to do. He was becoming even more sluggish. The vet had said there was nothing wrong with him as far as they could tell: just old age.

Emily knew the truth. He was mourning for Liam. He missed his oldest friend.

She sat on the edge of the bed and lowered Jamie to Rocky. Sometimes, her son stopped crying when Rocky began to softly lap at his cheek. But this evening it didn't work. Nothing did. She sang to him and rocked him and, eventually, she ended up bursting into tears herself.

They were pitiful and useless tears, but once she'd started she couldn't stop. Evil thoughts were twisting into her mind.

She imagined Liam on a beach someplace, maybe in Blackpool or maybe abroad, with a woman who never forgot to go to the gym and always wore the right amount of make-up and was a million times more glamorous than Emily. She saw them making love and laughing together.

There was no evidence he'd ran away.

And he'd changed. He really had. She hadn't doubted him in years.

But the police had found nothing. She was ringing them every day, demanding updates, but she was beginning to think there was nothing they could do. Without any witnesses or CCTV – and without a body to launch a murder investigation – they were stuck.

She cradled Jamie to her chest, sobbing. "He wouldn't leave us. He'd never do that."

But there was that doubt, niggling, taunting.

"Emily." Mum stood in the open doorway. She was wearing her disappointed face. Emily couldn't blame her. She must've looked like a wreck. Mum strode across the room and leaned down for her grandson. "There, there, my little angel. No need to make a song and dance of it."

Emily laughed shakily when Jamie immediately stopped crying. "That's impressive."

Mum frowned as she rocked him. "I know this is difficult, but you have to remember he can sense your moods. You need to try to be... not happy, exactly. But try to get on with it."

"Get on with it," Emily repeated dully, wiping her cheeks.

"I don't mean to sound cruel. But he has to come first. Don't get me wrong. I know you love him. I know you wouldn't do anything to intentionally upset him. It's just – oh, how is it helpful, crying like that? What does it achieve?"

Mum had always been the tough-love parent, but right then Emily didn't want to hear it. She returned to the window. The father and son had gone inside.

"I'm sorry." Mum's voice was low. "I didn't mean to upset you."

"You're right. I know you're right. I'm trying."

"I know you are."

"I just wish I knew, one way or the other."

"I thought you were certain..."

Mum trailed off, but Emily didn't need her to finish. She was going to say certain he'd been kidnapped or killed. And Emily had been. She really had. But her thoughts kept returning to that one incident, the event they'd put behind them, the one she'd rarely let herself think about until Liam disappeared.

"I was. But I don't know. Maybe it all really did get too much for him. Maybe I put too much pressure on him. If there's one thing Liam hates, Mum, it's being trapped. That's why he worked so hard to become a dog trainer. It's like he needed to be self-employed. He hates feeling boxed in. What if I made him feel that way?"

Mum joined her at the window, softly passing Jamie back to her. Emily winced as she took her son, but thankfully he kept sleeping, his breathing soft. "You don't know anything for sure."

"Do you know what he said to me when he passed his dog-training course? I can picture it now. He was so happy. He had that cheeky smile on his face, that beautiful smile. *I can go anywhere now, work anywhere.* That's what he said. *I*, not *we*."

"I don't think you should read too much into that," Mum said, stroking her hand over Emily's shoulder. "You'll go cuckoo if you go over every little thing. And we can't have that, can we?"

"Might be too late," Emily said, trying for a jokey tone.

But Mum didn't laugh. She wrapped her arm around Emily and pulled her close. Emily sighed and let her head come to rest on Mum's shoulder, knowing she was right: knowing obsessing wouldn't help anything. And yet it was like she couldn't stop.

It was an evil thought, but part of her almost wished for the phone call. The one that would tell her they'd found a body. At least then she'd know. At least then she wouldn't have to torture herself.

She held her son tighter, pushing the notion away. Liam was out there. He was a good man, even if he'd made a few mistakes.

CHAPTER THIRTY-ONE

Smith stood in front of the barracks building, his hands behind his back, reminding Harrison of the briefings he'd received overseas.

It was a few days after he'd beaten Liam with the riding crop, and nightmares had plagued Harrison every night. He kept hearing the way it cracked, only it was far louder in his dreams, like thunder. He'd beaten a man until the weapon snapped. And still he was here.

"Mr Pemberton wants us to be invisible during the dinner," Smith said to the assembled guards, all of them with their balaclavas on. None of them fidgeted or moved like Harrison did. "We'll be in the adjacent rooms, like normal, but the difference here is we're only going to reveal ourselves if *absolutely necessary*. Mr Pemberton doesn't want it to seem like he needs constant protection."

Harrison snorted. He was really starting to get tired of these rich bastards and their demands.

And yet he'd done it: he'd beaten Liam, an innocent man, painting his back in gore.

Smith looked sharply at him. Even behind the mask, Harrison could feel him glaring.

"Understandably, Mr Pemberton wants to keep this a private affair. Two of you will be acting as waiters. I'll go over it with you beforehand. You'll need to conduct yourselves like you're used to serving these sorts of people. But the basic point is this. Be invisible. They don't want to see you. They want you to serve their food, attend to their needs, but they don't want to know you exist. Okay. Back to your rooms."

The guards dispersed. Harrison looked around the grounds. It was a bright day, the midday sun beaming down. He didn't want to spend it locked in his room, but that was what they'd been doing ever since the beating. Harrison knew some of the other guards had been sent into the house, presumably to take Liam his meals, but otherwise they were waiting.

Smith stepped in front of Harrison. They were the final two outside.

"Are you good, lad?"

Harrison nodded.

"I don't want to have to keep reminding you of what'll happen if you do something stupid."

"Then don't. I've got the message."

Smith glanced over his shoulder. When he saw that nobody was watching, he pulled off his mask, revealing his silver hair and his ordinary features. Harrison shrugged and took off his mask too.

"Do you know why I picked you?" Smith asked.

"Because I've got military experience."

Smith laughed grimly. "You don't need military experience to do this job. You need criminal experience. You need a lack of morals. In fact, being in the military might actually make it more difficult."

"But *you* were," Harrison said.

"Who told you that?"

"No one. I can just tell. It's the way you hold yourself."

Smith nodded. "Maybe you're right. Maybe I served in the Marines once upon a time, before I became the Pembertons' head of security. And maybe I was involved in a mission that went wrong, and most of my friends died, and I was left wondering what the hell I was going to do with my life. And now maybe I have a family, a wife and a kid who live far, far away from all this nasty shit."

Harrison wasn't sure whether to believe him. But if it was true, it explained a lot. It might even make Harrison want to be his friend, in a different life: one where they weren't constantly doing terrible things. "Why are you telling me this?"

"Because if you fuck up, if you try to help Liam, I might have to kill you."

"You could always get one of the other men to do it," Harrison said bitterly. "Keep your hands clean."

"No, lad. No. I'd have to do it myself."

"Oh yeah? How would you go about it? A fair fight, or would you take me by surprise?"

"I'd order the men to restrain you, take you to a hole we'd already dug, and shoot you in the back of the head. Nobody would ever know what happened to you. Or we might make it look like a suicide, release the video on your social media account with a short message, implying you'd killed yourself. Nobody would ever find your body. They'd assume you drowned yourself in the ocean or something."

"You know he doesn't deserve this."

"You can't save him. All you can do is get both of you killed."

Harrison took a step, staring the older man directly in the eye. "I don't think that's true. If I really wanted to free him, I bet I could."

"Maybe. Or maybe we'd catch you. And even if you got away..."

"You'd release the video. You'd hunt me down. We're going in circles. Are we done?"

Smith suddenly grabbed Harrison by the shoulders, shoving him up against the wall. Harrison struggled, but Smith was far stronger than he looked.

"Don't throw this chance away. Don't be an idiot."

"I get it. You want me to choose the same life you did. Because then, what, it makes it all okay? It means you made the right choice? Get your hands off me." When Smith didn't, Harrison grabbed onto Smith's wrists. "I mean it. I'm not messing around."

A smirk touched the older man's lips, and he stepped back. "Fair enough."

Harrison straightened up. "So why did you pick me?"

Smith looked at him for a long moment, then shook his head. Pulling his balaclava on, he walked away.

Harrison sighed, watching him for a moment, and then pulled his mask over his face.

CHAPTER THIRTY-TWO

Liam was left on his own for the next few days. The guards brought him his food. The cuts on his back began to scab. Sleeping was difficult. He'd roll over, trying to get comfortable, only to wake a few minutes later with pain scorching up and down his skin.

He thought about what Madeline had said, about how they would have some alone time together after the meal. That would be his chance. He'd have to be brave.

Looking back on his time since his imprisonment in the cell, he realised something: he was becoming a coward. The fight was seeping out of him. He needed to remember who he was, remember Emily, remember his duty as a father and her partner.

One evening, the door opened and Bretherton walked in.

Liam peered across the room, feeling like he was staring at a ghost. The butler was wearing a three-piece suit, a gold chain dangling from the pocket. His hair was combed and he looked far more confident than Liam had ever seen him. "Hello, Liam."

"I thought you were dead," Liam muttered.

Bretherton smiled tightly. "My daughter and her games. No, I am very much alive."

"Your daughter?"

Liam rose to his feet. His legs were unsteady. He'd been working out every day: push-ups, pull-ups in the doorframe, squats. But he still felt weaker than he had in years. Nothing could replace being on his feet all day, every day.

Bretherton smirked. "Yes, my daughter. I'm afraid I haven't been particularly honest with you."

The truth hit Liam in the chest. These people were sick. "You're not a butler."

"Of course not. I'm Francis Pemberton."

Liam stared. It was like Francis wanted him to be impressed. "So why pretend to be a butler?"

"I enjoy the games in my own way. There's so much pressure in my life. But as sweet old Bretherton, things were simpler. And it gave me an insight into you. You speak much more freely with the help than you do with my daughter."

"That might have something to do with the fact she's keeping me prisoner."

Francis shook his head. "If I were you, I would stop saying things like that. Won't you ever learn your lesson?"

Liam stepped forwards. Francis frowned and took a step back, into the hallway. "What are you doing?"

Liam grinned. "I want to shake your hand, since we're properly meeting for the first time."

"I think you're fine where you are."

"Oh yeah?"

When Liam made to close the distance, Francis nodded to somebody in the hallway. A guard appeared with a folded-up piece of paper in his hand.

"Take a look at this first," Francis said. "It might calm you down."

Liam took the paper, unfolded it. He stared as a tremor

172

passed through his body. If he was alone, he would cry, but he couldn't let them see him like that.

The photo was taken at night. It wasn't clear. But Liam was able to make out Emily standing at the window of her parents' house, cradling their child. He thought she was crying, but it was difficult to tell. It didn't matter; there was proof, real proof that his child had been born.

Despite everything, a smile spread across his face. He was a father. It was all the more reason to get out of there.

But then darkness touched him. This was a threat. If he hurt Francis or Madeline, they were going to hurt his family. But what if he escaped without harming them? Would they still hurt her, hurt his child? He wasn't sure. Could he risk it? His mind was whirring. Francis had given him the photo to beat him into submission, but it only made Liam more certain he had to get home.

"Can I keep this?" he asked.

Francis scowled, as if this wasn't the reaction he'd hoped for. "If you must."

Liam went to the bedside table, opened the drawer, and placed it carefully inside. It was his most valuable object. He tried not to think about one of guards lurking outside Emily's parents' house. It made Liam want to fight. But fighting had got him nowhere.

"You know why I showed that to you," Francis said.

Liam turned. The guard had left the room, and now Francis stood more confidently at the threshold. But he still looked ready to dart away if Liam made any sudden movements.

"Yeah, I know."

"Madeline wants tonight to go well. She's taken an obscene liking to you, more so than..."

Francis trailed off. Liam mentally filled the blank. *More so than the others.* If that's what Francis had been going to say, it left the question of what had happened to the others. Not that Liam needed much imagination to work that out.

"She said she killed you," Liam said.

Francis was looking at Liam the way some of his posher clients sometimes did, like he was a curiosity, a different species.

He hated feeling like he was beneath these people. But there was nothing he could do. His thoughts kept returning to that idea: if he ran, didn't hurt Francis or Madeline, surely they wouldn't go through the effort of hurting Emily or his baby. It would be too risky.

Or maybe he was wrong. Maybe they were more insane than he gave them credit for.

"My daughter has an active imagination," Francis said after a pause. "Your presence is evidence of that. For reasons I will never understand, she seems to enjoy pretending you and she are engaged in some kind of romance. It's foolish and shameful, which is why I have given her use of this estate. At least she can indulge this nonsense away from prying eyes."

"Don't act like you're above it. You were playing along too. I bet you enjoyed it when the guards beat me. I bet you loved it when I had no clue who you really were. I bet you were laughing at me."

"It's true. All of it." Francis nodded. "But it was only a bit of fun."

"A bit of fun." Liam ground his teeth.

"Don't look at me like that. Not to put it too bluntly, but your life simply isn't as valuable as mine or my daughter's."

"How did you work that out?"

"People are made different. There are certain people who are... shall we say, invisible. Or perhaps immaterial would fit better. You see, my daughter is sole heir to a vast and significant estate. If she requires a man like you to keep her sane, to make it so she can fulfil her other responsibilities, then fine. I can live with that. As long as she doesn't get carried away. And yes, I had my fun. I enjoyed seeing you rage and fight as if you ever had a chance."

"What you're saying is, because you're rich and I'm not, you're better than me."

"Yes. We can do whatever we want with you."

Liam's back stung, as if Francis's words were reopening his wounds.

Too many memories passed across his mind: the way he'd felt at school when the other kids noticed he had holes in his trainers at PE; the laughter of the bosses at the warehouse as he left the office after being denied a raise; the sinking sensation in his gut when he and Emily had been looking for their first flat, realising they'd have to settle for somewhere with old dirty carpets and damp creeping up the walls.

"She told me what you did to her," Liam said. "I've seen the scars on her back. To do that to your own child."

"I have no idea what you're talking about."

"You hit her, beat her, your own daughter. And it turned her into a psychopath."

"There's nothing I despise more than people who blame every little thing on their childhood. For the record, I can assure you I have never laid a hand on my daughter. The scars on her back are the result of a childhood accident. She was climbing a tree when she was quite young, she fell into a thornbush, and she was so frightened she began thrashing around. It was half an hour before she was found. By then she'd torn herself up most terribly; she almost died from the blood loss."

"What if I don't believe you?"

Yet it rang true. Madeline was just the sort of person who'd pretend to be a victim. She'd love that. But it didn't matter. If she was a lunatic because of some childhood beatings or because she was born that way, he didn't care. All he cared about was returning to Emily and his child.

Francis raised his hands. "It makes no difference to me. I trust you're going to behave yourself during tonight's dinner? I don't want you upsetting our guests. They don't know about our... particular arrangement. As far as they're aware, you're a friend of Madeline's and nothing more."

Liam's heart thumped. This was a possible option.

"Yes," he told Francis. "You don't have to worry."

"Good man. I'll send somebody with your suit presently. Remember your manners. If you act like a pig, you'll get treated like one."

"I think I preferred you when you were a butler, mate."

Francis smiled tightly as he turned away, leaving the room without another word. The door slammed behind him.

Liam immediately went to the bedside table, taking out the photo and cradling it to his chest.

CHAPTER THIRTY-THREE

When the guards arrived with Liam's clothes, they weren't wearing masks. They were dressed in crisp white uniforms, like waiters, but Liam knew who – and what – they were from the way they were standing.

There was nothing remarkable about the men's faces, nothing to indicate they were the sort of people who'd keep a man prisoner and beat him. They were both around Liam's age, with short hair, their faces so generic Liam found himself actively looking for differences. One had a slightly crooked nose and was a tiny bit taller than the other.

"Did I do that?" Liam gestured at the man's face.

He stared blankly. "The lady wishes you to get changed and meet her in the drawing room. We're going to escort you."

The man laid the suit over the back of the chair and took a step away, hands folded across his middle. Liam studied him, wondering if he was hiding weapons in that clean ironed uniform.

They waited as he got changed, and then Liam turned around and offered up his hands for the cuffs. He did it without thinking; it had become a part of his routine.

"No need for that. The lady of the house wants to keep this civil."

Liam turned, feeling like a jackass. It was like he wanted to be their prisoner.

They led him down the stairs, past the paintings and the animal heads, and then down a corridor which had been locked the last time he'd seen it. They passed a suit of armour with a sword in the grip, the knight standing tall, proud. Liam grabbed the handle of the sword and gave it a tug, but it was welded into place.

"Stop fucking about," the guard grunted.

"Can't blame a man for trying."

Liam composed himself as they completed their journey. He had to play nice.

The guards opened the door into a room with a piano, tall bookshelves, a record player in the corner, a small bar, and a general sense of wealth.

Madeline fluttered across the room in her glittery dress. Liam fought the urge to move away from the dog-killing bitch. He could only hope she'd invented that story, like she'd possibly invented her abuse at the hands of Francis.

"Liam, you made it."

Of course he'd bloody made it.

She gripped his hand, staring up at him with glassy eyes. Whilst previously he'd wondered if she was on drugs, now he knew for certain she was. Either that or she was very drunk. Her smile was shaky and a sheen of sweat coated her skin.

"Olivia, Silas, this is my good friend, Liam. Father, I believe you've already met."

Francis was leaning against the piano, a glass of whisky in his hand. Olivia sat on a small chair, a woman with her greying hair woven into intricate patterns. The man was full-bellied and red-faced, dressed in an expensive suit, muttering a hello before he knocked back his glass in one gulp; his chunky gold wedding ring glinted at Liam.

The guards stood either side of the door, hands behind their back, becoming statues.

"Liam, a drink?" Francis said, pouring it before Liam had a chance to answer.

He strode across the room, handing Liam the glass. Liam took it, but Francis held on a second longer, staring. Liam remembered his warning not to say anything. Olivia looked kind, reminding him of his mother, with soft eyes. He wondered what she would say if she knew the truth.

He sipped his whisky, anything to make this easier.

Madeline pulled him across the room, hardly able to keep her footing. She sat Liam down on a chair and perched on the arm. What a perfect couple they made.

"I'm so excited you get to meet Liam. He's the most interesting man I've ever met."

"I think we'll be the judge of that." Silas knocked ice around in his glass, peering at Liam like his default mood was unimpressed. "So, Liam, what is it you do, exactly?"

"I'm a dog trainer."

Olivia made to talk, but Silas cut her off. "Why on earth would you want to do that?"

Madeline giggled, trailing her fingertips across Liam's neck. He didn't like it, the way it tickled his skin. "You see? People find it a very funny profession."

"It's just not the sort of thing I can imagine doing myself," Silas said, as though Liam was meant to care.

"Yes, but you've never worked a day in your life," Francis said.

Silas grinned. "But in theory, if I were to choose a vocation, training dogs would be far, far down on my list."

"It's rewarding." Liam shouldn't have cared if these people

wanted to criticise his job, but he'd worked hard to become qualified. He'd been so proud. "You take these dogs, some of them completely out of control, and you slowly introduce discipline. A lot of them have anxiety issues and you can help with that too, teach them they don't have to be afraid."

"What does a dog have to be afraid of?" Silas said.

Mad Maddie, for one.

"Lots of things. It depends on their upbringing–"

"I think we've heard quite enough about dogs." Madeline's laugh was the most annoying sound Liam had ever heard. "I must apologise. He can get a little carried away sometimes."

"I think it's fascinating." Olivia's smile was warm as she met Liam's eyes. She wouldn't approve of what Madeline and Francis were doing to him; Liam felt sure of that. Or maybe it was the alcohol. He'd only had a few sips, but his head was already swimming. "You must be a very patient man."

"It's easy to be patient with animals. They never do anything intentionally. It's just the way they've been treated, it shapes their behaviour."

Silas grunted. "Like people then."

"Yeah, I guess so. But animals can't choose. People can."

"Not all people have a choice, do they, Father?" Madeline's hand tightened on Liam's neck as she spoke, her fingernails digging into his skin.

"Not this again." Francis took a small sip of his drink. "I think you've been indulging too heavily, sweet daughter."

"Uh-oh." Silas chuckled. "Have we arrived in the middle of an argument?"

"My daughter has a passion for ancient history."

"How did you two meet?" Olivia cut in, but everybody ignored her.

"You know how Mummy died, don't you?" Madeline went on. "Cancer, eating away at her. She was such a lovely vivacious woman, so full of life, and it corroded her until there was nothing left. She was a shadow of her former self. Towards the end, when she was very weak, we had a—"

"Madeline, must you bore our guests?"

"We had a party." Her fingernails were buried deep in Liam's neck. He gritted his teeth against the pain, wondering what would happen if he addressed it. "Mother was horribly weak. But Father said there were going to be some important people there, and so it was up, up, up with her."

With each *up*, her grip tightened. Liam's hand shook as he brought the whisky glass to his mouth. He drank as much of it as he could stomach, senses dulling. Being imprisoned here had been the longest he'd gone without alcohol since he was a kid.

"She did her best. She always wanted to please you, Father."

Francis had finished his drink. He nodded to one of the guards, and they strode across the room and poured him another. He took it and the guard returned to his place.

"She died the next day," Madeline said.

"I'm so sorry," Olivia said. "That's awful."

Francis grunted. "It was nothing to do with the party. She was on her way out anyway."

"I don't think the party helped, Father."

"Enough, please. Why must you be so morbid?"

Madeline sprung to her feet, gouging her nails deeply into Liam's skin in the same movement. Liam let out a breath and then finished the rest of his whisky.

The evening went on like that for a time, the drinks flowing, the conversation moving around Liam. He only answered when they called on him, which was rarely.

They were talking about other families, about what position this or that man had taken, about a scandal involving the son of a prominent family, gossiping endlessly. Silas and Olivia were married, which felt like a weird match to Liam.

Silas was boisterous and casually cruel; Olivia seemed different.

Liam kept drinking. He studied Olivia, the only one who looked at Liam as though he was a human being.

His head was cloudy from the booze. How many glasses had he drunk? He wasn't sure. Time was doing funny things.

Whenever he finished a glass, the guards refilled it. It was so easy to keep knocking them down. Suddenly he didn't feel the cuts on his back, and the more he drank, the more certain he became Olivia was his way out of there.

It was her kind eyes; it was the way she smiled softly at him. The smile reminded him of his mum's when she'd told him about his dad moving up north to be with his new girlfriend, trying to put on a brave face, pretending it didn't bother her.

If Liam had been sober, maybe he would've realised that kind eyes and a soft smile weren't a good enough reason. But with the whisky in his system, he knew she would help him. He could give her a message to take to the outside world.

He bided his time. As more drinks flowed, he watched Olivia. Francis, Silas, and Madeline spoke to him as though he was hardly a person, beneath their attention. But there was something more humane in the way Olivia addressed him. He was sure he wasn't imagining it.

But he had no way of talking to her privately.

Then his chance came. Francis and Silas were incredibly drunk, even more than Liam. Silas could barely stand and Francis's face was bright red. Together, they were dragging Madeline over to the piano, jeering at her to play something. Madeline was laughing and shaking her head, but she was caught up in the moment.

Liam stood and walked over to Olivia. His legs trembled. He felt the guards glaring at him, but they didn't move from their place at the door. A quiet voice yelled from the back of his head, buried beneath all the whisky, telling him to stop. This was a bad idea.

He dropped down next to her as Madeline began to play, disjointed notes clanging in the air. "I hope you're having a good night," he said, voice artificially loud.

"Oh, yes, and it's only just beginning. I've worked up quite the appetite. I hope it's time to eat soon."

Liam chuckled, and then lowered his voice. He leaned closer. "I'm being kept here against my will."

Olivia stared at him for a moment, then smiled. "I know that already." She raised her voice. "Silas, Francis, you were right. The poor lad fell for the dough-eyed matriarch routine. How predictable."

"What's happening?" Madeline stopped playing. "What are you talking about?"

"Silly boy." Olivia rose to her feet. "Francis, be a dear and send for some bacon rashers."

"I warned you." Francis strode across the room, as Liam sat there with his mouth open and his eyes wide, struggling to understand how he could be so stupid. "Didn't you hear what I said? Act like a pig, get treated like one."

"Father, what is this?" Madeline demanded, stamping her foot like a little kid. "I thought you said they didn't know–"

"Quiet, of course they know. You think I'd risk it? Men, the bacon, if you will."

"Bacon, what for? Father, he's *mine*."

Liam rose slowly to his feet. All three of them backed away, as the guard stepped forwards, and more guards filed in behind him. They'd been waiting in the hallway. Harrison was there, as well as three others; unlike the waiters, they were all wearing their balaclavas, but Harrison's build stood out.

Francis grinned at one of them. "Sorry for the secrecy, good man. I wasn't sure how far Liam would get. I wasn't sure if we'd need you at all."

"No apologies necessary, sir." It was Smith's voice. "I serve at your pleasure."

"Where is that bacon?" Silas snapped, gesturing at Liam with his glass. "You just lost me half a million, you idiotic Oliver Twist fuck. Why did you have to say anything?"

Madeline was raging, tears in her eyes. "He's mine. He belongs to me. You *can't* do this."

"I'd finish that if I was you." Francis nodded at Liam's glass. "You're going to need it."

Liam knocked the drink back, then placed the glass down. He was finding it difficult to stand up straight. Olivia's expression had transformed completely. She was sneering.

The guard in the waiter's uniform returned, holding a silver platter with several rashers of bacon on it.

"Ah, here we go." Silas grinned. "Time for the fun to begin."

CHAPTER THIRTY-FOUR

Liam was an asshole. There was no way around it.

He should've kept his wits about him, but the lure of the whisky had been too strong. Forgetting, even for a little while, was too tempting. But now his vision was cloudy and he was struggling to make sense of what was happening. He felt far drunker than he ever had before, and he wondered if there had been something else in the alcohol...

The guards had been giving him his whiskies. He had no clue if they had come from the same bottle as the others. He had no clue what else they'd put in them.

What had he been thinking, asking one of these people for help? He'd believed Francis when he said the guests didn't know the full extent of the situation, which was a stupid thing to do.

Silas chuckled. "What a clever piggy. Look, Francis, he's learned how to stand."

Francis's smile was nothing like Bretherton's. It was difficult to believe they were the same person. Francis looked rich and ruthless, revelling in whatever was about to happen. "On the floor, piggy."

"Father, this isn't fair. Liam is mine. You can't—"

"Stop being such a bore," Francis snapped. "We're having a little fun. Don't worry. We won't break him... as long as he does what he's told."

"You heard him." There were two Olivias as she leered at him. Liam blinked and she became one. "On the floor. Naughty piggy."

When Liam was very young, he'd climbed into his friend's mum's car. His first instinct had been to move his hand to the lock, to click it into place, but then his friend's mum had turned and given him this pitiful sort of look.

"It has central locking," she'd told him. And even if Liam had probably imagined that look, it had always made him cringe to think about. It had always made him feel poor, like dirt, lesser somehow.

He felt the same sense of powerlessness here.

"No," he said, the word coming out slurred and shaky.

Olivia spun to Francis, as though telling him to fix the problem. That was Liam. A malfunctioning piece of equipment.

Madeline had given up trying to stop them; she sat in the corner, sipping from her glass, glaring around the room but otherwise not involved.

"Liam, don't be stupid." Francis scowled. "You know what happens if you disobey us. Get on the floor. On all fours. You don't want cold bacon, do you?"

"No." Liam tried to stand up straighter. His legs wavered. "I won't do it."

"You will." Silas gestured with the platter. "Or I'll break your skull with this, you cheap fuck. Who do you think you are. *On the floor, now! On the fucking floor!*"

He roared and began to chant, and then Olivia joined in, clapping her hands as her eyes flooded with glee. She looked like an excited little kid.

"*On the floor! On the floor! On the floor!*"

Liam was shaking his head, watching as Francis gestured to the masked guards.

"Please," Liam said, staring at Harrison. "Please don't do this."

"Nah-uh." Olivia stopped chanting. "Naughty little piggies can't talk. On your knees."

"Maybe we didn't give him enough," Silas muttered.

"Oh, so you gave him the concoction as well." Madeline huffed. "*Without* my permission. Father, honestly, this is completely unacceptable. Maybe I'll interrupt you next time you're with one of your whores."

"Try to enjoy it, Maddie. Jesus. It's just a bit of fun."

"You should've asked me first."

Liam's mind was working slowly. "Concoction?"

"He can hardly speak." Olivia tittered. "Is there any reason he's still standing?"

Francis gestured with his whisky glass. "Men."

Six guards crossed the room, fanning out around Liam.

"On your knees, mate." It was Smith's voice. "You're a pig. Pigs can't stand on two legs."

Liam coughed back a sob. Fuck. He couldn't cry in front of these people. "I'm not a pig."

"You are," Olivia said. "A dirty disobedient little piggy. On your knees."

"I don't want to get on my knees."

"I thought you said he was well-trained, Maddie."

"He is!" Madeline leapt to her feet. "But he only does what *I* want him to."

"Fine. Convince him."

Madeline approached, moving in that sickening way. It was like she thought she was the sexiest woman alive.

The guards fanned apart, following closely as Madeline

approached Liam. Liam tried to make himself fight, to explode into action, but it was an effort to stay upright.

Madeline paused just short of him, studied him for a moment, and then seemed to make a decision. She closed the distance. The guards surrounded Liam, trapping him on all sides. Olivia muttered something to Silas and the man guffawed.

Madeline brought her mouth to Liam's ear. Her breath tickled hatefully across his skin. "I'm sorry, but you have to do what they say. Father gets like this sometimes. I promise I didn't know. But if you don't – and I really am sorry, Liam, I am – I'll be forced to do very bad things to your family. You can't make me look like a fool, not in front of Daddy.

"I'll have the men bring Emily and your child and your little rat dog here, and I'll order them to rape Emily in front of you. And then I'll tie a rope around your dog's neck and hang him from the rafters. Finally I'll see about the child... I'm not sure if I have the stomach to kill a baby, but it will be an interesting test of my resolve. Please, Liam, don't make me do that. Just do what they say."

Liam was crying, tears sliding silently down his cheeks. He didn't sob, but he couldn't stop the tears. He felt like he'd wasted every good chance he'd had... but what was he supposed to do? He didn't know if Madeline was bluffing. He couldn't risk Emily's life.

Madeline returned to her father, resting her elbow on the piano. "He won't be any bother now."

"Is that right?" Silas called over. "Will you be a good piggy? I thought my lovely wife was mad when she said a few kind words would turn you into an idiot."

"It's the concoction," Francis said. "It does wonders for their inhibitions. I've used it dozens of times on my servants. It makes them ever so pliable."

"You could've warned me," Silas grumbled.

"Don't throw a tantrum over half a million."

With half a million Liam and Emily would be set for years, decades. He'd buy a house outright so he didn't have to pay the bank back. And, without a mortgage hanging over them, they'd be free to make improvements on their home. Maybe Emily could quit her job and Liam could expand his business. It was life-changing money, and they were talking about it like it was nothing.

"We're waiting, piggy," Olivia said.

Liam held the image of Emily and his child in his mind. As a sob escaped him, he slowly climbed onto the floor. He propped himself on his hands and knees, the sobs threatening to choke him.

He was filth. He was pathetic. He couldn't even afford a flat without damp on the walls; he couldn't even provide for Emily.

"Don't just kneel there. Move around. Even piggies need their exercise." Olivia was giggling as she spoke. "Come on. Move, piggy. Move."

Liam wept as he crawled around the room, over to the piano and back to where he'd started. They cheered him on, laughing and clapping as he made a circuit. The guards were never far away, ready to leap on him if he tried anything. But he didn't. He was beaten.

"What a quiet piggy."

"Make some noise, piggy."

"Oink, piggy. Oink."

He did what they said: he oinked as he crawled around. He started quietly, but they shouted at him and told him to be a proud piggy.

And so he became a proud piggy. He oinked as loudly as he could, and somehow this was worse than the rest of it. It was worse than the beatings and the whipping and his time in the dark cell. It was worse than everything. They didn't care that he was weeping as he oinked.

"Good piggy. May I feed him?"

Liam looked up to find Olivia holding some bacon rashers, pinching them between her forefinger and thumb as if she didn't want to get her hand dirty.

Francis smirked. "Of course."

The guards moved to let her through, and then closed in on Liam. He couldn't look at any of them, not when he was like this; he hadn't stopped weeping. He'd never felt like less of a man.

Olivia bent down with the rashers. "Nice and gentle now, piggy."

Liam took them from her hand in his mouth. He ate them quickly. He just wanted it to be over. Next Silas came. He shoved the rashers into Liam's mouth, sticking his fingers right to the back of his throat so Liam could taste sweat and skin. Liam coughed and almost choked on a stringy piece of fat, swallowing it down.

"Not going to indulge, Francis?" Silas asked as he walked away.

Francis shook his head. "Look at him. A real man would fight. A real man would do something. Even with everything at stake. That's how you know we're different. Would you ever crawl around like that, Silas?"

"Never."

"Exactly. And no, no, I'm not feeding him. If I had my way, he'd starve. Shall we?"

Francis walked to the door, and Silas and Olivia followed.

Madeline stood over Liam, her upper lip curled. "You didn't have to put so much passion into the oinking. And stop crying."

Liam bowed his head.

Madeline placed her hand on his back. "It's okay. I didn't

mean to yell. But you must try to have some self-respect. Father has completely spoiled my night, and I don't need you making it any worse. Go to bed and I'll come see you later... who knows, perhaps I'll even find a way to cheer you up."

Once Madeline had closed the door behind her, Liam slumped to the floor. He pulled his knees to his chest and cried.

CHAPTER THIRTY-FIVE

Harrison looked at Liam, hating that he'd ever agreed to meet with Smith, that he'd made the video, that he was a part of this in any way.

Watching Liam crawl around on the floor had been humiliating. Harrison had felt bad for him. But most of all Harrison had wanted to turn on them, Silas and Olivia and Francis, all three of them looking at Liam like it was a big joke.

Liam was completely deflated, sobbing uncontrollably as though all the pain from the past month was bursting out. He linked his hands around his knees, pulling them to his chest, hugging himself as he wept openly. He'd been crying the whole time he was crawling around and oinking, but he'd managed to keep the choking sobs at bay. Now he was like a small boy, desperate for his parents.

One of the other guards sniggered.

Harrison's gaze snapped to the man in the waiter's uniform. Unlike the four who had entered once the pig game begun, this guard wasn't wearing his balaclava. He had an ordinary-looking face, except for his busted nose. Harrison wondered if Liam had done it during one of their fights.

"Look at the big tough guy," the man sneered. "Crying like a little girl. Jesus Christ, is he ever going to stop?"

Harrison walked up to the man. It was one thing to do what had to be done. But to revel in it... He walked until he was face to face with him, staring right into the prick's eyes.

"Got a problem, big man?" he said.

Harrison nodded. "Yeah, I do. You're going to shut your mouth."

"Is that so?"

"It is."

"Or what?"

"I'll shut it for you."

The man chuckled. "Yeah, good luck with tha—"

Harrison didn't think. He couldn't even hear his own thoughts; all he could hear was Liam's crying, still going, like a dam had burst inside of him.

Harrison hit the man in the belly.

The man gasped and keeled over, and then Harrison was on him: hands on his neck as he threw him to the floor. They fell in a tangle and Harrison was hitting him, punching him in the face over and over, slamming his elbow into the side of his head. He roared and spit and made to headbutt him, but then Smith and another guard pulled him away, throwing him to the other end of the room.

Harrison roared. "Come on! Come on!"

"Enough, lad." Smith grabbed onto Harrison's shirt, glaring at him. "If they hear you, you're in the shit. Calm down."

"Sucker-punching pussy," the man said, climbing to his feet. Harrison was surprised to find the man's face largely unharmed. He felt like he'd hit him clean a few times, but he was unmarked except for a small cut on his cheek. "Let him go. Let's do this properly."

"Enough," Smith snapped. "Both of you. We can't have this."

"You said it was just going to be a dinner," Harrison said. "They wanted to have a meal. Not... not this."

"I didn't know. But it doesn't matter."

Harrison waved a hand at Liam, who was still curled in a ball. "How can you say this doesn't matter?"

"He's weak," the other guard said. "Doing what they wanted, fine. I get that. But crying like a little bitch? It's pathetic."

"I won't tell you again," Smith said. "And you..." He grimaced at Harrison. "If you want to play the Good Samaritan, go ahead. See where it gets you. Otherwise help us get Liam back to his room."

Harrison shrugged Smith's hand away. "I'm fine."

"You sure?"

"Yeah, I'm good. It won't happen again."

"It better not," the other guard grunted.

Harrison gave him a hard stare as he approached Liam, letting him know he was ready to go any time. Kneeling down next to Liam, he placed his hand on his shoulder. "It's all right, mate, you don't have to–"

Liam lashed out, pushing Harrison's hand away. He rose unsteadily to his feet. "Don't act like you're any different. You're just as bad as them. You're part of it. Don't pretend to care."

"I'm not enjoying this any more than you."

Liam snorted. His eyes were glassy and bloodshot. "You get whipped then. You make a fool out of yourself. You have your family threatened. You get put in a cell with no mattress or pillows or... you, *you* crawl around on the floor like a pig."

"I'm sorry."

"You're not. None of you are. If you were, you wouldn't let this happen."

Smith raised his hand. "Are you going to make this hard on us? We need to take you back to your room."

"Nah, it's all good." Liam rubbed his cheeks, laughing bitterly. "I'll be an obedient little piggy. Don't worry. Fuck me. What did they put in my drink?"

"I'm not sure," Smith said.

"But it was something, wasn't it? The concoction. You heard him."

"I'm not sure. Come on."

Smith took one arm and Harrison took the other. Liam's eyes never left Harrison as they exited the room. Harrison wanted to say something to make him feel better. But Liam was right; Harrison was part of it, as bad as the others... or maybe he was worse. Because he knew how wrong it was, he knew he had to help Liam. And still he did nothing.

"She said she's going to try to cheer me up later." Liam groaned, his words coming out garbled. He was clearly struggling with the alcohol and whatever drugs they'd given him. "I don't want to cheat on Emily. She can't make me, can she?"

Nobody answered. There was no need.

CHAPTER THIRTY-SIX

I t was difficult to be civil with Father for the rest of the evening.

He knew how important Liam was to me, and I suspect that's why he behaved how he did. The Bretherton business hadn't bothered me. That was one of his oldest games; he'd played it countless times growing up, pretending to be the butler with the servants, forcing them to treat him as though he was beneath them... and then punishing them for daring to do as he'd instructed.

That was fine. That was Father being Father. I was relieved when he'd left the estate and dropped the Bretherton routine. It had grown tiresome, and I didn't like to think about Father and Liam talking whenever he went to collect him. Father might overstep his mark... the way he had this evening.

Liam had liked Father when he was the butler; I was certain, because otherwise why had Liam asked after him? He'd lied and said Bretherton had offered to walk him around the grounds, which Father had never done. That was a problem. Liam had a bad habit of choosing the help over me.

No matter the mistakes Liam had made, Father was worse.

To lie to me about the nature of the meal, to pretend it was going to be a civilised affair, and then to ambush me like that. It was sickening. I should've suspected something when the guests arrived. There weren't many people involved in his games, but they were a lucky pair, and had participated countless times, always using false names just in case one of the servants got brave, not that they'd ever dare.

Father had promised: Liam was mine. He belonged to me.

But then the guards had started giving him glass after glass of whisky. I wasn't sure exactly what the concoction was made of, but I knew Father had hired a chemist years ago to produce the exact desired effect: massively reduced inhibition, increased emotion, paranoia.

It had turned Liam into a snivelling mess. That was why Father had done it. Perhaps he sensed my feelings for Liam were more than just some casual fling. Perhaps he thought I was going too far.

He didn't know that I'd been doubting Liam, little whispers at the edge of my resolve... but whenever I heard these traitor voices, I forced myself to remember how he'd looked the first time I'd seen him, the emotion which had flooded into me.

Love at first sight existed. I had experienced it.

But it had been difficult to feel anything positive for him as he crawled around on the floor, making those ugly snorting noises, humiliating himself. And me. The only possible reason I could forgive him was because he'd been under the influence of Father's concoction.

I could only hope its effects lessened over the course of a few hours, so he was ready when I visited him. I hadn't planned to throw myself at him so soon, but Father's trick bothered me. I had to assert my claim. I had to show Liam it was him and me against the world.

Liam was lucky. He was going to get to have sex with me far sooner than he should have.

As we were eating our main course that evening, Father turned to me. "Why did you tell the piggy I'd beaten you as a child? Why did you tell him that's how you got those scars on your back?"

"Because it's the truth."

Father frowned. "Do you really believe that, Maddie?"

Sometimes, when he looked at me like that, it was like he'd sincerely forgotten all the terrible things he'd done.

I knew the story he liked to tell. The old thornbush tale. I hated how stubbornly he stuck to it, even after all these years. His persistence even made *me* doubt it, as I thought back over my childhood, trying to hold the memories firmly in place.

Sometimes they flitted: I was in a thornbush, he was hitting me, back and forth, back and forth.

But no. He'd hurt me. That's why I was the way I was. That's why I found it so difficult to love and, when I did, I loved so intensely.

I had an excuse. I was a victim.

Father had once again tried to victimise me, by staking a claim in Liam, a man he had no business with at all. Father thought because he'd given me so much, he could treat me as abhorrently as he wished. But when Liam glided up inside of me – when our bodies fused – it would ignite what I'd felt the first time I saw him.

I'd forget his shameful oinking. I'd forget how tragic he'd looked when he was crawling around on the floor.

When we made love, everything would be perfect.

CHAPTER THIRTY-SEVEN

Snuggling into the chair, Emily wrapped her hands around her mug of hot chocolate and stared at the TV screen. The news was running a feature on a girl who had gone missing a few days earlier; there had been nothing about Liam, who'd vanished a month ago. An entire month... it was by far the longest they'd been apart since becoming boyfriend and girlfriend.

She craved him so badly. She sometimes woke at night, wrapped in the blankets, and managed to trick herself into believing it was his arms around her instead. But then those moments of sleep would fade, and she'd be left with the blunt reality.

"It's not fair," Emily whispered.

Mum and Dad tightened up on the sofa. They'd been doing that a lot lately, as though anticipating her every word. She wondered if she was coming across as a little unhinged. She wished she was stronger. But she couldn't stop thinking about him.

"Why should she get all this attention?"

"You don't mean that," Dad said. "She's a little girl."

"I know. If it was Jamie I'd want them to do the same. But..."

Emily placed her hot chocolate on the coffee table. The sound it made was far too loud. She slumped back and hugged her knees to her chest, wrapping her arms around herself. "But little kids don't run away, not when they're that young, not when their parents love them." Emily tightened her grip on her legs. "That's the difference. Liam could've run away. He could've abandoned us."

She hated the words: hated the thoughts. But she couldn't stop.

"I never told you he cheated, did I?"

"No, dear," Mum said softly, as the screen showed a photo of the bright-eyed vivacious girl.

"We'd only been together a few weeks. Liam was a little wild when he was younger. He freely admitted it. I guess it was hard, coming to terms with how many women he'd been with before me. But he promised he'd never stray. He swore."

Emily wiped away a tear. Dad rose gently from the sofa and walked over to her, kneeling next to the chair and placing his hand on her shoulder. She reached up and held on to him.

"Then one of his mates had a stag do." Emily watched Rocky as she spoke. The little dog was curled up on the back of the other chair. It was the closest to the window he could get, his head cocking slightly every time there was a noise outside. He'd never stop waiting. "Liam got so drunk. It was the last time he blacked out, he said. The next morning, he woke me up and told me one of his mates had seen him kissing a girl. He promised he didn't remember doing it."

Her parents said nothing, waiting for her to go on.

Emily wasn't sure why she was telling them. She'd never told anybody, even her closest friends; she didn't want to be known as the woman who got cheated on and took her man back. And yet keeping it inside felt wrong, especially now:

especially with what so many people were saying and implying.

Liam had left. The pressure had been too much. He didn't love her anymore.

"I asked him why he was telling me. He said he didn't want there to be any secrets between us. He cried and held me and promised he'd never get that drunk again. I loved him so much, even then, even in the beginning. It made me sick. We separated... for five days. But I couldn't be apart from him. I had to believe him."

"And?" Mum said. "Did he do it again?"

"Not that I know of. But what if I'm wrong? What if he found another woman and that's where he is now, with her? Maybe he got tired of me being pregnant..Liam is..."

She trailed off. She'd been about to say that Liam was a very sexual person. They'd always had a vibrant sex life. He'd never stopped lavishing her with attention, his hands all over her. But during her pregnancy, that had changed. Emily had expected it, but it was still a big transition. Maybe he'd gone looking elsewhere.

"He could've found somebody else." Emily glanced at the baby monitor, almost willing Jamie to start crying. "He was so excited, though. That's the thing I can't stop thinking about. Liam has always been such an upfront person, even with the cheating. I never felt like he was pretending with me. He couldn't wait to be a father."

"He's a good man," Dad said. "I know he made a mistake, but he told you the truth. Lots of men wouldn't do that."

"You've never cheated on Mum."

"No, I haven't."

"Why?"

"Emily..."

"It's a fair question."

"People are different," Dad said. "You said Liam had a wild side when he was younger. I never had that. I've always been, let's say... sensible." He grinned.

"Boring," Mum joked.

Emily couldn't remember the last time she'd laughed. It felt so good.

"But Liam overcame his demons, if we can call them that. He loved you."

"I know he does. I hope he does."

Suddenly Rocky sprung up from his sleeping position, yapping at the window. Emily leapt to her feet and rushed over to him.

"Hush. It's okay."

He couldn't stop, springing out of her hands any time she grabbed him. He was almost falling off the back of the chair. Dad walked over and grabbed onto him with his strong hands, hugging Rocky to his chest even as the dog tried to squirm free.

"What's gotten into you, huh?"

Emily looked through the window. There was a man standing on the other side of the street. Their curtains were open, but Mum had hung a white voile recently.

Emily could only make out the man's shape as he stood beneath the lamp post. It looked like he was staring at the house.

"Emily!"

She ignored Mum's cry as she sprinted for the hallway. Somebody was watching the house; maybe they had kidnapped Liam and now they were here out of guilt, or some sick pleasure. Or maybe it was Liam himself, visiting because he felt bad for running away. Emily rushed out the front door, running over the stones in her socks, barely feeling them as she ran onto the street.

The man was sprinting away.

"Stop!"

She still felt weak from the pregnancy. Plus she hadn't been eating much lately.

But she didn't care.

She ran as fast as she could. But he was fitter. He was outpacing her; he turned at the end of the street. She panted as she reached the turning.

He was gone.

"Emily, what the hell are you doing?" Dad jogged up the street in his slippers. "What happened?"

"There was a man."

Dad frowned. "A man?"

"I'm not making it up."

He approached her with his hands raised, gently wrapping his arms around her. "All right, all right. What did this man look like?"

She thought back to the chase. It had all happened so fast. "He was dressed in black, I think. And he was wearing a mask, no, like a balaclava. Or his hair was really dark. I don't know. I should've been paying attention. He was running away. Why would he do that if he didn't want me to catch him?"

"Are you sure he was running away from you? Maybe he was just getting some exercise. Lots of joggers run through our street. There's even a club."

"But he was staring at the house!"

"What?"

"Before, when Rocky was barking. He was standing across the street and staring at our house."

"Oh, Emily." Dad hugged her tighter.

"He was. I saw him."

"I'm not saying you didn't. But how do you know he was watching our house, specifically? Next door are selling, remember. He might've been looking at their property."

"No, he was standing across from *our* house." She winced at

203

the petulant note in her voice. She didn't sound like a mother, like a woman with her life in control. "We have to tell the police. Even if it's nothing. Just in case."

"Okay, that's fine. We'll ring them. How does that sound?"

There it was again; he was talking to her like she was crazy. Maybe he had a point. That was how she was starting to feel.

CHAPTER THIRTY-EIGHT

Liam spent the next few hours trying to sober up. He took an ice-cold shower and stood there naked, shivering as the water dripped down his skin. He wished he could open the window so it was even colder. He paced up and down the room, forced himself to do some push-ups.

Nothing worked.

It had been hours – at least he thought so – since they'd humiliated him.

He cringed when he thought about what they'd made him do. But it was worse when he remembered how he'd stupidly asked that woman for help. She'd given him a few looks, a few kind comments. His head had felt like it was full of cotton balls, and it felt that way now; it wouldn't end. Everything was cloudy, as if reality was behind a thick sheet of glass.

It was difficult for him to make sense of it. He'd never felt anything like this before.

The oinking noises replayed in his head, the looks of Olivia and Silas as they shoved the bacon into his mouth. It hurt worse than everything.

It had made him feel like a poor little kid, the same way he'd felt throughout all his childhood. His family had never been well off. Not destitute, but they'd gone without a lot. His mother was working full time and struggling to make ends meet. Liam's dad only helped when he felt like it. He never resented Mum, and he'd taken a paper round at twelve, working all through his teenage years to try to help.

But he could never shake that feeling, like he was somehow different from a lot of the kids he knew. His mum had always panicked about money, and it had branded him in some way.

He'd always expected disaster to hit any second. Maybe that was why it hurt so badly. Disaster had finally hit after so many years of waiting.

No more, he promised himself. He would never break down like that again.

But he hadn't forgotten Madeline's words. She was going to visit him tonight. He couldn't cheat on Emily, even to get out of there.

He'd taken his promise to her seriously. He'd never done it again. He'd purposefully avoided drinking too much for that very reason. There was some wildness in him, clearly, buried deep. He never wanted to hurt Emily again.

If she was here, what would she want him to do? Would she want him to go through with it?

If the positions were reversed, Liam would want her to do it. He'd hate the bloke who dared to put her in that position, but her life was too valuable.

Surely she'd feel the same.

The alternative was they'd kill him or hurt Emily or his child. He didn't know if he had a son or a daughter. That made tears rise to his eyes. He wiped them away. He needed to stop that bullshit. It wasn't helping.

Later, there was a knock at the door. Liam had been sitting at the window, staring down at his book, the words not sinking in. He still hadn't sobered up. He just wanted it to end so he could think clearly.

The knocking got louder.

"What?" he said, walking across the room.

"We've brought you some clothes." It was Harrison. "We're opening the door. Step back."

Liam did as he was told. He didn't have it in him to get in a brawl.

The door opened and Harrison stepped in, followed closely by another guard. The other guard stood against the wall with his arms folded across his middle, staring at Liam with narrowed eyes.

Harrison gestured with the coat hanger. A fresh suit hung from it; Liam had changed back into that night's one after the shower, except for the jacket.

"I guess she wants her plaything all fancied up." Liam took the hanger. "Has she told you what farm animal I'll be playing, mate?"

"Just take the suit."

Liam snatched it out of his hand and chucked it onto the bed. "Anything else?"

Harrison left without saying another word. Liam knew he should've been making an effort with him. Even if he hadn't helped, at least he'd addressed how messed up all of this was. But it didn't change the fact he'd just stood there as Liam crawled around, oinking like a pathetic piece of shit while the rich people laughed and clapped. He was a novelty. He was their circus freak.

He got changed. He had to be strong now, no matter what happened.

A short while later, another knock came at the door. It

opened and Smith strode in. Liam was beginning to be able to spot the man. He was similar height and build to many of the others, but he walked with more confidence, or maybe it was like he was trying to seem confident.

"The lady will be joining you soon," he said. "She's made the decision to be alone with you in the bedroom. My men are going to search it for any weapons. But just tell me now if you're hiding anything. It'll make this a lot simpler."

"I'm not. I haven't had a chance to."

"You'd be surprised. Prisoners can be pretty resourceful."

"Yeah, well, I'm not used to this."

"Get in the corner."

Liam dropped into his chair as three more men filed into the room. Harrison was one of them, and Liam made a point of staring at him as they flipped the mattress and moved all the furniture. They went under the bed and into the bathroom, combing every inch.

Harrison wouldn't look at him; he was purposefully staring anywhere but at Liam.

Finally Smith came to stand over Liam. "Got to search you too. Are you going to make it difficult?"

"When do I ever make anything difficult?" Liam rose and spread his arms. "Just a little obedient piggy. That's me. If they'd asked you to do that, Smith, what would you have done?"

Smith patted Liam down as he responded. "I would have done it."

"Would you have been happy about it?"

"I would've done it," he repeated. "All clear. I don't need to warn you about what happens if you hurt her, do I?"

"Don't worry. I won't do anything to spoil her rape."

Smith left the room, the men following.

Liam expected them to close the door, but they left it open.

Then Madeline appeared, dressed in what was supposed to

be sexy lingerie. A red bra and knickers, with frilly bits around the edge, stockings held up with red straps. If Emily had been wearing this, Liam would've lost his mind. But this woman had tortured him, imprisoned him, humiliated him; he wanted nothing to do with her.

If she'd heard anything he'd said, she gave no sign as she closed the door. She turned to him with a shaky smile, her eyes wide and manic.

"It's so nice to finally be alone, isn't it?"

Emily, Liam said in his mind. *Emily, Emily, Emily.*

He'd repeat her name like a mantra. That was the only way he was going to get through this.

"Yeah, it's a nice change."

She walked up to him, stopping with a melodramatic breath at the last moment. "To touch you... to be with you... and you do want it, don't you? I know things have been complicated between us, but you want this?"

He swallowed. "Yes, I want it so badly."

"Oh, goodie."

She threw herself against him, wrapping her arms around his neck and guiding his lips to hers. He kissed her, even as his body fought it; their mouths opened and she dragged her tongue along his, moaning and whimpering as though she was having the time of her life. He felt like he wasn't even there.

He was betraying Emily. He'd promised he'd never do this again.

Her hand snaked down his chest. She stopped the kiss when she pressed down on his dick.

"Is something wrong? You don't think I'm pretty?"

"No, I do. It's just... the alcohol."

"Hmm. I think I can fix that. Sit on the bed."

"Please."

She tilted her head. "Please, please what?"

209

He was going to ask her to please not do this. But he corrected quickly. "Please, I want it so badly."

"You already said that. Try to vary it up a bit. Don't you want this to be romantic and exciting?"

He groaned as she pushed him onto the bed. Then she was on her knees, her hands at his trousers. She unbuttoned him and took him out of his boxers. She stared at his limp cock for a moment, as though disgusted, and then with a sigh she took him in her mouth.

Liam stared down at her, trying to imagine it was Emily. If he couldn't do this... But thinking like that was only making it worse. He had to try to enjoy this on some fucked-up level. He had to make Maddie believe. But it wasn't working. She went at it for a minute, then two, three. Liam couldn't do what she wanted him to.

She let him go and sat back. "I shouldn't even be doing this. What's the matter with you? You said I was pretty."

"You are—"

"Then what's the *matter* with you? You managed to put a baby in that disgusting whale of a girlfriend. Are you really saying she's prettier than me?"

Liam stared.

"Well?" Maddie rocked onto her knees, placing her hands on his legs and digging her nails in. "Who's prettier, me or the whale?"

"Y-you," he stuttered.

"Exactly. So you need to get your act together. And don't even think about mentioning Viagra. If you can't get it up for the woman you're going to spend the rest of your life with, then, then maybe the rest of your life won't be very fucking long!" She stood, waving her hand. "I'm going to freshen up. Compose yourself."

She marched into the en suite. Liam pulled his trousers up, walking over to the window.

He couldn't do this anymore; it was killing him, one little piece at a time. He couldn't make himself attracted to this woman, and the drink wasn't helping. There were only going to be more problems if he was here when she returned.

He took off his jacket and wrapped it around his hand.

After the first *thud*, he heard movement outside the bedroom door. But with the second strike, the glass shattered. The hole wasn't big; he would have to drag himself through.

People were shouting. The lock was rattling. Liam heard the en suite door fly open behind him.

But he was already halfway through the hole. The glass scraped his legs, digging into his thighs, cutting into his back and catching onto his shirt as he pulled himself through.

"Quickly! Quickly!" Madeline shouted.

Liam hauled himself the rest of the way, grabbing onto the window frame. The glass cut into his palms. Blood wept down the frame. Liam stared at them all, at Smith and Harrison and the other guards, at Madeline.

And then he let go.

CHAPTER THIRTY-NINE

L iam roared as his ankle rolled. He fell onto his side, the stones biting into his bicep. He made himself stand and duck his head, running for the trees.

His ankle throbbed and protested with each step, threatening to give way again. His body tingled from where he'd cut himself clambering through the window.

But he didn't let himself stop. He ran as fast as he could.

He ducked behind a tree and peered around it, looking back at the house. The guards were rushing out the front door.

Madeline jogged out in a silk nightgown, waving her hands. Liam had closed the distance quickly, especially considering his injuries; her voice came to him only dimly. She seemed very far away, and he wanted to keep it like that.

He began to make his way doggedly through the trees. It was funny how he only noticed his feet were bare when a sharp twig stuck him between the toes. He leaned against a tree, pulled it loose, and added it to the list of pain which bothered him with every step.

Breaking through the trees, he growled as his ankle tried to roll again. It felt like his shin was sitting atop a mass of uneven bone, constantly trying to slip out of place. But he couldn't go back there: to the oinking and her lips wrapped around him, the look in her eyes when he couldn't do what she needed him to.

He had to press on. He had to find Emily.

The pounding in his head wasn't helping. He wondered if he'd hit it when he jumped from the window. With the haziness of the alcohol – and whatever drugs they'd given him – it was difficult to believe he'd jumped from the third storey. Maybe he was dead. Maybe this was Hell.

He ran.

Engines purred in the air all around him. Liam was standing in the middle of a field when he spotted the high beams cutting across the grounds. He froze, watching as they got closer, and then dropped to his belly and laid himself flat against the grass. It wasn't a great hiding place, but it was the best he had.

His legs twitched, trying to get him to stand and run. But the car was getting closer. He would have to wait.

It passed close by him, so near he was sure he felt the earth tremble. He winced as it drove away. Leaning up, he looked around and, when the only lights he could see were in the distance, he climbed unsteadily to his feet and kept on the way he'd been going.

He crested the low hill and scanned the horizon. The night was too dark to make anything out clearly. They really were in the middle of nowhere.

He'd hoped to see some city lights, or the flicker of a town, or a village, or something: any civilisation, any place he could aim. But there was nothing but the seemingly endless dark, punctuated with the high beams combing up and down the fields.

There was a car to the far left, so Liam headed right, to what he prayed was the corner of the estate. Once he'd reached its boundaries, he'd be able to decide what to do. If it was a wall, he'd climb it. If it was a river, he'd swim across, even if it meant snapping his ankle clean off the bone.

Tears rose in his eyes with each step, but these weren't the pathetic sobs from when he'd crawled around. These tears meant something; he was pushing through the pain; he was going to get home.

The night was so dark he didn't spot the wall until he was almost standing beneath it. He stared up, craning his neck, as a sinking feeling hit him right in the gut.

There was no way he could climb this. It was at least fifteen feet tall, and it was completely sheer, with no handholds Liam could see.

He approached, ran his hand over it, hoping to feel some unevenness. It was like the stone had been mechanically sanded, leaving it smooth to the touch.

Liam rested his forehead against it, as his body tried to make him sit down, take the pressure off his ankle. It felt like it was swelling. He wouldn't look at it, in case it was worse than he thought and he lost his nerve.

Moving away, he walked alongside the wall, searching for any weak spots, anything he could hold on to. There must be a way. If he had a rope, maybe... but it didn't matter. He didn't have a rope. And even if he did, there was nothing to tether it to.

The cars were making another circuit. Liam limped into a patch of longish grass and pressed his cheek against the earth, watching as high beams panned across the grounds. It wouldn't be long before they found him. And then what?

He couldn't think about the consequences. He'd made his choice.

Once the car passed, he stood and limped alongside the wall. The adrenaline was fading, his body suddenly feeling weary, the pain more pronounced. The grass was becoming more and more welcoming; to lay his head down, close his eyes, sink into oblivion, that would be heaven.

The wall gave him nothing. It was smooth. It was a perfect jailor's tool.

But then, after walking for what felt like hours, he came to the other end of the estate.

The trees had been allowed to grow closer to the wall here. One had grasping branches, almost reaching to the top of the wall. Liam studied it. He'd have to climb the tree, crawl along the branch, and then jump to the wall. Then he'd have to lower himself down and drop, like he had from the window.

His ankle pulsed at the thought, as though getting him ready. He had no doubt he would break it.

Bright lights shone behind him. He spun. Men were walking at him on foot, holding heavy torches. They were silhouettes in the darkness, hiding behind their blinding torchlight. Liam lifted his hand to shield his eyes.

"He's here! We found him!"

Liam made for the tree. The branches were high, the shortest one taller than him. He stood below it, judging the distance. He would only have one chance. If he jumped and missed it, his ankle would shatter. It felt like a swollen ball already, about to burst.

In his mind, Emily was smiling at him. She'd just found out she was pregnant and the smile was a little shaky, a little unsure, as if she wasn't certain how he was going to react. When his smile mirrored hers, she let her true feelings of pure joy out, throwing her arms around him.

Liam jumped. His hands clawed for the branch.

He missed.

White-hot agony shot up his leg.

Stumbling, his face smashed into the tree trunk. Splinters bit into his cheek. He somehow righted himself. He had no idea where the strength came from, but he limped to beneath the branch again, staring up at it, as the guards rushed him.

They were so close. He could hear their boots in the grass.

He leaned heavily on his good ankle, bent his legs, and jumped again.

This time he managed to hook one hand around the tree branch. His muscles protested, feeling like they were ripping off the bone, as he hauled himself up. He grabbed the branch with his other hand and pulled with all his strength.

The guards were directly beneath him, leaping for his feet. He kicked wildly as he thrashed his way onto the branch.

"What's your plan, you idiot?" a guard snapped. "We've got backup coming. The other side of the wall isn't going to be any safer than this one. Come down now and maybe she'll forgive you."

Liam climbed the tree. He had to drag his wounded leg behind him, glad that his arms were cooperating at least. Every time his ankle bumped into the trunk or a jutting branch, fire shot through his body.

But he kept climbing. This was it. This was who he truly was: a man who'd do anything to return to his fiancée, his child. He wasn't a coward crawling around on the floor.

He climbed until he was where he needed to be, the highest he could go without risking his weight on the lighter branches. Wedging his back against a thick branch and his good foot against another, he judged the jump. The jutting branch looked far skinnier from up here, and everything seemed higher.

A car approached and stopped beneath the tree. Madeline stepped out, still in her nightgown. The driver followed her. Liam thought it was Smith, from the way he moved, standing at his lady's side like the loyal weasel he was.

"Tell him to come down," Madeline snapped.

"What are you thinking, Liam?" Smith called. "There's no way out of this. Get down."

Liam ignored him, willing himself to start walking along the tree branch.

"I can't believe he'd do this to me. I thought it was real. It *is* real. But he won't learn his lesson. We fell in love. I felt it. I know he did too. This isn't fair. This isn't *fair!*" Madeline was pacing up and down the base of the tree, wringing her hands together. "Do the phone thing. Make him understand."

Liam was manoeuvring into position when a phone started to ring on loudspeaker. He looked down to find Smith holding a mobile, aiming it at Liam as though it was a gun, the square of light shining up at him.

"Hello?"

Liam's body trembled. It was Emily. Her voice. The voice he knew so well. He knew he'd missed it, but he hadn't realised how much. He was almost crying again.

"Who is this?"

"Emily," he called, voice torn.

"It's on mute, mate," Smith said.

"Who is this?" Emily snapped. "Liam? Is that you? Liam?"

"I'm here!" he shouted. "Emily, Emily."

"Didn't you hear him?" Madeline said. "She can't hear you. Why won't you stop disappointing me? This isn't how it's supposed to be at all. This isn't what *you're* supposed to be."

"Liam, if it's you, please just say something. Please let me know you're okay."

"You get the point," Smith said. "Don't make me say it."

"Say it!" Liam shouted. "Fucking say it. Say you'll hurt my fiancée if I don't pretend to love this lunatic. Say you'll gang-rape her in front of me. Say you'll slit my child's throat. Is that it? Is that what you'd do?"

Liam stood on the branch, holding on with one hand. He

slammed his other against his chest, over and over. "You're all scum. That's it. The lowest of the low."

"Liam!" Emily was shouting, her voice frantic. He wanted to hold her and tell her it would be okay.

"We'll do all of those things," Smith said. "But we don't want to. Don't make us. Come down."

"Last warning. Or I'll give the order. I swear to God I will." Madeline stared at him from the base of the tree. "You'll need to be taught a lesson, but I won't hurt the whale or the kid. That's the deal. But this is your last chance. I mean it."

Liam eyed the branch, and then a car began to move towards the wall from the other side, filled with two masked guards.

Liam had no choice. He'd failed. Again.

He climbed down the tree, which was far more difficult than the journey up had been. He slipped and fell from the lowest branch, screaming when he landed on his ankle. He fell and began to shiver.

Madeline stood over him. For a moment, Liam thought he saw her features soften. But then they hardened, and he wondered if he'd imagined it.

"Beat him and take him to the cell."

"How severely, miss?" Smith asked in a businesslike tone.

"As severely as he deserves."

"I understand."

The guards converged on him.

Liam lay still as boots and fists pounded his body.

CHAPTER FORTY

Harrison and Smith were carrying Liam down the hallway which led to the stone cell. Liam was hardly moving, except to wince every time his foot brushed against the floor.

Harrison's grandfather was in his head, the man's wrinkled skin, his hard eyes. His words were in his head. "Always do the right thing. No matter how hard it is. No matter what the consequences are. My dad was ready to die on that beach. He wouldn't have thought anything of it. Because it was the right thing to do."

Harrison tried to shut down his emotions. He couldn't let himself think about what he'd done, what he was still doing: the part he was playing. As the guards had beat Liam, Harrison had tried to stand off to the side. But then Madeline had noticed.

"What's the matter, soldier boy? Think you're special?"

Smith had grabbed him and tossed him at Liam, and Harrison had joined in. He'd kicked Liam in the stomach and punched him across the face, and even if he tried to put as little strength as possible into each strike, it didn't change the fact he'd done it.

Madeline had made a point of ordering Harrison to help

carry Liam to the cells. She wanted to break him: to break everybody around her.

They paused when they reached the door. Liam was groaning. His face was swollen and his legs dangled; he was no longer able to support himself. His hair was matted with blood. A couple of the other guards had taken their chance to get revenge on him, kicking him brutally, so hard Liam had coughed up big phlegmy balls of red.

"Hold him while I unlock the door."

"He needs a doctor."

"I know," Smith said, as he pushed Liam onto Harrison.

Harrison caught him, almost hugging the other man, his back straining as Liam became a dead weight. Blood was all over Harrison's hands and clothes, but it wasn't his. Liam was seeping from dozens of places, his arms shredded, the cuts on his back causing his shirt to stick to him. His feet were lacerated from his barefoot run across the grounds.

Smith opened the door with a loud metal crank.

"I didn't mean it," Liam moaned, his words barely discernible in his pained noises. "Didn't even remember it. Never do it again. Promised. Kept it too. And she tried. She tried. But I love her. I love her and I love my kid and I love her. I love her. Please tell her I love her."

Strength came into Liam's body. Harrison felt him tensing up.

"Tell her." Liam's voice rose. "Tell her I love her. Tell her I love her."

"It's too late for that." Smith sighed. "She won't believe you."

"He's not talking about Madeline," Harrison said. "He's talking about Emily."

"Yes, Emily! Tell her. Please tell her."

"This isn't helping anything." Smith grabbed Liam and,

with Harrison's help, they guided him to the rear of the cold damp cell. Lowering him softly, they backed away to the exit, as Liam hunched over and began to sob. "None of his injuries look severe."

"Unless he has internal bleeding."

"That's a chance we're going to have to take. We'll keep an eye on him."

"How long will she keep him in here?"

"All of this is new to me, truth be told. There've been games before. I won't lie... but I will make you pay if you repeat my words."

"And the games have never lasted this long?" Harrison asked, ignoring the threat.

"No. This is by far the longest. I miss my kids." Smith stood up straighter, as though toughening himself. "But we've got a job to do. However long it takes, we'll do our duty."

"I just want this to be over."

"Don't start whining again."

"How the fuck is it whining–"

"If you want it to be over that badly, go in there and strangle him until he stops breathing. We can tell Madeline he died of his injuries. She'll believe us."

Harrison looked at the wretch in the cell, hunched over and muttering under his breath between sobs. "Tell her I love her, tell her I love her, tell her I love her..."

"You know I can't do that," Harrison said.

"No, I don't know that. There's plenty you say you can't do. You're always ready to take the moral high ground. But when it comes down to it, you're the same as the rest of us."

Smith slammed the door and turned the key. "What? Nothing to say to that?"

Smith was right. Harrison might pretend. He might rage. He might act as though he was somehow better than them. But he wasn't wrestling Smith to the ground; he wasn't stealing the key. He wasn't opening the door and doing whatever it took to get Liam out of here.

Instead, he walked down the hallway, leaving Liam locked in the cell.

"What do you think your kids would say, if they knew what we were doing?"

Smith punched Harrison in the side of the head. It was a vicious strike, thrown without warning, and Harrison slammed against the wall. He fell. Smith leapt on top of him and punched him on the other side of the head.

"Don't ever talk about my kids."

Smith stood and walked away. Harrison lay there awhile, his head ringing, wishing he was more like his grandfather.

CHAPTER FORTY-ONE

It had been two days since Liam rejected me. I'd gone to his cell soon after the guards had taken him there, cracking the door and waiting for him to say something, to do something, to prove he was willing to put an effort in.

Surely this couldn't be it, all we'd been building up to: his limp dick in my mouth, his sobs broken by his cries for the tragically average Emily Taylor.

He said nothing, just stared at the floor, hunched over like some kind of beast.

Perhaps it would've been better to end him. I could've ordered Smith or one of the other guards – maybe that fence-riding soldier – to go in there and slit his throat. It would've been a simple thing. But I couldn't stop thinking about the first time I'd seen him: the love, the potential. That was the only thing saving him.

I was at my London flat, drinking far too much, partying far too hard. I'd taken a medley of pills last night as we went from club to club, trying to make myself feel something, anything.

I'd even kissed somebody on the dance floor, a stranger, grinding my body against his... And there was nothing; I'd felt nothing. It was so seedy, so sad, so unlike what I'd dreamed Liam would give me.

It had always been this way. Feelings had always been difficult to, well, *feel*. But I did my best. I was trying with Liam, trying to recreate what I'd read in so many books, what I'd watched in so many films. I'd done my part, provided a wonderful setting for our romance, given him all the necessary motivation so he could forget about his former life.

And how had he rewarded me?

I cringed every time I thought about going to my knees in front of him. I shouldn't have even been doing that.

The second he saw me in that outfit, he should've been solid. I understood alcohol and drugs could slow a man down somewhat, but this was plain ridiculous. He hadn't shown me even a hint of excitement. It was humiliating.

And then, to make matters even more offensive, he'd tried to run. He'd rather cut his body to pieces than be with me. Not once did he stop to think about how it would make me feel.

I wasn't sure how long I was going to leave him in there; perhaps I'd let him starve to death. I hadn't made my mind up yet. But he had to know he'd behaved in a completely unacceptable way. He had to understand that his previous life no longer existed; he was mine, mine alone, and no amount of crying or oinking or bleeding would change that.

He would learn or he would die.

CHAPTER FORTY-TWO

L iam woke with his body laced in pain. He rolled over and clawed out for Emily, his fingernails scraping across cold stone.

Sleep left him and he moaned for the dream, for Emily's face, to take away this agony. He grunted and climbed to his knees, opened his eyes... and there was only darkness. He couldn't even see his hand when he waved it in front of his face.

His body gave out and his ankle rolled over. His cheek smashed into the stone wall and his jaws throbbed. Finally he managed to climb down to his side, where he lay, shivering as his ankle felt like it was tearing in half. Memories of his escape returned to him: trusting Olivia, the alcohol, the jump out of the window.

"I'm done."

His voice was far too loud.

That was something he was going to learn well over the coming months, if they were months: the silence and the dark.

The darkness lasted all day and night, every day and night.

Even when the guards slid food into the cell, it was from a greater darkness. Liam began to lay with his eyes open, staring at nothing, feeling like he was floating in a black sea. The food they gave him was nothing like when he'd first arrived; now they gave him a tin of chilli con carne or tuna to eat with his hands. Once it was done, he had to leave it near the door.

One time, he refused to do it. He kept the can huddled to his chest and roared at the door. "You're not having it. You braindead motherfuckers. I've got a kid. I've got a—"

The door exploded open and they rushed in.

They were wearing goggles, big and chunky, and Liam guessed that was how they saw in the dark; he could only see them because a faint light emitted from around the edge.

It was more light than Liam had seen in weeks.

They looked like threatening insects as they closed in on him. It only took one guard to hook an arm around Liam's waist and shove him up against the wall. His spine cracked and the breath went from his chest. Another guard picked up the tin, and they were gone.

Memories like that came and went, thoughts of the early days when he'd been imprisoned there.

Time was a strange thing. In school, one of Liam's mates had a sick grandad. It was dementia, Liam now knew, but he didn't know that as a kid. He'd be around his friend's house and the grandad would suddenly look up, with a little boy's eyes, as if shocked to find himself in an old man's body. And that was what Liam felt, as his nails grew and his hair grew and his face was covered in a thick tangled beard. He was ageing, but he didn't know how much.

They gave him less and less food as time went on. Sometimes they gave him a single tin of soup. Whether this was once a day, twice a day, or three times, Liam didn't know. He'd tried counting and his mind had wandered, dancing away to waking dreams.

Sometimes he was with Emily. They were standing at the

edge of a pond as their daughter trotted ahead in her pink coat. It was always a daughter in this fantasy, in her bright pink coat with flecks of mud on it, from where she'd been jumping in the puddles. She turned to Liam and her face lit up, and Liam smiled at Emily; she beamed right back at him. He tried to hold on to those fantasies, but too often they warped. Then it was Madeline.

She was standing over a cot with her hair hanging lankly around her face, staring with that creepy grin on her lips. The smile that said: she owned you, and she'd always own you. She could do whatever she wanted.

What day was it? What time? How long had he been there?

This was the usual rush of questions which entered his mind the moment he woke up. But now they went away easier. He rose with an effort. His cuts had become crusty and scabby, but his ankle was only getting worse. He wept with the agony sometimes, contorting himself on the floor to try to get it into a comfortable position.

He wanted to stay strong. Every time he woke, he promised himself he'd walk a little bit. If he could work up to a few laps every day, then he could get healthy again. Maybe his ankle wasn't as bad as he thought.

He moaned and fell onto his side. He caught himself on the wall, slid down, wheezing and panting.

The cell stank. It reeked of sweat and shit and piss. The bucket in the corner was changed at a random schedule, it seemed to Liam. Sometimes it overflowed. Portions of the wall and the floor must've been covered in flecks of shit. But Liam couldn't see it. That was one time he was thankful for the imposed blindness.

227

He got used to it. He never gagged anymore. He never choked on the stink.

Squatting over the bucket was the main problem, adding a burden to his shredded ankle. Since he'd been put there, they hadn't given him toilet paper. He was sleeping in his own filth, all the time. He'd tried wiping it on his clothes and they'd simply left him that way; he thought they might give him fresh ones. They ignored him when he cried, begged, screamed at them for anything: for food or toilet paper or clothes or a few seconds of light.

It was like they were robots. Liam began to wonder if that was it.

Madeline had used her money to build robots with big insect eyes. He almost longed for them; the tiny flicker of light which lit their goggled faces... it was like the sun breaking through the clouds on an autumn day. He'd kill for a candle, just a candle. He wanted to see. He started to wonder if any of this was real.

Maybe he'd gone to get those beers and he'd passed out, a brain aneurism or whatever they were called. He'd hit his head and now he was dreaming up all this crazy stuff.

She couldn't put him in here, couldn't do this, make him an animal, just because he didn't get hard when she gave him a blow job. What sort of madness was that? Liam refused to believe it; she would have to view him as not even a person. Not even real.

He was real, wasn't he?

"I'm real," he whispered, as his belly felt like it was gnawing itself.

His chest was becoming concave. His ribs jutted from his chest as he ran his fingertips over them. They were ridged, and he thought of the time he and Emily and little Jamie had gone to see the alligators at the zoo. Jamie had walked right up the glass, pointed, turned and smiled at them. Emily rushed for her phone and took the most beautiful photo of their son smiling.

That was a memory. No, it hadn't happened.

The door opened and a tin slid in, scraping along the stone floor. He never bothered with the tins anymore. When they gave him half a bottle of water – a plastic Coke bottle, battered like it'd been repeatedly stepped on – he drank as much as he could stomach. But food didn't interest him.

He wanted to return to the zoo, or the pond, or the climbing centre. Liam could take his wife and his children, and then they'd go for a meal...

Only now Madeline was smiling at him. That was happening too much lately. Madeline's face was melting into Emily's, like she was infecting the memories, the fantasies. Liam tried to push her away but then she rushed at him.

She was with him, in the cell. What the fuck?

She had him pinned against the wall and she was driving her crotch against his. She was doing it hard, aggressively sitting down on his lap over and over. Liam grunted as his groin ached. She kept hammering it, dragging her fingernails down his chest, opening deep gashes which seeped blood.

Liam begged her to stop, but then her tongue was in his mouth. She reached down and forced him to get hard and–

Liam gasped, punching himself in the chest. He remembered a man who could bench a lot at the gym. He'd been fit once, hadn't he? He remembered a man who could spend eight hours running up and down the fields with a full schedule of dogs to train. It seemed so distant. He couldn't imagine being a man like that.

Even his chest punch was weak. It had felt so real, like she was really in there with him. Liam thought about how he'd fought when he first came there, before he knew Rebecca was a fake. He'd grabbed her and brought a knife to her throat. He'd failed.

Would he do it now if he got his hands on Madeline? Would he slit her throat?

He wanted the answer to be yes. But he didn't know if he'd be able to drag the knife across, if he'd be able to apply enough pressure. He felt like his body would give out on him.

When had he become so pathetic?

When he was eating the tins, he'd had some fight in him. He was sure of that. He'd kept that tin the one time, and they'd had to come in here and wrestle it away from him. It hadn't been much of a fight, sure, but he'd done his best.

What was in today's tin? Maybe he would eat, get his strength up. He whimpered as he crawled across the room, and then the whimpering got louder, deafening with everything else silent.

He couldn't get the tin. He kept doing this: forgetting about his plan.

He was going to starve himself until these bastards had to make a decision, these bug-eyed motherfuckers. That was it; he was going to waste away, and see if they'd let him die, let Madeline's precious toy become useless. They wouldn't risk angering her.

That was what Liam had to believe. He returned to the other end of the room.

He had to remember that. He felt like he was floating in some impossible place, between fantasy and reality.

Suddenly Emily returned to him; her whole face lit up. "I forgive you. I forgave you a long time ago. I know you'd never hurt me again."

"I'm so sorry." Liam cried as he smothered his face with his hand. "I wish I could take it back."

Her hands were on his shoulders, so soft, so warm. "It's okay, baby. I know you'll never do it again. I know you love me."

"I do, so much."

He broke down completely, sobbing so hard his wheezy chest rattled. He sounded like an old man, like he'd been in this place for years.

He knew it was more than weeks, possibly months, but he'd never thought about years before. He remembered his mate's dad, the old man with the little boy's eyes, shocked to find himself in the elderly body. Liam might leave this place in his sixties, seventies, eighties. Maybe the family would keep him around as a weird curiosity.

What would starving achieve?

Liam pressed the back of his head against the stone cell.

Something; it would do something. That was all he could do. Something instead of this cold dark endless nothing.

CHAPTER FORTY-THREE

"Peekaboo!" Emily moved her hands aside and smiled down at Jamie. He was getting so expressive, giggling every time Emily revealed her face. He was five months old, and already so eager, rolling from his back to his belly and clawing his hands and feet like he wanted to crawl. "Are you cold, sweetheart?" She pulled up his blanket and looked around the park.

It was a gloriously sunny day, with a January frost in the air. It had been autumn when Liam disappeared. It seemed like such a long time ago. And yet it seemed like only yesterday too.

The park glistened, the dew catching the sunlight. Emily felt Liam's absence trying to shroud her, like he was hugging her from behind. But she couldn't think like that.

She was doing better: looking to the future, focusing on her son. Rocky was galloping around in the grass, chasing an insect, and that gave her hope. They were getting back to normal.

A new normal, Dad had called it. "I'm not saying it'll be better, or even as good. But it will be steady. You'll have a routine."

She hadn't thought about going back to work yet. She didn't know how she was going to face that. She would have to ask

Mum and Dad to help with Jamie. Maybe Liam's parents would help too. They'd been in contact, meeting with Jamie a few times. They were interested but not like her mum and dad; they weren't crazy about him.

They seemed a little distant to Emily; they always had, slightly cold. Liam had been like that in the beginning, able to shut himself down in arguments, so Emily would rage and shout and he'd just stare at her.

Jamie pawed at her. She picked him up. He held her so firmly these days, properly growing up.

He had Liam's smile. Everybody said that. Emily saw Liam in his eyes too, bright and wide. She wondered if Jamie would agree when he was old enough to see the pictures. If he would think he looked like his dad.

Emily sat and Rocky padded over. He sprung onto the park bench and curled up next to Jamie. They sat together for a while. It was good to do this, to slow down, to take these little moments to focus on what was important. She might quit the call centre and get a part-time job. Mum and Dad said she could live with them until she was ready. That would be best for Jamie, if she was going to be at work.

She didn't want to think about a life without Liam, but she couldn't let herself go the other way. She'd been going crazy a few months ago, with that jogger outside the house, and the phone call... Mum and Dad had said it was probably just a prank caller, but she'd known it was something more.

"Why would he ring you and not say anything?" Dad had said.

"Because he can't talk. I don't know."

"He can't talk? Then how is he ringing you?"

"I don't know, Dad!"

"Do you think he's being held hostage?"

"I. Do. Not. Know."

That had caused a stalemate, as they glared at each other across the kitchen partition. That was before she'd decided to get control of herself.

A man and his son entered the park from the other direction. The man was tall and lean. Emily had seen him before. He was probably a few years older than her, with brown hair cut short, and a confident smile. His son was maybe eight or nine, running behind him, as they threw a tennis ball back and forth. The man had a youthful smile and bounced easily on his feet.

He looked over, and Emily moved her gaze away. She didn't want him to think she'd been staring at him.

The ball thudded over on the grass. With a yapping bark, Rocky sprang down and leapt at it. He scooped it into his mouth and started running around, tail pricked, as the man chuckled.

Emily felt her cheeks getting hot for no reason. She smiled at him as he grinned and offered his hand to Rocky.

"Not going to take my hand off, is he?" The man laughed.

"No, you should be fine. He's already had breakfast."

He laughed again, and she laughed with him. It was far easier than it should've been. He softly took the ball from Rocky and then stood, tossing it from hand to hand. "Have I seen you here before?"

"Maybe. I come fairly often."

"More in the mornings, right?"

He was standing over her, head tilted, stance wide. It was like he was ready to jump on her. She cautioned herself to calm down; she'd seen this person many times. He wasn't the man outside her parents' house. He hadn't hurt Liam.

"Yeah, pretty much."

"Ah, okay." He nodded, moving closer. "I was going to say, I've never seen you here in the evenings."

Emily hugged Jamie to her chest. Rocky was standing off to

the side, looking suspiciously up at the man. Was Emily going mad, or was he acting strangely? He kept moving closer.

She didn't know what to say. She glanced at his son; he was standing back near the entrance, as if he knew to stay away when his dad was talking to a woman. It was suspicious, how that boy was standing: sort of turned away, sort of anticipating something. Was this what he did, assaulted women with his son present?

"What did you say?" the man snapped.

Jamie let out a soft cry.

"Nothing," Emily said.

"That's what I thought. Don't say a lot, do you?"

"I'm sorry."

He laughed gruffly. "Sorry." He stepped forwards; he was blocking the sun. Rocky let out a low growl. "What're you sorry for?"

"Just..."

"Just? Just what?"

"Please."

"Please?" He took a step back. "What're you on about, darling? I'm just talking to you."

She nodded, trying to believe him, but there was a mean glint in his eye. "You don't know who I am, do you, Emily?"

She flinched when he used her name. She hadn't given it to him. "I don't remember."

"We've never met, but I knew Liam in school. My sister did, anyway. They were together when my sister and him were fourteen." The man chuckled. "What are the chances I'd run into you, huh? I saw that appeal you did on the Facebook page. That was hilarious. Did somebody make you fake cry?"

His words bit into her, but he said them in such a light-hearted tone of voice. He smiled widely, as though convincing her to take it as a joke.

"No, I was really crying. I miss him."

"Liam bloody Knight. Yeah, he was a beast in school. Played for the rugby team. Could handle himself off the field too. Liked to *play* the field, even when he had a girlfriend..."

He closed the distance again, his smile becoming a grimace. His hand was clenched tightly around the ball, his knuckles turning white. "My sister turned bulimic for six months after Liam cheated on her. I tried to make him pay, but he jumped me, the little prick. He used a cheap tactic."

Emily felt the deranged urge to laugh. Liam was gone: the father of her son was gone. And this man thought teenage drama mattered. "Liam isn't a teenager anymore. People change."

"You know what people say, don't you? How opposites attract?"

"I'm with my son." Emily's voice shivered; the man's tone had become husky, weird. She didn't like it. "Please don't stand so close. I'm sorry. But come on."

"Come on, what? I'm just talking to you. Have you heard that phrase, that opposites attract?"

Emily had to answer. "Yes."

"See, I don't think that's true. I think people like to be with similar people. What would you say?"

"I'm not sure."

Emily wanted to scream at him to go away. He had no right to make her feel small, but he hadn't done anything overtly aggressive yet.

"If you see Liam, say hello."

Emily's mouth fell open when the man grinned. With a shrug – as if none of this mattered – he jogged back over to his son.

Emily busied herself getting Jamie into the pram. As she clipped Rocky to the handle – the little terrier would dutifully trot next to Jamie – she reminded herself to calm down. It was just that man, bothering her. What a horrible thing to do.

If you see Liam, say hello...

After spotting the other man outside her parents' house, she had pursued the police every single day for months; she had put out online campaigns and emailed the local newspapers. She had spent her mornings walking the streets, putting up photos of Liam. The police had discovered nothing linking the jogger to Liam's disappearance, and they couldn't do anything with the phone call.

She never wanted to lose hope, but hope made her feel weak. If she wanted to take good care of her son, she might have to stop wishing for Liam to return.

He was dead. Or he was gone and he'd never be coming back.

She couldn't think about the day he'd wrap his strong arms around her again, hold her, run his fingers through her hair.

Wiping a tear from her cheek, she pushed the pram down the lane.

CHAPTER FORTY-FOUR

It was so difficult to enjoy life after I left Liam in the cell.

I wanted to teach him a real lesson, one he would never forget; I was willing to play the long game if that's what it took. But as time passed, I thought about him less. I wondered if perhaps I'd been a little hasty, the way I had in the past. Toys and servants were only useful for so long.

But I wasn't decided yet. Liam might emerge from his cocoon completely transformed. Perhaps he'd learn to push away what had already happened between us, to force it to the far corner of his mind.

Then we could pretend, and just be happy. That was all I wanted, what any woman longed for: a happily ever after, a perfect match. I wasn't a monster for wanting that.

Lately I'd been watching men. As the months passed, I'd been spying the New Yorkers and the Italians and the Spaniards and the clubbers in London. I'd felt their gazes on me at parties, restaurants, when I was walking the streets. I had been loyal to Liam so far, but I wasn't sure how much longer my patience would last.

I could free him and see if he was ready to fulfil his role. But Smith had informed me there would be a rehab period.

Apparently his ankle was in some kind of bother and he'd starved himself down to a skeleton. I would need to give it a month or two after release so he could become a person again.

There was something else. This feeling of knowing he was in there, it did something to me. Every time Smith asked if they should let him out, or feed him more, I said no. I was in charge: not Father, not my dead mother, not anybody else. It was just me. He belonged to me. So let him rot a while longer.

After, if he performed his rehab and did as I told him – which was only reasonable – we'd see if we truly shared the connection I'd thought we did. I'd always believed in love at first sight, but what if I'd misread the signs with Liam?

He had to find a way to prove it to me. Perhaps I'd give him a nudge, a test, and have one of the guards wear a microphone so I could hear his answers.

He loved me, or he loved me not.

It was time for him to make up his mind.

CHAPTER FORTY-FIVE

Harrison spent the months in training.

He used the gym for his maximum allowance every day and did push-ups and sit-ups in his room. He shadowboxed until he could barely move his arms. Anything was better than thinking about what they were doing to Liam.

The second they'd put Liam in the cell, Harrison knew it was a mistake.

He'd been looking for a way to get him out ever since, but Madeline had apparently ordered that Harrison not be allowed on solo guard duty. "She questions soldier boy's loyalty," Smith had told him a few days after Liam's imprisonment.

"So what am I supposed to do?"

"Wait. It'll only increase your salary. Overtime was in the contract, lad."

"But..."

"Stop whining. Getting paid hundreds of thousands to hang around and do fuck all. People would kill to be in your position."

Harrison thought about Liam. He hadn't seen him yet, but he sensed it was bad from the way the other guards behaved when they returned. It was in their faces, their eyes staring from the masks.

Harrison no longer cared about the blackmail video. He realised that on another of those endless days, lying on his bed, staring at the ceiling.

Liam was being broken, piece by piece, a man who had a fiancée and a son. Harrison had seen Emily with her boy, in the park, but only ever with Smith there. Madeline still liked to receive the photos, as though feeding on the woman's misery.

He would tell the truth. It was such a simple concept. He would tell his family everything, and if some people doubted, Harrison would stick to his story. He'd admit it all, even his own involvement. That was what would make his parents and his grandparents truly proud. Do the right thing, his grandad had always said, and Harrison knew what that was. He'd done the wrong thing for so long; he'd become muddled up. He was done with that.

One afternoon, he took his chance.

Smith was talking to Madeline on the phone. Harrison knew it was her from the commander's tone of voice. He always sounded more eager to please. Harrison approached him, where he leaned against the barracks wall.

"He can't do it, miss. Yes—I know. Of course. Yes, I understand that, but the lad is—"

The lad.

"Are you talking about me?" Harrison said.

Smith glared at him, but Harrison stood his ground. Smith sighed. "Yes, he is."

He shoved the phone at Harrison. Harrison's hand trembled slightly as he took it. Despite his convictions, he knew the video wasn't the only thing he had to worry about. He could end up in a cell, just like Liam. Or worse.

Harrison took the phone. "Hello."

"Aren't you a nosy boy," Madeline said.

"I'm sorry."

"I have a little activity for Liam. I know he must be so starved for stimulation. I have a photo album I'd like you to show him, to prove your loyalty. And there's something else. You can refuse, if it makes you feel like a man. Refusal, however, will not give you what you want."

"What do you want me to do?" Harrison asked.

Harrison had taken his chance, and it had led him here.

He was staring down the corridor at the cell. With the naked bulbs turned on, the yellow light was stark. It shone on the damp-stained stone walls. The door was heavy and metal, the surface flaky and brown with rust.

Harrison tucked his items under his arm and tried not to gag as he unlocked the door and pushed it open.

The light switched on, and Harrison stared down at the animal who'd taken Liam's place. His body was covered in brown stains. His beard was scraggly and long, his hair wiry around his cheeks. Most of all he was thin, not at all like the man who'd come there. He'd shrunk. He looked old.

Liam moaned and stared up at the light. "Is this it? The end?"

Harrison wanted to yell at him, ask him why he hadn't been eating, but that would make it seem like he cared. He reached down and grabbed Liam by the arm, hauling him to a sitting position as softly as he was able. Touching him made Harrison want to cringe away. He reeked. His skin was thick with grime.

Harrison pushed the instinct down; it wasn't Liam's fault.

"I've got a couple of things you need to see."

Harrison quickly grabbed the folded-up piece of paper and flashed it at Liam.

She is listening.

He'd quickly scrawled it with a pencil he'd found on the grounds, on the back of his electric toothbrush's instruction manual. He held it up higher when Liam only stared, like he couldn't see.

"Is this the end?"

Harrison swallowed. He couldn't delay any longer. He'd wanted Liam to play along, to give her what she wanted. "I've got this knife for you, Liam."

"A knife?"

Harrison pressed the blade into his hand. Liam could barely take it. His hands were shaking so badly. Eventually he managed to curl his hands around the hilt, but then he looked around with childlike eyes, blinking as though he didn't know where he was. "Why a knife?"

"Madeline has an offer to make you. But first she wants me to show you something."

"So hold on to the knife?"

"Yeah, for now."

Harrison couldn't stand Liam's gaze for long. It was like he didn't even know who Harrison was. But if he hadn't been eating, living there, with only his thoughts... it would make anybody crazy. Harrison had let this go too far, but Madeline was listening through a microphone on his shirt.

He couldn't do anything. Not now.

"Look at this."

The photo album was bound in leather, thick, though there were only nine photos in there. Harrison moved so he was sitting against the wall with Liam. He felt giant against the emaciated man. Liam gazed down dumbly at the album.

"Do you know what this is?"

"A photo... album. We're always meaning to make one. A proper one. But we upload all our photos. But when the kids come, yeah, I think we'll make one. It'll be good to have something solid to hold on to."

Harrison nudged him, reaching over and grabbing the piece of paper. He showed it to Liam again. This time, Liam's eyes glimmered with something like his old self. But then he slumped against the wall.

"My eyes hurt."

"There are only a few photos."

Harrison didn't know if Liam had taken the message. Was he saying his eyes hurt because he couldn't read Harrison's words, or because the light was too painful?

Harrison flipped the first page, and at the same time he reached down and began to slowly and carefully take off his belt.

Liam stared at the faces. There were three of them: all of them had black hair with a light beard. All of them had rugged stubble and a certain look in their eyes, recklessness maybe, something that set them apart. They looked like Liam, and they had big red crosses running through them.

"She's done this before," Liam muttered, running his blackened fingernails over the page. "These men are me."

"They look like you."

"No, they're me. We're all the same. To them. It doesn't matter."

Harrison flipped the page. "Do you know why I'm showing you this?"

"You didn't do shit. You didn't do a thing." Liam laughed in a strange high-pitched way, grinning sleepily as he leaned against the wall. "But it doesn't matter now. I'm going to be with them soon."

"Look at the photos," Harrison said sternly, even if there was so much else he wanted to say, needed to.

"More photos of me."

"Madeline doesn't want you to end up like these men."

"And how did they end up?"

Harrison swallowed. Madeline had given him the details, as if wanting Harrison to rub it in, but he hadn't planned on telling Liam unless he asked. "Some were shot in the back of the head and buried. One was fed to starving dogs while he was still alive. Another was slowly poisoned to death. A couple have died in this cell."

"But why?" Liam groaned. "Why does she get to do that? Why doesn't anybody stop her?"

"She doesn't want you to end up like them," Harrison snapped, sliding his belt free in the same movement. "She wants you to prove how much you love her."

"But I hate her."

"Liam..."

Liam grinned madly. "It's the truth. I hate her on every level. She thinks I'm a toy, pop some batteries in me and off I go. But I'm a person, Harrison, like you're a person. I don't... I don't oink. I'm not a pig. I'm not. Am I?" Tears glimmered in his eyes. "Am I what she's made me?"

Harrison stood, closing the photo album. "There's a final test, a way for you to free yourself."

"Yeah?"

"If you stab me, if you kill me, they'll let you out of here. That's what the knife is for."

Liam stared up at him. He seemed determined for a moment. The illusion shattered when he tried to stand, groaning as he wobbled on his ankle. It was swollen, purple and grotesque. Harrison wondered if it would need amputating. Draining. Something. It looked like a big sack of puss.

Liam took a shaky step, aiming the knife. "You're as bad as the rest of them."

"I know."

"Why didn't you help me?"

Harrison swallowed. "Because I'm loyal to the lady of the house."

"Oh, yeah, yeah." Liam nodded, his beard brushing against his bare and grimy chest. "We can't upset Her Highness. So that's why you're here alone, then? Just in case I go feral."

"Yeah, you're free to kill me."

"And it will set me free."

"Yeah."

Liam took another step, wincing. "Why didn't you do anything?"

"Because I'm loyal to the—"

Liam lurched. Harrison ducked back, hands raised, instinct kicking in. But Liam had only lost his footing. He wasn't lunging. Harrison rushed forwards, offering his arm. Liam dug his fingernails into Harrison's skin and leaned heavily against him.

"Why, Harrison?" Liam wheezed. "Why aren't you helping me? The truth, please."

"Because I'm a coward. That's the truth."

Liam slumped to the floor and dropped the knife, lying on his side. "I can't fight. I can't stab you. I can't even stand up. Just fuck off. Let me die."

Harrison left the cell, leaning down on his way out. As the heavy metal door tried to swing shut, the belt wedged it into place, stopping the latch lock from automatically closing behind him.

The door was open. Harrison had completed step one.

He walked out of the basement and another guard

approached him. Harrison recognised him as one of the nasty fuckers, always ready for a fight. "Where's the knife?"

Harrison had to pray Madeline wasn't listening now. He wasn't sure why she would be.

"I already gave it to Smith."

"Oh yeah? How's that? Smith's in the garden."

"There's another exit..."

"Bullshit—"

Harrison sprang at the man and grabbed his head in his hands, spinning and smashing his skull against the wall. The man gasped and his eyes flooded with tears, his legs giving out as he slumped to the floor.

Harrison looked around. The man wouldn't stay unconscious for long. They were in the supply closet, the room which led to the hidden hallway, which in turn led to Liam's cell.

There was rope. Harrison would have to move quickly.

CHAPTER FORTY-SIX

Liam stared at the door. The light was still on, his vision pulsing. Everything was far too bright. It jabbed at his eyes, worked its way into his skull. A tension headache had been gripping him the moment the lights turned on. But he saw the belt: wedged in the doorway, preventing it from closing.

Madeline had tested him before. Maybe she was purposefully leaving him here, the door open, waiting for him to make the so-called right choice and pick her instead of freedom.

She was probably waiting outside the door. She was with all the guards, the cruel ones who enjoyed beating him, or maybe with her father and their friends. They were here to play another game.

Gripping the knife, he crawled across the room. He couldn't believe these hands belonged to him, so dirty, so ancient. He wasn't sure if they were wrinkles or cracks in the dirt on his skin. His fingernails were long and thick.

The door whined as he pulled, and then clattered shut. Liam's shoulder was pumping with the effort. It was heavier than it looked, and yet Liam remembered a time when he'd be able to throw it open easily. He groaned as he climbed to his feet, working his fingernails into the gap and pulling with more force.

He slipped, almost fell, nearly cut himself on the knife. No guards came. Madeline wasn't laughing. Maybe they weren't waiting outside; maybe this was his one chance of escape. He had to take it. Whatever happened.

What else could they do to him?

Suddenly, the door swung open, almost smashing into his face. Harrison rushed into the room. It was the first time Liam had ever seen him without his mask on; just now, with the photo album, he'd been wearing his balaclava. He was young, with freckles across his cheeks, his dusty brown hair matted to his forehead.

"What's happening?" Liam said.

"We're going. Do everything I say."

"But–"

"Everything I say. Understand?"

Liam nodded, and Harrison took the knife. He grabbed Liam's arm and threw it over his shoulder, helping him to walk to the door. Liam hobbled after him.

Harrison opened the door with one hand, making it look easy, as Liam struggled to limp on his one good leg. They moved down a corridor, lit by bright yellow light.

"Where are we going?" Liam said. "Is this a trick?"

"I'm getting you out of here. It's not a trick."

"How do I know?"

"You don't."

They said nothing else as Liam limped down the hallway. At the bottom of the stairs, Harrison bit down on the blade and then turned to Liam. Liam tried to tell him no; he could do it. But then it was too late and Harrison already had him in his arms.

The younger man took the stairs easily, nudging the door

open with his shoulder. Liam found himself relaxing into his grip, even as he fought the feeling. It was so much better than the agony of walking.

Maybe Harrison sensed this. He didn't drop Liam as he walked into a storage closet, with ropes and tape and supplies everywhere. A man groaned from the corner, a rope tied around his mouth, trapping it open, his hands tied behind his back and his ankles tied to his hands. He was contorted on the floor, glowering up at them.

"Ignore him," Harrison grunted.

"Your mask. He'll know who you are."

Liam knew, if he was Harrison, he would never want anybody knowing who he was, that he'd ever been there.

"I'm done hiding," Harrison snapped.

Harrison carried him up another flight of stairs and then into a small outhouse. He pushed another door open and then they were outside. Liam heaved in a breath as Harrison placed him down. He limped over to the wall and gripped onto the windowsill, staring at the grounds.

There was so much *stuff*. It was an icy day, morning, the sun low in the sky. The grass had never seemed greener. The sunlight had never looked more beautiful.

He stared, captivated, wondering if this was a dream. Emily would walk out from under the trees with her hands raised, beckoning him to join her. He'd been seeing Emily a lot lately, visiting him in the darkness, telling him it was so much better in the light with her; maybe this was the light.

"Liam."

He turned to find a small vehicle sitting there, like a groundkeeper's buggy, with a plastic roof and no doors. Harrison climbed into the driver's seat and scooted over to Liam, handling the vehicle deftly.

Liam fell into the passenger seat, sitting awkwardly on his

side with his hip bone digging into the chair. He adjusted as Harrison sped away.

The wind rushed too quickly into Liam's face. "What's the plan?"

"I was going to steal a proper car. Put you in the boot. But there's no time."

"What happened?"

"I didn't expect another guard to be waiting for me." Harrison spun the buggy to the side, driving over the grass and up the hill, the house receding behind them; any second somebody could look in their direction and spot them, but at least the vehicle was quiet.

"He was probably there just in case you went through with it, to get the knife back. I don't know. Fuck."

Liam took the knife from Harrison's hand; he was holding it clumsily as he handled the steering wheel. Harrison let him have it without comment. Liam gripped it hard and told himself this was it: his time to be useful, his time to stop being so pathetic.

He wasn't the beast in the cell anymore. He was outside, in the sun; Emily was out there somewhere.

Wasn't she?

Suddenly he panicked. "Harrison, Emily, my child..."

"Emily and Jamie are fine, as far as I know."

"Jamie." Liam croaked, faltering on his son's name. "I have a son."

"Yeah, you do. But don't get all mushy on me. We've got to stay focused."

Harrison sped them past the trees and then turned onto the field, putting the trees between them and the house. As they crested the hill, the tall walls revealed themselves, marked out in the otherwise unbroken countryside.

The wheels churned and the cart bumped up and down,

Liam's ankle bashing against it, but he said nothing. None of this mattered. If he had to lose his legs to return to Emily, he would.

Harrison joined a gravel road, guiding the buggy towards a large black iron gate. There was a small booth off to the side, and as they got closer a figure walked out of it. Another one followed: two guards.

"Smith," Harrison said.

Smith and one unknown, maybe one who'd beaten Liam senseless before, or who Liam had hurt, a man who wanted revenge. Smith walked into the middle of the road, his hand at his hip: ready to reach for a needle or a gun or a baton or a walkie-talkie, to gather more guards.

"What are you doing, lad? We've got men on all the gates."

"Why?"

"Because Madeline ordered it. You failed her test. You idiot. Why did you have to do this?"

Harrison began to slowly back up the buggy. "You're going to kill me, are you?"

"I told you I'd have to do it myself. Don't make us chase you. Get out of that thing. Be a man."

Liam urged Harrison to back the car up, but suddenly Harrison stopped. He took his hands off the steering wheel and looked at Smith. Liam squeezed the knife harder, twisting the hilt between both of his hands. They couldn't hang around here, but what if they really did have all the other gates covered?

"You're not going to kill us, Smith."

Smith crept closer, reaching into his cargo pocket and pulling a thick knife from a sheath. The other guard did the same, and Liam tensed up. Harrison stared at Smith, tracking his movements as he got closer.

"You're not a murderer."

"That's where you're wrong, lad. I wasn't lying when I said Rebecca was the first person Madeline ever killed."

"It was you," Liam whispered. "The other men. The other Liams."

Smith looked sharply at Liam. "You sound mad, mate. Fucking mental."

"Don't come any closer," Harrison said. "We're leaving."

"You're not."

"You say you have a wife, children." Harrison placed his hands on the steering wheel again. "I don't understand how you can do this if that's the case. Liam doesn't deserve this."

"Lots of people don't deserve a lot of shit. I already told you before. You think too much."

Harrison shouted as he pushed down on the accelerator. Liam yelled and held on, twisting his hips painfully as he struggled to stay in the seat. Harrison was driving around them, heading for the gate.

"The booth!" Harrison roared, as he brought the car to a screeching stop in the gravel, kicking up dust and stones. "Open the gate. Go, Liam. And give me that."

Harrison snatched the knife from his hand and jumped from the buggy. Liam clambered out, his ankle screaming at him to stop, his whole body trying to drag him down as he limped for the booth.

CHAPTER FORTY-SEVEN

Harrison wrapped his hand around the knife and squared his shoulders. Smith was fanning out to his left, the other guard to his right, both holding blades much chunkier than his; he'd taken his from the kitchen, hiding it just outside the barracks, where he was sure there were no cameras. But they'd found him anyway.

"Don't do this." Harrison wanted to turn and see how close Liam was to the booth, where he could flip the switch to open the gate. Smith and the other guard were getting closer. "Smith, please. You don't want this."

"It's not about what I want."

"The lady of the house," the other guard muttered, making it sound like a religious phrase. "You're disturbing the lady of the house. Let's stick him, sir."

"We will," Smith said. "Take him from the other side."

"Better radio for more guards," Harrison snapped, spinning as he tried to keep both of them in view. "You two pussies don't want to risk it alone."

Smith grunted. "No, lad. You're a coward. You failed overseas and you failed to redeem yourself and you failed to make your family proud. You couldn't even save your friends. You had a chance here, an opportunity to make something of your life, and you fucked it."

The gate began to open with a mechanical whine. All three turned, spotting Liam hobbling back to the buggy. He looked so out of place, wearing only his shit-stained underwear; he didn't even look human.

"You fucked it for... *that*."

"We're all in the wrong here. Look at him. You have to see that."

"Wrong is getting killed and robbing my kids of their dad. Wrong is not providing my wife with the life she deserves. That *thing* is a small price to pay."

Harrison was spinning almost continuously, trying to keep them both in sight. "We should've freed him the second we realised what was really going on."

"Everybody knew." Smith tossed his knife from one hand to the other. "You were the only one who didn't. I wanted to ease you into it. You're not the sort of person we usually choose for a job like this."

"Then why..."

"You were very close with one of my boys over there. All right. There it is. My Martin, he served with you. He spoke about you sometimes."

"Martin?" Harrison shook his head, searching the names of all his squad mates.

Smith waved the knife. "He said his nickname was Chewie because he was so hairy."

"Oh, right. Yeah."

Harrison had known Chewie as the recluse of the group, lurking at the edges. But he was loyal and always spotted trouble up ahead. Harrison had watched as his neck opened and blood gushed out like syrup, his shirt torn open to reveal his muscled and lacerated flesh.

"He was your son?" Harrison said.

"He said he felt like he had to look out for you, for all of you. When he died, and you were the only one left, I knew I had to do something. Think about it: why would we hire soldiers? All these men are hardened criminals, used to the lady's desires. I stuck my bloody neck out to get you this job."

"You think Chewie would've wanted this?"

"I did the best I could."

Smith paused a few feet away, reached up and tugged on his mask. The gate had finished opening, the mechanical whir becoming silent. Harrison looked over his shoulder, tensing up when he saw how close the other guard had moved.

"Now it's my loyalty being questioned. That's how it works. I brought you on. You betrayed me. I have to show I'm willing to rectify that."

"Which is what your son would've wanted, is it?" Harrison said. "I knew him. He was a brave man. He was a good man. He did the right thing, like I used to think I always would. He never wavered. So shut up, Smith, about your son. If you think he'd be okay with this, you never knew him."

Smith inched forwards. "Motherfucker."

They all turned as the buggy raced at them. Liam twisted the wheel and slammed it into the guard; he bounced off the bonnet and fell onto the ground, moaning and rubbing his head. Liam yanked the wheel and spun around, staring at Harrison, willing him to get in the car.

Harrison moved. Then the knife punched into his side. He grunted and keeled over when it punched into him again, a solid jab of hot metal slipping between his ribs.

He gasped and blood bubbled up his throat, and he was being stabbed again, as Smith and the other guard converged on him; he'd quickly climbed to his feet after the buggy hit him, and now he was aiming his rage at Harrison.

He fell onto his side and the buggy's wheels made a screeching noise as they left Harrison in the dirt, or maybe that was his imagination; the noise screeched through his mind each time they stabbed him, shanking him over and over, until it didn't hurt anymore.

He began to get afraid at the end, when the darkness started to fall, blurring his vision.

He wanted to be with his mum: his mum who had hugged him so tight when he joined the Army. She had held him and wept, and he'd felt all the pride in the world bursting out of him. He disappeared into that hug; he faded away.

Smith rolled over his body with his boot. "That's the last time I do a good deed."

Liam drove that little buggy until the engine began to chug. He rode it as fast as he could through the countryside, always certain the guards were going to be waiting for him at the next corner or clearing.

He never stopped. He heard them; he heard engines, and shouting, and he took wilder and wilder turns, getting lost in the narrow passages, big enough for his little car but too small for theirs.

The engine began to croak and finally Liam was forced to walk. Crying, grinding his teeth, he eventually found a branch he could prop under his armpit on his bad ankle's side. He hobbled like that as the sun set, often hiding in the trees, flinching at every car noise, every bird's cry.

What had happened to Harrison? Liam hadn't waited to

see. He couldn't risk it. He'd seen the other guard stand up, though, right before he'd sped away.

He was weeping by the time he walked onto the side of the road. There was a garage up ahead, the lights shining into the dusk. It was like a beacon, like the sunlight coming through the trees at the pond when he and Emily had gone together. He kept that thought in his mind as he limped at it, his ankle pulsing with each step, his belly cramping with hunger.

He walked up to the garage door and fell inside. A bell rang loudly and an elderly man glared at him from across the counter. For a second the man stared, angry at the intrusion, and then his eyes widened as he took in Liam's full state: his grimy skin, his near nakedness.

"Bloody hell. What happened to you?"

"Please. The police. You have to call the police."

The man had a shaved head with a tattoo behind his ear, a portrait of Maddie with her lips parted in a crimson smile. Liam could see it when the man turned to scratch his face. "The police. Eh. That's not really going to work."

"Please."

"You see, mate, the lady of the house needs to be satisfied. She doesn't like it when naughty boys try to run away."

Liam was yelling and thrashing, roaring at the man to get away from him; he flung his arms out to catch the guard across the face. But there were more of them, suddenly, as if they'd been waiting here all along. They kept coming, relentless as they clawed at him. Liam screamed Emily's name and told the men to get away from him.

The old man was talking, hands raised. He was trying to get Liam's attention.

Where had the guards gone?

Liam was on the floor, he realised, the same way he often ended up in the cell. In make-believe fights, hitting phantoms who weren't there, except he was here, he was safe; he wasn't with them anymore. He wasn't in the dark.

"The police are on their way."

"I'm sorry."

"What happened to you?"

Liam sat up, pushing away any notion that this man was somehow involved in it. Was he a friend of the Pembertons? Maybe he'd alerted them that Liam was here, and that was who they were really waiting for. Liam didn't have the energy to move. He sat, leaning against the shelves, with his head bowed.

Then sirens touched the air, and, not long after, police officers' shoes were walking towards him. He tried to remember the last time he'd worn shoes; it had been the oinking night, the night he'd run, except he'd stupidly decided not to put them on before jumping out the window. He'd made so many mistakes.

"Sir, hello, can you hear me?"

"I want to see Emily," Liam said.

"That's fine. We can do that. But let's get you checked up first. Can you do that for me?"

Liam was about to tell the police officer he didn't have to talk to him like an idiot, but how else was he supposed to? He was a shit-stained beast; people around here would talk about the state of him for years to come.

"Yeah, yes," he whispered, as his voice tried to crack with sobs. "I can do that. Thank you. Thank you so much."

CHAPTER FORTY-EIGHT

"He was a cripple. In a buggy."

"Miss..."

I was angriest with Smith. When he told me about Liam's escape, I raged at him down the phone. It didn't make any sense. Liam had been partially crippled, apparently, driving one of the groundskeeping buggies. He'd only been able to get out of the gate because Smith and another guard had wasted time with the soldier boy. And fine, yes; they'd done the right thing and tied up that loose end. But they'd let Liam get away in the process.

"I'm just trying to get this clear in my head." I was gripping the balcony railing, staring down at London, as the wind whipped at me. My other hand clutched my phone tightly. If Smith had been there, I would've slapped him. "He had a crippled leg. He was malnourished. He was on his own. And somehow you let him escape."

"There's a lot of land around the estate, miss. We tried to cover as much as possible. But he got away."

"So where is he?"

"We've had reports he's with the police."

"Reports? What reports?"

"He was spotted at the station. I sent a few men down, just in case he ended up there."

"This is truly ridiculous. I hope you can see that. Have you told Father?"

"Yes, he knows. We're putting a plan in place now to cover our tracks."

"I'd like to know the details. Unless it's too inconvenient for you."

I kept repeating the phrase in my mind. *A cripple in a buggy.*

I'd never have believed it if another of the guards had told me, but – while allowing for so-called quality time with his joke of a family – Smith had been with us for as long as I could remember, a fixture during the games with the servants and the other men: my sweet other men, all of them failures, like Liam had turned out to be.

I had been planning to order Liam's death, anyway, after he'd given such disappointing answers during the interview with soldier boy. It had been clear Liam was never going to see sense.

Smith told me about the plan. There was no way for Liam to prove we'd done the things he would undoubtedly tell the police. Smith and the others were already stripping the estate clean of any sign of Liam's occupation. Every room he'd ever stepped in would be sterilised from top to bottom. There was no visual evidence of him being at the estate; Smith and the men would burn everything in his room.

"But it's not ideal," Smith said. "It will be his word against ours."

"Our word is worth a hundred of his. He'll sound like a madman."

"That's what we're hoping. But if there are any loose ends you need to tell me about..."

"Like what?" I didn't like being questioned. Smith sometimes forgot he was a hired hand: that just because he helped us with certain things, he wasn't one of us.

"Anybody you've spoken to about this, even if it's just a few comments here and there—"

I laughed harshly. "I'm not an idiot. I suppose you're going to tell me there's nothing we can do to him, for revenge."

"To Liam?"

"Who else?" I yelled, my voice travelling across the London skyline.

He paused, and then said quietly, "No, miss. We gain nothing by trying to get to him now. If we try and fail, the consequences will be severe. It will only make us look guilty."

"I'm not suggesting that Father march up to Liam's house and stab him himself. But perhaps a few months down the line, once this has all blown over, a mugging gone wrong… Maybe Liam should've looked twice before he crossed the road, a tragic accident. That sort of thing."

"Oh." Smith sighed. "Yes, miss. That's an option we can explore, once we've reassessed our position. But I'll have to get clearance from your father."

"Yes, yes."

They always needed clearance from Father. I'd had to get the same clearance when I started this latest game, and now Father was blaming me for this mess. He came to visit me at my London apartment soon after the phone call with Smith.

"You got carried away, Maddie."

"Father, I—"

He raised a hand as he strode into the apartment. "We need to make that clear from the beginning. You got carried away. You were never meant to kill that girl. But fine, I understand; sometimes things go too far, no matter how we plan them. You picked her well. Nobody will ever know her name. But this latest one..." Father rubbed his temples. "What was *his* name? I feel like it's been years since I even thought about him."

"Liam."

"Ah, yes, and I was Bretherton. Oh! From the dinner with Oliver and Selene."

"Silas and Olivia, you mean."

He was talking about the night when Liam had humiliated himself and me: the first of his humiliations that evening, before the embarrassment in the bedroom and his stupid jump out of the window.

"Don't pout at me, Maddie. This is your mess, not mine. You've dragged me into it. And please forget this nonsense about somehow getting to Liam."

"Do we know what he's doing?"

"It doesn't matter what he's doing. All that matters is anything he says is completely and utterly insane to you. You cannot even begin to comprehend why he would say such a thing. As long as there are no loose ends, we'll be fine. I have already established alibis for us, so we can be elsewhere when he claims we were in Lincolnshire. There's nothing to tie us to him, is there? You were careful."

"Yes, Father. Obviously I was careful. I only ever laid eyes on him myself once, before... before he came to the estate. And I'm sure your men didn't make any mistakes when they were performing their reconnaissance."

"We'll make it through this." Father placed his hand on my shoulder, a rare sign of affection. "And then perhaps we can put all of this behind us. The games, I see the appeal in them."

"You started them."

He squeezed my shoulder. "Yes, I did. But where you've taken them... It has become too elaborate, too much of an obsession. I'm beginning to wonder if you enjoy these little distractions more than your regular life."

I laughed and turned away, so he wouldn't see the effect his words were having on me. He was right. The games *were* better than real life. But he was making it sound like a bad thing.

Father sighed. "No loose ends, Maddie? You can assure me of that?"

"Yes, I promise."

That was a lie; there was one loose end, a small thing, tiny really. Nothing would come of it.

"And perhaps you can stop telling people I struck you as a child. It reflects very poorly on me."

"Sometimes, Father, I think you truly believe you didn't do it."

"That's because we both know I didn't. I'd never lay a finger on you. You're my heir. You're a Pemberton."

I shook my head. He was always trying to worm his way into my mind, make me believe I'd been this way since birth, as though it was my fault, not his, as though I wasn't a victim.

But I was; I'd been hurt. *He'd* hurt me.

"I'm going now. I love you."

"I love you too, Father."

CHAPTER FORTY-NINE

E mily never wanted to let him go. It had been three weeks since she discovered he was alive, but this was their first night in the flat together. Emily was careful not to hold him too tightly, but it was difficult; she kept digging her fingernails into him, as though confirming he was really there, until he laughed softly and told her she might want to ease up a bit.

"I'm sorry," she whispered, laying her head against his shoulder. "It's just so good to have you home."

"It's good to *be* home."

He didn't sound like the old Liam.

She understood it was going to take him some time to readjust, especially after he'd told her all that had happened. He hadn't been able to speak properly for two days after collapsing in the petrol station, in Lincolnshire, on the other side of the country.

Emily had left Jamie with her parents and raced over to him as fast as she could, sitting at his side until he was awake, holding his impossibly skinny hand in hers.

He'd looked terrible, his cheeks concave, his eyes dark holes. His beard and his hair were longer than she'd ever seen them.

He looked like he'd been starved for weeks, months, and sometimes, when Emily looked at him, she struggled to believe it was really Liam. But then he'd woken up, the strength returning to his body. His eyes blinked open and he started to cry.

"Emily," he'd moaned, as she laid her cheek tenderly against his, not sure how fiercely she could hold him. "Tell me it's you. Tell me you're real."

"It's me." She was sobbing. "I'm here."

"Tell me something. Something only you would know."

"Liam, it's me." She could barely push the words past her crying. To hear his voice, even husky and dehydrated, it was heaven; it was more than she could wish for.

"Please."

"You once ate a whole bowl of Coco Pops at one o'clock in the morning after coming home from a night out. See? Nobody else knows that."

He broke down like she'd never seen him do before, crying so hard his chest began to make a wheezing rattling sound. It was like all the pain was bursting out of him.

Emily wondered if she should get a nurse or a doctor, but then Liam slowly began to calm down. Wrapping his skinny arms around her, he held her as tightly as he was able. He felt so weak, so unlike Liam. But it didn't matter; he was here, and she would help him any way she could.

After Jamie's bottled milk had run out, Mum and Dad brought him up to Lincolnshire, renting a small house through a website.

Emily would never forget the moment Liam had first seen his son. It was after he'd spoken to the police, and he was sitting up in bed, his hand trembling as he struggled with his porridge.

He dropped the spoon when Emily entered the room, staring wide-eyed at her, with that dreamish look he'd had ever since he'd returned; it was like he was expecting to wake up back there any second.

Liam's hair and beard had been cut, making his face look even sharper, even more severely emaciated. But when he smiled, it was Liam, her Liam, the man she was going to marry. He held Jamie so tenderly, smiling through tears as his son made babbling noises and reached for his hand.

"Do you know me, little man?" Liam whispered. "It's me. It's your dad."

He moved his face close to Jamie's and let him paw at his features, and then he kissed his forehead and sat back, cradling him to his chest, staying that way for a long time.

Now, Liam reached for the TV remote. He winced as he sat back. Jamie was sleeping in the next room, and Rocky was curled up at Liam's side. The Jack Russell hadn't left him alone since he'd returned.

Liam turned on the TV and an advertisement for a luxury cruise played.

He glanced at her, his lips shaping into one of his old smiles. He was beginning to put on weight, slowly, but he still looked like a different man sometimes; she was so used to his wide shoulders and thick arms and general bulkiness.

But when he smiled, he was Liam. When he laughed and kissed and held her, he was Liam.

"I'd rather be here." He gestured at the TV, at the tropical paradise the cruise ship was gliding through.

"Me too. Just me and you and Rocky and Jamie. That's all I need. Liam... we don't have to watch this."

"I know. I want to."

The police had disagreed with Liam taking his story public, but he'd insisted on it. He'd said these people had been getting away with this for a long time, and the world needed to know who they truly were. He said he wouldn't hide away. "I won't do what they want me to. Not anymore. Never again."

So Emily had held her phone camera as, still in his hospital bed, Liam had told his story. He'd told it right from the beginning, going into detail about how that crazy bitch Madeline had tried to seduce him, the sick games she'd played: the way they'd laughed as he snorted and oinked. He told the world about Rebecca's murder and Harrison's help at the end.

"I'm sorry," Liam had told the camera. "I don't know if he's dead or alive. I ran. I was so scared."

The Pembertons were giving an interview to defend their case. The police hadn't been able to get a search warrant for the Lincolnshire property, and they still hadn't located Rebecca's family, any of the guards, or the commander, a man called Smith.

But they *had* found Harrison's family, and they had corroborated certain basic facts, like that Harrison had moved away for work. That was it. Otherwise, it seemed as if the Pembertons were going to get away with it, like they got away with everything.

The adverts stopped and they appeared, Francis and Madeline Pemberton, the older man sitting upright in a fancy suit, a chain snaking from his pocket. Madeline was dressed like she was going to church, trying to act all prim and proper when she would've raped Emily's fiancé if she'd been able to.

Emily hated her. She didn't doubt Liam's story for a moment, even if the Pembertons public image didn't fit with everything he'd told her. They were a family from old money, often appearing at parties. Madeline volunteered with several charities – or at least hung around long enough to have her photo taken – and she was often seen in nightclubs in London and Paris. They seemed like any other ultra-wealthy family, living their high-flying lives.

But Emily didn't buy Madeline's disarming smile for a second.

Liam sat up as the interview began.

"Let me start with the most obvious question. Did you do this?"

Madeline looked at her father, and her father smiled as if to say, *What are these people like?* He turned back to the interviewer. "No, we did not imprison a total stranger for half a year. We didn't make him... what was it? Crawl around on the floor and oink like a pig. Frankly, every claim this man has made is absurd."

"He said you wanted to seduce him, Madeline."

"Oh, yes. All my life, I have *longed* for a complete stranger with a fiancée and a child. I'm sorry, but my father is right. This is a joke. Why on earth would I randomly select a man off the street to... to *torture*? The very thought is unbelievable."

"My daughter is too proud to say it, but she actually works with a charity who helps victims of this sort of alleged abuse."

"So where was Liam Knight? And why, if his account is false, has he gone to the trouble of telling this story in such detail?"

"I'd have to be as mad as Mr Knight to answer that question," Francis said. Liam tensed up, and Emily wrapped her hand around his. "Perhaps it's a publicity stunt. Perhaps he thinks he's going to get a reality television show. Who knows when you're dealing with a person like that? All I can do is tell you the truth. Before I saw his offensive and despicable video, I had never seen this man before in my life. Neither had my daughter."

"It just seems like such a random thing to invent–"

"So we are to be hostage to every fanciful thing any person on the street dreams up?" Madeline snapped. Emily wished she could slap her across the face; she was far too convincing. "We

269

aren't saying this Liam person hasn't been through something. Clearly, he has. But to say that my father or I had anything to do with it – I'm sorry, but it's unthinkable."

Liam switched off the TV. "That's enough of that."

"They're such good liars."

Liam looked at her sharply. "You don't believe them, do you?"

She held his face, pressing her palms against his cheeks, feeling his jagged cheekbones. They stared into each other's eyes. "No. But the way they lie... it's like they've been doing it their whole lives, like it's the norm."

"It's the norm for them. She thought she could make me love her, Emily. She genuinely believed it. She didn't see it as abuse, or assault, or whatever you want to call it. They're not just lying to the world. They're lying to themselves."

Emily rested her head on his shoulder, hugging him. "They sound very miserable."

She glanced at their reflection in the TV, as Liam wrapped his arm around her and Rocky curled up next to them. They looked like a family. They looked like they were home.

CHAPTER FIFTY

"Father says I have to be done with the games now. There's too much risk. But I spoke to him and I explained, very reasonably, that you're not an *extra* risk. You've been with us for months; nobody knows where you are. Your family are making efforts to find you, it's true, but they won't think to look here. How do you like it?"

Harrison could barely make out the woman's voice. His thoughts were fuzzy. He remembered when Liam had hit the guard with the buggy, but then Smith had stabbed him, and the other guard had recovered and joined in with the attack. And then everything had gone dark.

After that, he recalled little, flashes here and there: somebody was telling him to keep his eyes open, holding a rag to his belly. Harrison thought it might be Smith, and then he remembered something else: what Smith had said. About Chewie, his old mate overseas, Smith's son.

"I hope you're comfortable," Madeline went on, leaning down over him.

Harrison's head felt like it was floating. He could vaguely feel his body, and he was so grateful when he was able to twitch his fingers and toes. At least he wasn't paralysed. But there was hardly any sensation, and suddenly he wondered if he had imagined the movement.

He tried to look down; his head was pinned in place with a hard strip of leather, and he was sure he felt similar restraints on the rest of his body.

"Never fear, soldier boy." Harrison could just about make out her smile through his hazy eyes. "You're quite heavily medicated. A necessity, they tell me, because of all those stab wounds you received. Nineteen, in total. I think Smith got a little carried away. But then we all did. I've promised Father to keep this game far more contained."

She laughed. "And it's so nice to have somebody to talk to! I could never share this with Father, or any of my so-called friends, but you'll listen, won't you?"

She trailed her fingertips across his cheek. Harrison tried to shout, but there was a rag stuffed in his mouth.

"I truly thought Liam might be the one. I truly thought we might be able to make something of ourselves. It was the first time I saw him that convinced me. I was simply dying for a coffee, and so I braved one of the chains in the city centre. There was a park across from the café, and Liam was there, training the most disobedient dog I have ever seen."

Her fingernails were scraping along Harrison's forehead. He shivered, and tears welled in his eyes, but there was nothing he could do. Liam was safe; he'd done the right thing. Wasn't he? Liam had got away? Harrison had no way of knowing.

"That's a sign, I believe, of how hard I fell for him. I hate dogs. I've always hated animals, but dogs are worst of all, loud attention-seeking ugly things. But even when I saw that training dogs was clearly his job, it didn't stop me. I watched him for a while, and then, finally, he looked up. He saw me. We met eyes. He smiled, this very particular sort of smile... it was like he was saying, *Come get me, come free me from my regular boring life.*"

She let go of Harrison and walked out of view. He couldn't turn his head, but there was a metallic clattering noise, as though she was rifling through a toolbox. Was she going to take a hammer to his drugged body, a scalpel, a blowtorch?

Harrison strained at the bindings, but his body didn't respond. Strangely, he felt the tears most of all, as they streamed sideways down his face. They were hot and they stung.

"After that," Madeline went on, as the clattering stopped; she'd selected her tool. "I spoke to the woman whose dog he'd been training. She was a disoriented sort of person, you know the type; they never have their act together. They're always on the verge of a disaster. Maybe that was why her dog was so wild. I pretended I needed a dog trainer too, and she gave me his name."

Madeline returned to the table. Her hands were out of view. Harrison wished she'd just show him what it was, so he knew what to expect, what type of pain she was going to inflict.

"That's the one loose end. That woman. I've tried to find her, but it seems she didn't contact him through his public Facebook page. I didn't get her name. But it's been weeks now, and nothing has come of her. I think, dear soldier boy, we're going to get away with it."

Something cold began to trail up Harrison's leg. It felt like the edge of a claw hammer, or the point of a screwdriver. He couldn't be sure. She wasn't applying a lot of pressure yet.

"Father asked me, a few years ago, why I always choose men who look alike. He's always looking for reasons, my father, always trying to sort the world into a neat orderly system. The truth is, I don't know why my type is my type more than anybody does."

She paused with the metal object pushed against the inside

of Harrison's thigh. He made a muffled noise as he tried to beg, but the rag was stuffed too deeply into his mouth. He just wanted to know what it was. Was she going to scrape skin away, stab, what?

"I discovered something during this most recent game. I have been lying to myself. I suppose we all do, in one way or another, but my lie has cost me a great many years. I used to think I was searching for love, that I would be happy once I found a man who wasn't a constant disappointment to me. But now I see that was only an excuse. What I'm really searching for is pain."

She began to twist something. Harrison's skin burned, but the sensation was distant, numbed by the drugs.

"That's why I asked them to take Liam when his child was due to be born. I told myself it was merely for the leverage it would give us, but honestly, I think I just wanted to make him squirm. And make her squirm, the bitch he impregnated. In fact, I think I'd like to make as many people squirm as possible. I'm done pretending."

She twisted the tool around and around, and Harrison's vision began to waver. Even if the feeling was faraway, his body didn't want to stay awake. But he was afraid to sleep. He didn't know what he'd wake up to.

"My medical advisor assures me this won't cause any permanent damage, but the agony, once I taper you off your medication, is going to be excruciating. I'm so happy you get to go on this journey with me. I'm so excited to discover myself, fully, all of me. Thank you, Harrison. Thank you so much."

CHAPTER FIFTY-ONE

L iam still found it difficult to be outside. It had been a month and a half since he'd escaped. His ankle was slowly beginning to heal, but he knew the days where he'd no longer need his walking stick were a long way off. He leaned on it heavily, as he reached into Jamie's pram and softly stroked his son across the cheek.

Rocky was running around the park like a madman, playing with all the other dogs and generally making a fool of himself. Liam loved to watch his old friend play. He'd never stop appreciating it, any of it: life. He would never stop savouring the way Emily looked as she smiled up at him, ready to take on the world, ready to move on, ready for their lives.

Liam had to glance over his shoulder; they were near the park railing, and he knew it would be easy for somebody to sneak up and grab one of them. But the field behind them was empty, as it had been the last time he checked.

Emily frowned but then let her gaze drop. Liam knew she didn't want him to be paranoid all the time, but there was no other choice.

They were out there, the masked men, the men with the needles, ready to hurt him if the lady of the house commanded it.

There had been little progress on his case. After several weeks, the police had managed to secure a search warrant for the property. Of course, they'd found nothing. The Pembertons weren't idiots. They'd been doing this for a long time. They'd hidden or destroyed all the evidence. When Liam had asked the police if they'd found the cell, the officer had sighed down the phone, as though her belief was straining.

The best they'd come up with was a payment into Harrison's bank account, for hundreds of thousands of dollars. But there was no way to trace the funds to the Pembertons, apparently; he'd been paid by an oil company overseas. As far as anybody knew, he might still be out there, choosing not to make contact.

Liam hated and loved Harrison.

He hated the bastard for not doing something sooner, for not acting when he had the chance. But he also understood that, without Harrison, he wouldn't be here. The breeze wouldn't be blowing softly against his skin. The sunlight wouldn't be shining down on him and his fiancée and his child.

He hoped Harrison had died during the fight; if he was alive, terrible things were most likely happening to him.

He'd died, surely. Madeline wouldn't let him live after his betrayal.

Liam flinched when the dog barked from behind him. He turned and almost fell, but managed to catch himself with his walking stick at the last second. The dog was a gorgeous greyhound, with long legs and kind eyes. Liam looked at him for a moment, as the dog stared back, no longer barking.

"I know you, don't I?" Liam said, limping closer to the fence. "Did I train you, huh? Is that it?"

Leaning against the railing, he reached over and gently lowered his hand. The dog sniffed a couple of times, reminding Liam of Buck in that book he'd read, in the early days of his imprisonment; he would've killed for that book in the cell, an escape, even if it was only in his mind.

He pushed those thoughts away. He was here now; he'd never be there again.

The dog play bowed and then rolled over, pawing at the air, whining at Liam. He chuckled. "I can't chase you, I'm sorry."

"No offence," Emily said. "But if you trained him, you did a terrible job."

Liam laughed. He loved when Emily felt comfortable enough to tease him, just like the old days, before everything changed: before he started waking up screaming in the middle of the night, before he flinched at every little noise. But he was getting better. He was determined to get better. For his family.

"You're right about that. I wonder where the owner is. Ah."

"Ah?"

Liam nodded down the path. He remembered the woman because she had the same hair. It was like something straight out of the eighties, a fuzz ball spiralling in all directions. She was dressed in similarly outlandish clothes, with leopard print leggings and a black T-shirt with a cartoon of the prime minister taking a shit on it.

"Granger, what are you doing?"

"That was it." Liam smiled down at the dog. "Granger. Do you remember me, boy?"

The dog whined and then began to lope around the field outside the gate, ducking his head and sprinting all over the place, too much energy to contain. It was clear the woman hadn't been keeping up with his training exercises. But that was okay. He was happy and free, and that was all anybody could ask for.

"Wait a sec." The woman raised her hands to her face, shielding the sunlight. "I know you, don't I?"

"Yeah, we have a mutual friend." He nodded to her dog. "I trained him about a year and a half back."

She clicked her fingers. "And you were on the telly, right? Sorry. My head's always in a million places. I'm a poet, you see, and I'm always thinking of interesting things I could be writing about. And then there's the heroin. Can't forget the heroin. Ha!"

Liam chuckled at the heavy sarcasm in her voice. "Sure, can't ever forget that."

"You know, it's the funniest thing." She approached the railing. "I was talking to my boyfriend about you last night. He was telling me I should go to the police."

"The police?"

"It's the strangest thing. You know that posh lady, the one you say kept you prisoner?"

Liam stood up straighter. He was gripping the handle of his walking stick hard. "Yes."

"I met her, towards the end of when we were working together. She said she had a dog that needed training, but maybe she just wanted your name or something? I don't know. Do you think it could be important?"

Liam struggled to stay upright, his head rushing. This woman clearly didn't think what she was saying had any significance; she was already turning back to her dog, as though getting ready to walk away.

"Wait. Yes, yes. It's important. I'm sorry, but you need to talk to my contact with the police. You need to tell them exactly what happened."

"I don't have my phone on me. Hey, Granger! Get out of there!"

Liam went for his pocket, to grab his phone, but it was in his bag on the bench. Emily handed it to him with a soft smile on her face. As Liam took it, their fingertips brushed.

THE END

ACKNOWLEDGEMENTS

(The following has been left unedited at the author's request.)

This book was very difficult to write. The certain type of pain Madeline inflicts on Liam hits close to home for me. And it's for that reason I'd like to thank my friend, who I won't name. It was through conversations with him I was able to partially understand the sensation of being Madeline-ized. It's an attack of a man's spirit as well as his body and his identity, and of course I exaggerated it.

It's with massive thanks to Bloodhound Books that I was able to do that. They gave me lots of creative freedom, and special thanks is to submission readers (there is a fancy term; I can't remember it) who accepted my book. I would also like to say *merci* to Betsy Reavley, Fred Freeman (no idea if I'm spelling these surnames right and I'm not proofreading this), and Tara Lyons (I know this one's right). They are all great to work with. Fred is quick to respond and Betsy is always understanding. Tara is all-around positive and I'm always happy when I see her name in my inbox because it means I get to go on this amazing journey again, of writing books.

Writing is a lonely endeavor, but luckily I'm popular as fuck and I've got loads of friends. There's Marshall who lives in Krakow and Jake who lives in my parent's house (he's also my brother), there's Kane with curly-wurly hair and 'Sunglasses' Rhu at the skate meet; there's Lewis and Neil and Tom and Matt and another Matt and I'm pretty sure there's a third Matt. There's James, who I've known since primary school. I've clearly left friends off, but if I see you one a semi-regular basis and we have a laugh, consider yourself well and truly thanked. Oh there's John too, Swampie-face John, Mr Chicken 'Laid the Egg' John...

(*I bet you're wondering right now, what in the actual fuck am I reading. Well, basically, I wasn't going to write an acknowledgements for this book. But then I thought, hey, it's Sunday, it's raining, I can't go Rollerblading, I'm hungover and feeling very ready to melt into my bed. I might as well have some fun with this. So keep reading if you want to watch my slow descent into insanity.*)

I'd like to thank my wife, Krystle. Without her I really wouldn't be a writer. Krystle is my Emily. Liam is the closest to me of any of my protoganists, and Emily is very clearly *his* Krystle. We met when I was 21 and didn't have my life together. She supported me as I became a writer, the same way Emily supports Liam to become a dog trainer. We both also love dogs; we have a Jack Russell called Loki, very much a little Rocky, and also a Chiuauaua (I can't spell) called Gizmo. Without Krystle, I honestly mean this, I wouldn't have published a single book. She taught me work ethic, pride in what I do, inspired me in so many ways.

Mum, Dad, Ben, anybody else I've forgotten: *You're thanked pals, thank-ee very much, take your pat on the back and stuff it where the sun don't...*

Morgen Bailey, as always, was fantastic to work with. She is the best kind of editors. For my first book, she had a LOT of notes, and I was like, damn, I must be a terrible writer. But then with my second book I improved, and there were far fewer. This one had the perfect amount, in my opinion, but perhaps readers will disagree; perhaps they'll wish I was edited into the ground, so they could free themselves of the drivel to which they have just subjected themselves. But yeah, thank you, Morgen!

Lastly, I'd like to say *gratias tibi* to two writing friends who started as merely work buddies, I guess you'd call it, a couple of biddies to pass the time of day with at the water cooler, except the water cooler is Facebook Messenger. But over the months since we met – over a *year* now; time really does go far too quickly—I feel we've become real friends. I know I could call either of these biddies up if I needed help; the biddies would a-come running. Keri Beevis actually wrote a book about friends helping each other hide a body, called *With Friends Like These* (which is really very excellent, and I think you'll love it if you enjoyed this even a little bit, though she's probably better, which is acceptably because she's also far older...) and I remember thinking, I'm glad me and Keri are better friends than these sociopaths. Patricia Dixon also wrote a book sort of connected to this, called *#MeToo*. It shows the female-male violent or sabotaging behavior types. Mine is notched up to a higher degree, sort of like a bargain bin Squid Games (if you're a reviewer steal that). But the general message is there, if there's a message at all. Patricia Dixon is actually now, as I write this, halfway through the book. She says she loves it so far. She might be lying, but hey, that's what friends are for: to lie to your face and tell you you're excellent no matter what. No, I'm sure the book is good. Did you like it, dear reader, mad person who's somehow made it this far into this ridiculous time-wasting rant? Did you like my book? Please go to www.IlikedNathansbook.-

com/mentalbreakdown to confirm that you liked it. Thank you ever so much.

Lastly, I'd like to thank my publisher for allowing me to include this frankly insane note; I'm not reading this back. I'm going to trust my gut. I'm sort of curious how long I can make this and have them still put it in the book. Are they realistically going to put the ramblings of a bored madman into the back of a book? Or do they *have* to because the book is mine?

If you're reading this, you know the answer.

A few key moments

The line between comedy and drama—I was walking this pretty carefully through a couple of scenes. One was when Liam gives Madeline the massage, and she does that massively over the top fake orgasm, and it's clearly ridiculous and sort of sad and pathetic and tragic at the same time, and I wanted to demonstrate that, while still maybe having some comedy in there. The other was when Liam recites his shit poem. The *Evan*, and Liam gets angry, and I wanted there to be some conflicting feelings there.

Liam's long haul in the cell—He had to be broken down. It had to go to its logical conclusion. I was in that cell with Liam, imagining my mind breaking down, the visions tempting me... but it also couldn't mess up the plot of the story. Three chapters, I gave it, one for Liam sandwiched between a Harrison and an Emily; that way, the passage of time is felt, and all the characters are situated for the final act. The only downside is you lose some of the sense of time; there is the challenge. *How can I show the reader in 1,800 words this man's mind and body have broken down over a few months?* Then it becomes a matter of choosing the most impactful statements, weird or interesting or relatable scenarios. I hope I succeeded.

Liam and Madeline are going to have sex—Evil scene, so

horrible. Madeline is almost too narcissistic, in her complete disregard of him, but these types of people exist. True evil would seem like comic book fare to many people; their non-sociopathic minds simply can't comprehend somebody indulging so freely and so carelessly in sadism. But people do, and part of Madeline's journey is discovering she no longer wants to make excuses for her true desire. She's not going to use the guise of love anymore; she's going to luxuriate shamelessly in the act of inflicting pain. Part of that pain is in this scene, with Liam, where she is committing a sex act on him, and Liam can't perform. It's a horrible scenario for any man even in the best circumstances, but with the shame and the abuse mixed in, it's so much worse. That's why he jumps. He has to. There's no choice left. She's stripped him of everything.

The bacon feeding—For anybody who's spotted the similarities, this scene is a direct and purposefully reference to the brilliant TV show *Succession*. There's a scene in that called 'boar on the floor' where the tyrannical and excellently portrayed Logan Roy forces some underlings to crawl around and debase themselves, as a power play. I needed something similar for a scene, but the objective would be pure and casual cruelty, rather than existing within the structure of *Succession's* power hierarchy. So I thought, I'm going to do the same, because it works and I love that show and it's different enough, and in a massively different context, that I think fans of my books and the show might find it kind of cool.

Emily in the park/weird writing quirks—There's a scene where Emily is in the park and a man approaches her. It's slow and not much happens, existing as a sort of stop-gap before the final racing pace of the conclusion. When I was writing this scene, I sort of slipped, and a scenario takes over as if often does; this can be gold dust at times, but destroy a story at others. Mine would've destroyed had I not edited it; Emily was, in this old version, going through a psychotic breakdown, and she had imagined the man in the park. The problem was, this was near the end of the book... Am I really going to introduce such a massive plot element so late, only to solve it/ignore it almost immediately? There were other moments like that; there was even a part, early on, when Liam was sort of attracted to Maddie. But I didn't like it. I appreciate Liam's loyalty. He's a good man, my favorite character I ever wrote. (Incidentally, I just noticed this is in US English, and the rest of the book is in UK; grammar pedants, I hope you are screaming and raging at me right now ahhahahahahahaah!)

Female-male abuse: You may have noticed Liam think things like *I wish she was a man* in response to the abuse he is suffering. This plays on one of the most common aspects of this kinds of situation. Madeline, a skilled sociopath, knows that Liam was probably brought up to never hit a woman, as I was, and as most of my male friends were. So she knows how to play this, to goad him, to make him doubt and hate himself for it. Liam can't help but be resistant to the idea of harming him; it's in his bones, ever since he was a little kid. Probably toddler Liam pushed a girl and an older man, maybe a man he looked up to, shouted at him, maybe slapped him around the earhole. He can't stop seeing her as *woman* and start seeing her as *human being I need to kill/capture to escape*. This is why, in my opinion, he is locked in a stasis of sorts for the middle section of the book. He is constantly on the *edge* of acting, but always pulling back, never allowing himself to fall over the edge. That is not to say he should've have hurt her. It's difficult for any person to know what they would do in Liam's situation. It all depends on who they are.

Male-female abuse—If this book gets popular – which would be awesome – and you find yourself thinking (*you* being whatever lunatic has made it this far)... *oh, this NJ Moss only writes about women hurting men*, please go and read, or read the blurb of *Her Final Victim*. The main character in that is a woman called Millicent, who was raised in a cult, and I take great pride in how I constructed her to show the instinctual response of vulnerability, protectiveness, violence, and sadness certain types of abuse can cause.

Bretherton—I loved the idea of this man pretending to the butler. There's some class stuff in this novel, for sure, because Liam trusts his own – or who he perceives to be his own – way more than any upper-class person. It's understandable considering the circumstances, but I think it would be true for Liam anywhere he went. It's a story of classes taken to the extreme, pushed to maybe ridiculous levels – and I'll understand if people judge the slightly surreal aspects in that way – and Liam can't escape. Madeline can't escape, not really. But her *dad* does, playing the butler, controlling everything.

The situation/suspension of disbelief—If you found yourself jolted out of the story at certain points, for whatever reason I can't foresee – if I could, it wouldn't be there for you to notice – please no the choices and mistakes are mine. There are certain things I know may seem unrealistic, but the story always comes first, and I am always so grateful to those readers who can come with me, trusting I won't take the piss *too* much.

(*Like writing a 2,000+ word note at the very end of your book, forcing people to finish it. Now THAT would be taking the piss.*)

To whoever has made it this far, thank you. I hope you had fun. It's been a great couple of hours for me.

A NOTE FROM THE PUBLISHER

Thank you for reading this book. If you enjoyed it please do consider leaving a review on Amazon to help others find it too.

We hate typos. All of our books have been rigorously edited and proofread, but sometimes mistakes do slip through. If you have spotted a typo, please do let us know and we can get it amended within hours.

info@bloodhoundbooks.com

Printed in Great Britain
by Amazon

82378101R00171